DARKNESS AT FAIR WINDS

Suddenly Varina found herself in Andrew's arms, but her hysteria deepened as she remembered the charge she had heard against him: wife-beater and murderer. What kind of monster was this man?

The slap of Andrew's hand across her face brought her to her senses long enough to realize that she had babbled her thoughts aloud. "Are you going to beat me, too?" she asked.

Andrew flinched, as if she had landed a physical blow. He grasped her by the shoulders and forced her to look him in the eye. "It would be a lie to say I did not want to kill them. But with God as my witness, Varina, if I could have thought of a way to save ourselves without hurting them, I would have done it."

One part of her wanted to believe him, wanted to throw her arms about him in gratitude for rescuing her, but another part that had swayed between reason and terror for the past few weeks was not convinced. But how soon would it be before she knew the truth? Either this man was a heinous murderer, or he was not. And how could she be sure?

CHARLOTTE DOUGLAS

DARKNESS AT FAIR WINDS

This book is dedicated with love and gratitude to Butch and Button.

Book Margins, Inc.

A BMI Edition

Published by special arrangement with Dorchester Publishing Co., Inc.

Printed in the United States of America.

ACKNOWLEDGMENTS

Accurate portrayal of historical events and actual people and places would have been most difficult without the gracious assistance of:

The Dunedin Historical Society
The Pinellas County Historical Society
The Ybor City Museum Society
The Henry B. Plant Museum
The Edison Winter Home
Roy Leep, chief meteorologist, WTVT, Tampa
The William M. Douglas Military Museum
Carl James Decker, military historian
Hampton Dunn, Florida historian
Dr. and Mrs. Richard C. Boyd, First Presbyterian
Church of New Bern, North Carolina

Although Henry Scharrer, Manuel Menendez, Kate Johnson, Thomas Edison, and Mr. and Mrs. Henry B. Plant are real people who were alive in 1894, all others are completely fictitious, and any resemblance they might bear to persons living or dead is completely coincidental.

DARKNESS AT FAIRWINDS

Chapter One

Varina watched her uncle ascend the stairs of the central elevated pulpit, his ecclesiatical majesty unmarred by the perspiration glistening on his forehead. Although a cool early-autumn breeze wafted through the open windows of New Bern Church, the minister's somber black robe and passion for his topic generated much heat. Like a beneficent dark bird perched atop a mountain crag, he stood high above his congregation, opened the huge Bible, and began to read in a sonorous voice, his slender index finger punctuating the air above his head.

" 'Now it is high time to awake out of sleep . . . The night is far spent, the day is at hand: let us therefore cast off the works of darkness, and let us put on the armor of light.' "

Aunt Mae, sitting beside Varina in the family

pew, turned her face toward the pulpit, like a sunflower tracking the sun, following each word her husband spoke, his elocution honed to a sharp edge.

If love is an armor of light, then Aunt Mae is well-clothed, Varina thought, observing the adoring sparkle of her aunt's bright blue eyes.

An uncharacteristic pang of jealousy nipped her as she thought of Mae and William's happy marriage and their brood of noisy children. Irrationally, Varina felt very much alone. Her own parents had died when she was five years old, and Mae and William had taken her in and raised her as their own. Her boisterous cousins thought of her as their older sister, and her life in New Bern had been secure and happy, surrounded by loving relatives and friends, but today something was missing. Suddenly she was gripped by a yawning emptiness, an uncharacteristic longing for something that she could not identify, that eluded her when she attempted to name it.

She pushed the uncomfortable feelings from her mind, attributing her feverish dissatisfactions to an approaching cold, and returned her attention so diligently to Uncle William's sermon that she was unaware of Aunt Mae's studying sidelong glances creasing the brow of her kindly face.

When the service had ended and parting greetings had been exchanged with members of the congregation, Mae and Varina performed their weekly ritual of removing the massive arrangements of bronze chrysanthemums from the pulpit vases, and, exiting by the church's rear doors, walked across its back lawn, through the gate of a high white picket fence, and into the back yard of the manse.

An aura of peacefulness filled the deep expanse of yard, its grass now burned brown from early frosts, the scuppernong arbor a mass of bare intertwined ropes of vine, and the vegetable garden empty and mulched for winter. Varina tried to imagine these peaceful surroundings as the war zone they had been thirty years ago when the last Yankee troops had withdrawn from New Bern. During the war, the Union Army had used the church as a hospital and quartered their soldiers in the homes of the town, but today serenity reigned not only in the back gardens but throughout the community, and war seemed a distant and fading nightmare.

Her own name—Varina, after Varina Howell Davis, the First Lady of the Confederacy—was a constant reminder to her of that disastrous conflict. She didn't know why her parents had named her after Jefferson Davis's wife, but she was proud of the name. Varina Davis had been a beautiful woman of great courage and spirit, and Varina Cameron struggled to live up to her namesake's standards.

The day was cloudless, and the sapphire blue of the sky was broken only by a chevron of migratory birds, heading south for the winter. As Varina watched them disappear over the horizon behind the towering white steeple of New Bern Church, she felt again the nameless yearning that had gripped her earlier.

"Is anything wrong, dear?" Mae called from the back steps of the manse.

Varina stood where she had stopped to watch the flight of geese, her trimly booted ankles deep in the fallen golden leaves of the manse's sugar maple. She threw her aunt a reassuring smile.

"I'm thinking that it's too pretty a day to spend inside." Reluctant to articulate her thoughts, even if she could identify the longings she felt, she shook the leaves from the hem of her dress and followed her aunt into the house.

Varina hurried into the hallway to remove her Sunday hat, a confection of teal-green velvet and tulle which set off her russet hair and large hazel eyes of changeable hues that glowed sometimes brown, but more often radiant green. She hung her dark green suit coat on the mirrored rack and adjusted the high collar of her crisp white shirtwaist.

"Rina," Mae's oldest son Andy called to her teasingly from the landing. "No need to check that mirror. You are still the prettiest girl in New Bern."

The fifteen-year-old galloped down the last flight of stairs and lifted his lovely cousin off her feet in an enthusiastic hug, twirling her dizzily around the hallway.

"Andy McLaren, you behave yourself!"

Varina's tone was stern, but affection for the young scamp shone in her eyes as she patted her hair back into place and waited for the room to stop spinning.

"Your mother needs wood for the kitchen stove, and your father won't be home for another half-hour. You'd better go give her a hand."

Rolling up the sleeves of her shirtwaist, Varina returned to the spacious sunny kitchen to help with preparations for Sunday dinner. The luscious smell of warm cinnamon from the apple pies cooling on the windowsill filled the air. Mae, hatless now and aproned, mixed spices and flour to batter chicken for frying, while Varina peeled potatoes. Efficiently but without haste, the two worked in companionable silence at the accustomed rhythm of their chores.

"Varina," Mae said as she removed the last piece of crusty golden chicken from the pan and placed it on a large hand-painted china platter, "you are as dear to me as any of my own children. You do know that, don't you, dear?"

Mae had a habit of speaking in non sequiturs that Varina had long ago learned to interpret, and she felt a tiny spasm of fear at her aunt's words. Usually a declaration of affection preceded some pronouncement that Mae knew Varina would find unsettling. Varina tried to squelch her feelings of alarm. She looked across the familiar room at her aunt whose expression held such seriousness, and at any other time Varina would have laughed at the smear of flour across the tip of her aunt's nose. Instead, she took a dish towel and wiped the older woman's face clean, planting a kiss where the flour had been, reassuring herself with the gesture that her aunt had never caused her pain.

"Darling Aunt Mae, of course I know you love me. You and Uncle Will have been mother and father to me for fifteen years, and no one, not even my own parents, could have made a happier home than you have made for me."

She surveyed the cozy kitchen where she had spent so many enjoyable hours. Pots of fragrant geraniums crowded the south windows, and the well-scrubbed table, center of lively family conferences, study sessions, and informal meals, bore scratches and gouges like lines in the palm of a familiar and beloved hand. Blue Willow plates gleamed in the rack that bordered the pale yellow walls, and just off the porch, visible through the windowed back door, stood the dogwood tree, red-leaved now, but glowing pink as a cloud at sunset when it blossomed in the spring. Varina loved this room and the family it sheltered.

"I don't tell you often enough of my appreciation."

"Lawh, child," her aunt said, "I'm the one who should be thanking you. However could I have run a household with four small children if it hadn't been for all the help you've given me? That is why it is going to be so difficult—"

The older woman stopped, turning her attention to the pots on the stovetop, but not before Varina could witness the dismay on her aunt's face. That look intensified Varina's feelings of alarm.

14

"What, Aunt Mae? What's going to be difficult?"

Mae set down her long stirring spoon and looked across the kitchen at her niece.

"Your uncle and I wish to talk with you after dinner. We have a favor to ask of you, dear. But it must wait until we feed this hungry family of ours."

Having firmly closed the subject, she began bustling about the kitchen in final preparations for the meal.

Throughout the elaborate Sunday dinner for which the entire family gathered in the large dining room, Varina's thoughts returned to the upcoming conference and what it might mean. She watched her adopted family as they laughed and talked, burning pictures of them into her mind with a strange foreboding.

Andy, the oldest of her cousins, tall and lanky like his father, had a sharp intelligence and a predilection for mischief. The twins, Molly and Margaret, were two years younger and as like their blond, blue-eyed mother as they were each other. Harris was the baby, although at eleven could hardly be called a baby any longer. Already he was beginning to lose his childhood pudginess and showed signs of long-leggedness that ran in the male side of the family.

Varina watched Aunt Mae closely, hoping she would drop a hint about their upcoming discussion. The small plump woman was a domestic wonder, keeping track of her children, the workings of the manse, her husband and his ministry, and still maintaining her sunny disposition. As she had many times over the years, Varina wondered whether her mother would have been like Aunt Mae, her only sister, had she lived. Varina had only vague, shadowy memories of her natural parents and had long ago accepted Aunt Mae and Uncle William as her true family.

"Molly and Margaret," Aunt Mae instructed after the apple pie had been eaten, "clear the table, put the food away, and do the dishes. Andy and Harris, you boys carry the flowers down to the hospital for the nurses to distribute in the wards. And don't dawdle on the way or the chrysanthemums will wilt. Varina, come with us."

The cheerful and ready manner in which the children accepted and carried out their responsibilities was evidence of the firm and loving upbringing they had received. Complaining was not acceptable in the McLaren household. All were fully aware that their lot in life was a happy and secure one, and they thanked God for it.

Varina followed Aunt Mae obediently into the front parlor and Uncle William came behind, closing the double doors into the hallway.

"Sit down, my dear."

He motioned to the plush horsehair sofa and Varina settled on it, wishing she could settle her nerves as well. Never had she been the center of one of the "parlor conferences," as the children referred to them with awe. Many times Andy had been the focus of these discussions, usually after one of his pranks, such as hiding in the church balcony during the women's prayer meeting and pretending to be the voice of God. Whatever the point of this discussion, however, Varina knew that it did not involve any misconduct on her part; her conscience was clear. Her life was too uneventful to be sinful.

"Varina," William began in the rich mellifluous voice that so often mesmerized his congregation, "you have been like our own daughter for the past fifteen years and we love you as our own. You have returned our love with yours and given Mae more assistance than can ever be counted. Our home will always be your home—and it would not seem like home without you."

Varina sat quietly, knowing from experience that a response was unnecessary when Uncle William was speaking in his sermonizing tone. When he wanted her opinion, he would ask for it.

"I have said all this, my dear, so that you will not—you *must* not in any way interpret what we are about to say as wanting you to leave."

Leave echoed through the pounding of blood in her ears, and for a moment Varina thought she would faint. Aunt Mae sat next to her and placed her arms around her.

"Dearest girl, please listen carefully. The decision must be yours. We can only present you with the facts and let you make up your own mind."

"Do you remember Andrew?" William asked, throwing Varina into confusion by the rapid shift in subject.

"How could any of us forget Andrew?" Varina said, remembering fondly Uncle William's handsome younger brother. "We always had such fun when he visited us between his trips abroad."

"I miss him," Aunt Mae said. "We had such lovely picnics at the shore whenever he came, and what tales he told us about his adventures in the Orient and South America and—"

Uncle William cleared his throat meaningfully, and Aunt Mae abruptly ceased her reminiscences. "Sorry, dear. Please continue."

Varina thought of Andrew's visits that stood out as milestones of her childhood memories. With a love of adventure and a laugh that warmed the entire house with its resonance, Andrew had never seemed to mind the hours he spent entertaining his young cousins, even though he was fifteen years older than Varina. He held advanced degrees in botany and horticulture and was regarded internationally as an authority in his field, but when he was with his family, he was always simply Andrew, unassuming and fun-loving. He had gladly taken them on nature walks through the pine forests and tidal flats, pointing out birds and plants and comparing them to exotic species he had encountered in foreign lands. The manse at New Bern had been his home when the wanderlust was not upon him, and everyone rejoiced at his coming and mourned his departures.

But seven years ago the visits had stopped. That New Year's Eve Varina had been allowed to stay up to usher in 1888, and even more important, to await Andrew's arrival. Then only thirteen, Varina had perched on the window seat, her coltish legs hugged to her skinny frame in restless anticipation, her chin on her knees, watching the rain-drenched street through lace curtains for the first sight of him.

Over the previous years, between Andrew's frequent visits, Uncle William had read all of Andrew's letters aloud to Varina and her young cousins, and that night Varina's mind had reeled with images of the gallant young botanist who traveled the world from the Amazon basin to the islands of the East Indies in search of new and valuable plant specimens. Now he was on his way to set up an experimental plantation on the west coast of Florida, but he would be visiting his family first.

When his carriage finally pulled to a stop in front of the house, Varina had raced to let the others know that Andrew had arrived, then had run back to the door to be the first to welcome him. She had smoothed her white pinafore over her dress, too short in the sleeves and skirt for her rapidly increasing height, and run her fingers through her russet mane, wishing for the thousandth time that her hair was straight and smooth instead of a riot of uncontrollable brown curls.

As she had thrown open the wide front door, Varina was oblivious to rain and cold, for Andrew McLaren, tall and tanned, with drops of rain glistening in his sun-burnished hair, looked down at her, laughter dancing in his deep brown eyes.

"Varina!" With all the exuberance of his care-free character, he had grabbed her up in a rough embrace and swung her off her feet. Varina had felt the strength of his arms, and her head went giddy from both the movement and the rush of pleasure that reddened her girlish cheeks. But the intoxicating moment was short-lived. After he returned her to her feet and released her, he had stepped into the hallway, turning to pull someone in behind him.

By that time William and Aunt Mae had joined them, and Andrew drew his companion before him.

"I have a surprise for you." His voice was buoyant with pride. "This is my wife, Theodora."

The sight of Andrew's wife had hit Varina like sheets of cold rain, making her feel childish, awkward, and incredibly sad, as if she had lost something that could never be found. Standing in the light of the hallway, the petite woman, extraordinarily lovely, was dressed entirely in white, from her expensive fur bonnet and wool-en cloak to her immaculately dainty boots. Her hair was so blonde that it shimmered like silver, and her blue eyes glittered like frozen water.

An ice maiden, Varina had thought, and the image had strengthened when Theodora spoke, her tone cold and biting, expressing no pleasure at meeting Andrew's family. But Andrew hadn't seemed to notice. Over a late supper, impervious to his wife's aloofness, he had regaled them all with tales of his foreign adventures, throwing frequent loving glances toward Theodora, who had somehow remained apart from all that surrounded her. In contrast, Varina had absorbed every word he spoke, following the gestures of his strong slender hands and the gamut of expressions of his charmingly boyish face.

When the tall case clock in the hallway had struck midnight, the family had exchanged kisses and wishes for a happy and prosperous New Year, and Varina, in a paroxysm of adolescent ecstasy, had feared her heart would stop and that she would never breathe again when Andrew kissed her cheek.

She had then discovered herself torn between her youthful fascination with Andrew and jealousy of his unapproachable bride. To Varina's relief, her agony was brief, for she was to see Andrew only once more. The following morning when she was on her way downstairs to breakfast, she had heard Theodora speaking through the open door of the guest room and found herself drawn toward the door, her curiosity about any aspect of Andrew's life outweighing parental injunctions against eavesdropping.

"We can't stay here, Andrew. The woman doesn't even have a maid! Surely I can't be expected to make my own bed, nor can I allow my hostess to do it."

Then the whining tone of the feminine voice had increased in volume and pitch. "You have placed me in an impossible situation here, and we must leave as soon as possible."

Standing on the stairs, caught up in the woman's complaints, Varina had heard the stamp of a tiny foot.

"Theodora," she had heard Andrew reply in a patient and even tone, "William and Mae and their children are my only family, and I haven't seen them for months. I've been looking forward to this visit and had hoped you would enjoy it, too. If it's a problem for you, *I'll* make the bed."

"Oh, Andrew, you never listen to what I say."

The timbre of Theodora's voice had grated like metal drawn across glass, causing Varina to shiver involuntarily at the sound, as well as from the knowledge that her own conduct was unacceptable in Uncle William's house.

"Isn't there a good hotel in town where we can have the service we're used to?"

"This *is* what I'm used to, dear."

The strain could be heard in his voice. At that moment he had stepped from the room into the hallway, and Varina had glimpsed the pain clouding his eyes. But he had laughed when he saw Varina.

"Well, my little niece-by-marriage, it looks as if you have big ears to match those big eyes of yours."

At that, Varina had fled in embarrassment to the safety of the kitchen, descending the stairs at a speed dangerous to both limbs and dignity. After breakfast that morning, Andrew and Theodora had moved to the hotel downtown, and the next day they were gone. No one in the family had seen either of them in the seven years that had passed since that unfortunate visit.

Varina's thoughts and attention snapped back to the present at the sound of Uncle William's ominous throat-clearing.

"The last time that Andrew was here," William continued, "was when he surprised us all by marrying that New York Vandemere heiress with the strange habit of dressing in white."

Varina had almost forgotten that idiosyncracy. But now she remembered Aunt Mae telling her that Theodora was so horrified of dirt that she never wore any color but white, so that soil would show immediately and she could change her clothes at the first sign of it. No wonder she had seemed like an ice princess.

Varina was trying hard to pay attention, but she could not see how Andrew and his wife could have any bearing on her. Impatiently, she attempted to focus on what Uncle William was saying.

"The letters I received from Andrew were extremely enthusiastic about his work in Florida, for he was meeting with great success, including some crossbreeding he was doing with various types of citrus. His happiness seemed complete when his son Jamie was born. Let's see, that must have been almost five years ago now."

Varina felt like screaming. Would Uncle William never finish with Andrew and deal with what concerned her? The tension mounted until she could stand it no longer.

"But what has all this to do with me?"

23

"Patience, child, you'll see." Mae patted her arm.

"It has been over a year since I have heard from Andrew, but I was not worried," William went on. "I thought that if there had been bad news, we would have heard. That, however, turned out to be an erroneous assumption. Yesterday I finally received a letter from Andrew. It is strangely disjointed and most pathetic. Over a year ago, Theodora died of yellow fever. Since then, Andrew says, he has been unable to concentrate on his work, and he is worried about Jamie."

"How terrible for Andrew—and for the poor little boy with no mother to care for him." The gravity of the news drew Varina's thoughts away from her own anxieties.

William and Mae exchanged the look of married couples who know each other's mind. Then William continued, "Jamie was the main concern of Andrew's letter. Since his mother died, the boy has been cared for by a housekeeper, but Andrew feels he needs his own kin, his own flesh and blood to care for him as no one else can. He wants to send the boy to us."

Varina leaned back upon the horsehair settee with a sigh of relief.

"That's a wonderful idea. I'll be happy to help Aunt Mae look after him—"

"No, Jamie isn't coming here," Uncle William said in the tone his family knew as intractable.

Varina stared at him in confusion and amazement. Her kind, compassionate uncle turning away his own nephew? She couldn't believe it.

"It isn't what you think, my dear," Mae assured her. "William and I talked of this until the early hours of this morning. We would love to have Andrew's Jamie here, but there are other considerations."

"Yes," William said. "We have to consider whether this is really what's best for both Andrew and Jamie. Here's a young lad who's just lost his mother. Do we take him away from his father and the only home he's ever known? Do we leave poor widowed Andrew alone without his son? No, bringing the boy here simply is not the solution."

"Then what is?" Varina asked.

"It's a very simple one really," Mae answered brightly. "William and I were very pleased with ourselves when we thought of it." She glanced at her husband and he nodded for her to continue. "We will send *you* to them instead."

"Oh," was all that Varina could answer.

Any objections she might have made had already been countered by William's logic.

When their discussion ended, Varina excused herself, pulled on her coat, pinned her green hat to her russet curls, and hurried down the broad front steps of the manse. Walking briskly, she headed toward the center of town. Uncle William had insisted that she take a week to make her decision, but she already knew what that decision would be.

She looked back with amusement and some

Charlotte Douglas

embarrassment on her adolescent fantasies of
Andrew. Maturity had laid those silly feelings
to rest long ago. Now she regarded him with
the familial fondness evoked by pleasant memories and happy associations, and embraced the
opportunity to repay the many kindnesses that
he had shown her as a child. At the same time,
she could love the small motherless boy who
needed her. The more she thought of under-
taking that responsibility, the more it appealed
to her.

The thought of traveling was also appealing.
Perhaps the unnamed longing she had felt that
morning had been a desire for new places and
new experiences. She pictured Florida as a jungle paradise, filled with exotic plants and animals, romantic beaches and cypress lakes, full
of lurking dangers and incredible beauty. For
a young woman who had lived her entire life
at a placid pace on the coastal plains of North
Carolina, the lure of travel and excitement was
inescapable.

That lure, however, was firmly counterbalanced by her love of New Bern and her
reluctance to leave behind all that was dear
and familiar. After decades of hardship and
deprivation following the war, prosperity and
contentment had finally returned to her town.
As she walked, she passed large comfortable
homes with spacious neighborly front porches
furnished with inviting rocking chairs and wide
swings, all set among trees now ablaze with the
fiery colors of autumn. Leaves rustled beneath

her feet, and the air contained an invigorating crispness and the tang of woodsmoke. For every home she passed, Varina could name the family who lived there, knew how they earned their living, and who their relations were. Such knowledge gave her a sense of belonging and permanence that many never achieve in a life-time. If she went away, even if only for a year, would she feel the same about the town when she returned?

She reached the Episcopal church grounds and wandered into the church, admiring the proudly polished silver communion service presented by George III to the congregation when New Bern had been under the governance of the British Crown. Turning toward Tryon Palace, seat of the first colonial governor of North Carolina, she meandered through the formal gardens. The entire town was steeped in history, even to the very house where she lived, which had served as quarters for Union officers during the War Between the States. Every so often, Andy or Harris would dig up a musket ball or a picket pin in the yard or from behind a panel in the attic. Varina felt herself a part of the flow of history in this place, with deep roots in the sandy soil of the Carolina pine forests.

What would it be like to go from here to a place that had no history? Other than the Indians, the earliest settlers had been on Florida's West Coast for only about fifty years, the same age as Uncle William. Then came a thought even more daunting. What would it be like to go to a place where she had no sense of belonging, where all would be strangers?

As she retraced her steps toward home, Varina pondered over living in a place where she had no relatives, no one to whom she belonged. Andrew and Jamie were related to her by marriage, but that didn't really count. Andrew was a pleasant but faded memory, and Jamie she had never even seen. To whom would she turn for advice or affection? Seven hundred miles was a long way, even by railroad, from those she loved.

Having come full circle in her trek and in her thoughts, she stood on the front steps of the manse and watched another flock of birds headed south, flying so high they looked like tiny dots in a vee formation. Longing for faraway places tugged at her again, and Varina knew that she must spread her own wings and leave this comfortable and familiar nest soon, or she might never leave at all.

With a sharp sadness for all she would leave behind, she looked ahead to the opportunity to help Andrew and Jamie, to travel, and to be on her own with new responsibilities. Then she went inside to tell her aunt and uncle her decision.

Chapter Two

In the following weeks the level of activity in the manse resembled that of a fortress preparing to undergo a seige. William, Mae, and their children made and gathered gifts for Jamie; and Varina, Mae, and the local seamstress worked furiously to prepare her clothes for an indeterminate stay in the semi-tropical climate.

A telegram had been dispatched immediately to tell Andrew of her planned arrival, and his return letter had stung Varina with its bluntness:

Dear William,

My deepest thanks for your quick response to my letter. I have mixed feelings over your decision. I know that Jamie would be happy in the security and comfort of your home and that you would love him as your own, yet I am gratified that he will not have to leave me. As for Varina, I remember only a tall scrawny child with big eyes. Are you certain that she will be able to handle the responsibilities of a difficult five-year-old? If not, I warn you, I will send her and Jamie both back to you.

> Your loving brother,
> Andrew

"There now, dear," Mae consoled her wounded pride. "You've had enough experience in caring for my youngsters that Jamie will be no problem for you. Andrew couldn't have a more qualified person for Jamie's care. And as for Andrew himself, I can assure you that he is in for a surprise."

Varina was standing on a hassock in her bedroom for the final fitting of a forest-green silk gown, and she could see her reflection in the mirror above the bureau. The gown's snug bodice with its high-necked yoke of illusion, tucked and trimmed in cream-colored lace, brought out the healthy flush of her cheeks and the green highlights in her eyes. The skirt, fashionably narrow at the hips and pulled into a modest bustle, widened at the knee into a pleated flounce that accented her tiny waist and trim figure. Her thick brown hair, arranged in a bouffant coronet about her oval face, escaped here and there in rebellious wisps of curls. She turned to see Aunt

Mae watching her with a glow of maternal pride, and she wondered if Andrew would think her pretty.

"That's the last of it, miss," the seamstress mumbled through her mouthful of pins. "When I hem this, your clothes'll be ready." Varina felt the time rushing by to her departure.

That evening the family gathered in the sitting room after supper as had been their custom every Friday night since Varina had come to live with William and Mae as a five-year-old. Andy had been only an infant then, and Varina remembered Mae knitting beside the fire with Andy tucked in his cradle beside her. Uncle William had held his small niece on his lap as he read in his wonderfully expressive voice the stories of Cinderella, Red Riding Hood, and tales of Moses and David from the Bible.

Now the family circle included the twins and Harris as well, and the reading matter, which Uncle William allowed the children to choose by turn, had graduated from fairy tales and Bible stories to poetry and novels. Last week he had finished Andy's request for *Sir Gawain and the Green Knight*, and tonight he began Molly's favorite, *Jane Eyre*. Molly and Margaret, mirror images of one another, sat across from each other like bookends as one held skeins of deep blue yarn draped over her extended hands, and the other rolled it carefully into a ball. Andy toasted pecans, dipped in butter and rolled in cinnamon and sugar, in a wire basket over the open fire, and the spiced butter hissed as it dripped into the burning logs and filled the air with its rich scent. Harris sat with his back against his mother's skirts, staring into the flames.

Varina felt her throat constrict with sadness as she realized that in just two weeks they would all be gathered here as usual, except her, and she thought for the first time her decision to leave home was a terrible mistake. Perhaps it was not too late to change her mind.

Uncle William closed his book quietly after finishing the chapter, and Aunt Mae looked up from her sewing with a smile for her niece.

"These evenings won't be the same without you, my dear." She echoed Varina's thoughts. "In fact, it pains me so to think of your going that I'm almost ready to beg you to stay."

Varina's heart leapt with hope at her words.

"But that would be selfish of me," Mae said. "When I see all of us gathered about like this, I think of Andrew and Jamie so alone and unhappy in the Florida wilderness, and know how fortunate I am. Knowing the happiness your presence will bring them eases the pain of your leaving."

"There now, Mae, it will only be for a year at the most," William reminded her. "Perhaps by then Andrew will have found himself a new wife, or else Jamie will be old enough to leave his father and come live with us for a while. Although I must admit"—he rose to knock the ashes from his pipe into the fire, his back to Varina so she could not see his face—"a year without Varina in the house seems quite a long time indeed."

Varina feared that she would burst into tears of premature homesickness if the conversation stayed on its present course. "Remember the time Andrew brought a special plant for Andy?" she asked.

Andy's face contorted with the memory. "Yes, a stapelia from South Africa. He said it was a man's plant, nothing sissy like violets or lilies. He said I should put it in a sunny window in my room and wait for it to bloom."

"Did it?" Molly asked. "I must have been too little to remember."

"How could anyone forget? The blossom was a huge hairy brownish star-shape, the most evil-smelling living thing I've ever known." Andy laughed at the joke his uncle had played on him. "It took days for the smell to air out of my room. Then I received his letter informing me that the common name for my special plant was carrion flower."

Mae, years removed now from the disgusting odor that had permeated her home, could smile at the memory. "I made you bury it in the compost heap, and when Andrew came again, he was horrified at the demise of his valuable specimen."

They laughed at memories of Andrew until bedtime, and Varina climbed the stairs to her room with emotions battling within her. She turned down the covers on her canopied bed, but knew that sleep would elude her in her present state. After changing into a warm flannel gown, she sat on the window seat, brushing her thick curls and watching the starry sky through the bare lacy branches of the sugar maple. As she thought back over the evening, she knew that leaving home would be the hardest thing she had ever done. Then she thought of little Jamie, five years old, the same age she had been when Mae and William had brought her to the warmth and security of the manse and filled her life with so much love that all the terror she had felt at her parents' deaths had gradually vanished. Even though she had never met him, she felt a growing kinship with the boy, knowing from her own experience what he must be enduring now. A few months to a year away from home was not too much to ask in order to attempt to do for him what others had done for her. She slipped into her familiar bed, at peace once more with her decision.

The following week, while waiting for her wardrobe to be delivered, Varina packed her books. As she handled each well-read volume, she realized what an excellent classical education she had received from Uncle William, studying Greek and Latin as well as a wealth of literature. Seeking out her knowledgeable uncle as he prepared next Sunday's sermon in his study, she asked him about the Florida town where Andrew lived and worked.

"Where did it get its strange name? I've never heard of Dunedin before."

"Andrew writes me that it's Gaelic, the original name of Edinburgh, Scotland. The town was founded by Scots, so you should feel right at home with all the good Scots blood you have running through your veins."

"Dun–ee–din." Varina rolled the syllables on her tongue, their foreign sound conjuring exotic visions. "But how strange for a tropical town to be named after a cold Scottish city. What else has Andrew said about the place?"

"It's really little more than a settlement, less than a hundred people. The commerce there was originally Sea Island cotton, but today there are rapidly expanding citrus and tourist industries, both booming now that the railroad has reached the area. When Andrew first went there, it was so remote that he had to sail down the coast by steamer. It was either that or take an exhausting journey by stage overland through virtual wilderness."

"Thank goodness for the railroad."

They both smiled, knowing her notorious reputation for seasickness.

"You must write me often and tell me all about the place—and especially how Andrew and Jamie are faring. Andrew's last letters have not been at all like him." William's face above his clerical collar was grim. "I'm worried that Theodora's death has caused him . . . Well, I don't know what it's done to him, but I can tell you that he has changed. And he hints of problems with Jamie, but he doesn't say what they are. I need you to find out and let me know

35

if there is any way that I can help him. Will you do that for me, my girl?"

Varina's watched her uncle's anguish over his brother etch deeper lines in an already furrowed brow.

"Of course," she promised, feeling a panic of inadequacy at the task she had set for herself.

The November day of her departure dawned cold and drizzly. As the family waited with her on the station platform, Varina was keenly aware of her connectedness with them and prayed that the miles would not unravel the skeins of affection that bound them close. She hugged each of her cousins to her fiercely, sorry at the last moment for the decision that would take her away from them.

"Ow, Rina, you're breaking my ribs!" Harris protested, trying to act grown up and refusing to be kissed.

Mae, overcome with grief at Varina's going, couldn't speak, but embraced her fervently, then dabbed at her tears with a delicate linen handkerchief.

William, never an outwardly emotional man outside the confines of his pulpit, cleared his throat and blinked away suspicious moisture from his eyes.

"Please remember, Varina, that if for any reason you are unhappy in Florida, you are to return to us at once. This journey is not an exile, but a mission of mercy of your own choosing. If you find that it is a mistake, don't be too proud to admit it. However, knowing you as I do, I believe you are going to have a wonderful time with Jamie and Andrew, and they are certainly fortunate to have you."

Varina suppressed a smile at William's tendency to turn all events into a sermon, hugged Mae once more, and boarded. As the train pulled away from New Bern station, she stayed at the window, waving to the beloved familiar group on the platform until she could see them no more. Then she settled into her seat for the trip to Raleigh where she would change to a southbound train, allowing herself a good cry at leaving home before yielding to the excitement of her journey.

Hours later, when she had disembarked at Raleigh station and was boarding the southbound train, she was startled when a strong hand gripped her arm.

"Allow me to assist you."

The owner of the voice with strong Spanish accents was a tall, strikingly handsome man with dark hair, smoldering eyes like lumps of glittering coal formed deep beneath the pressures of the earth, and a flowing moustache. Had it not been for his speech, he could have passed for any well-dressed, respectable Southern gentleman. But a respectable Southern gentleman, Varina reminded herself, did not force his attentions on young women. The conductor had been there to steady her up the steps of the railway car, so the man's action was not only unnecessary but impertinent.

She chose to ignore his intrusion and went to her seat without a response or a backward look. The stranger, however, was persistent. He followed her down the aisle and took the seat next to her.

"Permit me to introduce myself, *senorita*. I am Estaban Duarte."

The man's smile was warm and his manner charming, but Varina had been firmly instructed by Mae not to talk with strangers. She nodded coolly and turned her back to him to gaze out the window. Duarte, however, was not discouraged.

"*Senorita* Cameron, I am going to Florida on this train, as are you, and surely you can speak a few words to me. I had hoped we might assist one another in whiling away the long monotonous hours of our journey."

Varina turned to him, astonished and frightened that he should know her name and destination. She saw that his eyes held a glint of mockery behind his sauve manner. Angered and afraid, she did not speak, but gathered her bag and book and stepped past him into the aisle, moving toward the ladies lounge to discourage his following her.

There she ran cool water over her wrists and splashed her heated face, hoping to still the trembling that the ominous *Senor* Duarte had caused. How could he know so much about her—and why? When she had stopped shaking and regained her composure, her head cleared and she used logic to banish her fears. Perhaps he had seen a tag on her luggage, or even been at New Bern station and heard someone call her by name. And guessing that she was on her way to Florida was an easy assumption. After reassuring herself that she had nothing to fear from the ill-mannered Duarte, she slipped into a seat in another section of the car. She was engrossed in her reading when a snarling voice at her elbow made her jump.

"I do not take kindly to being ignored, *senorita*. Besides," Duarte added, his voice laden with innuendo, "you should be glad of the protection of an escort. There are many dangers for a beautiful lady traveling alone so far from home."

As he spoke, Duarte had again occupied the adjacent seat. His look was menacing as he leaned toward her, so close that she could see the glint of gold in one of the fillings of his teeth. Furious at his unbelievable insolence, Varina forgot her former trepidation.

"How dare you threaten me! And what right have you to force your company upon me simply because we are passengers on the same train? I don't know where you come from, sir, but here in the South, gentlemen are taught better manners than those you exhibit."

Her fiery temper, a burden that she had struggled with all her short years, rumbled within her like a gathering thunderstorm, ready to unleash itself. Passengers in the other seats had turned to see what was happening, murmuring among themselves over the disturbance, when the conductor interrupted her.

"Anything wrong here, miss?" He looked at Duarte, then to Varina, whose flare of anger was dissipating.

"No, everything is under control, thank you. This gentleman was just returning to his own seat, were you not?"

With more bravado than she felt, Varina threw a challenging look at the intimidating man in the seat beside her. For a passing instant, she thought he would explode with rage. Then he threw back his head and laughed.

"*Si, senor,*" he assured the conductor, "I am returning to my seat." He stood, bowing arrogantly to Varina before he moved away.

"Let me know, miss, if he causes you any problem, you hear?" the conductor insisted.

"Yes, thank you." Varina's heart had begun to beat wildly with fear as she imagined the reaction her outburst might have provoked. She must remember to keep her temper and tongue under better control or she would quickly find herself in circumstances better avoided. Leaning back against the starched white linen that covered the cushion behind her head, she was slowly lulled into relaxation by the monotonous cadence of wheels on the rails. She pushed Duarte from her mind and turned her attention to the passing countryside.

As the train plowed through endless miles of forest and farmland, Varina wondered about her welcome. How different would Andrew be? With the tragedy of his wife's death and the unidentified problems of his small son, he had undoubtedly changed from the fun-loving, carefree young man she remembered.

The piercing whistle of the train roused Varina from her memories, and she looked out to a changing landscape. Georgian marshes, sweeping expanses of waving grasses, threaded by narrow aisles of dark water winding seaward, were barely visible in the gathering twilight. *The marshes of Glynn*, she thought, remembering how Uncle William had often read the poems of Sidney Lanier before the fire on a winter's night. The tranquillity of the scene was like a tonic and her excitement over her journey returned.

Chapter Three

After dozing fitfully through the night, Varina awoke to the conductor's call of Dunedin as the next stop. As she stood to gather her belongings, she brushed against a passenger in the crowded aisle and looked up into Duarte's face. He greeted her with a cold smile.

"So *Senorita* Cameron is stopping at Dunedin, too? How convenient. Perhaps you will grace me with your company yet. I promise you that I will see to it."

With a look that caused Varina to shiver in the heated carriage, Duarte turned and left the train. Shakily, she attempted to thrust him once more from her thoughts, refusing to allow him to spoil the beginning of her first real adventure.

As she disembarked with a number of other passengers, the novelty of her surroundings caused Duarte and even Andrew and Jamie to be forgotten momentarily. The train station was on the eastern edge of the village so small that its entire business district could be seen at a glance. Less than three short blocks to the west the waters of St. Joseph Sound sparkled at the end of a dusty street lined with a canopy of oaks. A general store, a drugstore, a feed store, and stable, all built of rough wooden planking and connected by boardwalks, gave the town a frontier atmosphere. To the east of the train station, the sandy road disappeared into a forest of thick pines and palmetto bushes.

Varina breathed in the morning air, fresh and clean with a hint of salt. Gone was the invigorating chill of autumn, replaced by the moderate warmth of a summer day. Above in the cloudless azure sky, seagulls wheeled and dived, screaming a raucous welcome to the newcomers.

I followed the wild geese, she thought with satisfaction. *I hope I won't regret it.*

Abruptly, she remembered Andrew, and looking for him, noticed a man striding back and forth across the wooden planks of the loading platform above her. Tall, tanned, and well-muscled, he was dressed in riding breeches and a collarless shirt, its sleeves rolled to the elbow. The cordovan leather of his riding boots creaked as he marched up and down, scrutinizing the face of each arrival.

His wide-brimmed hat threw a shadow across his face, but when he turned toward her and the sunlight illuminated the classic planes of his nose and cheekbones and his deep brown eyes, Varina recognized Andrew. Her heart lurched as she saw that he was as astonishingly attractive as ever, even with the dusting of gray at his temples. His formerly jovial manner, however, had disappeared, and a heavy solemnity, foreign to her remembrances of him, had taken its place.

Varina smiled at him in welcome, but his glance passed over her without recognition as he walked to the other end of the platform, still searching. Resignedly, Varina lifted her skirts and climbed the stairs, crossed to the man who was looking west down the main street in his frustrated search for his charge, and placed her gloved hand lightly on his arm.

"Andrew, I'm the one you're looking for."

He turned to her, his eyes puzzled. "What did you say?"

"Andrew, it's me. I'm Mae's niece, Varina Cameron."

"Good God!" Andrew sputtered, looking as if all the breath had been knocked out of him.

Varina's reply caught in her throat as she looked up into Andrew's eyes. For a brief instant they had shone with warmth and approval as well as surprise before the light left them and his face again became expressionless, hard, and impersonal. Varina felt a desolating sense of loss, seeing the Andrew she had known vanish and a cold distant stranger take his place.

"Thank you for meeting me," she stammered, disoriented by his swift change of mood. "I have only this bag"—she held it up for his inspection—"and my trunk."

"Gordie will see to that."

He turned abruptly, calling to a man who waited alongside the platform on the bench of a large wagon hitched to a matched team. The driver was middle-aged with the leather complexion of an outdoorsman and a full red beard spotted with gray. Above his ruddy cheeks his gray eyes reflected good humor. Clucking to his team, he snapped the reins and backed the wagon to the platform, then alighted to assist Andrew in loading Varina's trunk. But first he approached her, wiping his hand carefully on his rough trousers before extending it to her in welcome.

"Aye, lassie, you're a welcome sight. Me and the missis, that's Mr. McLaren's housekeeper, are glad you're here. I'm Gordie Roth, and if there's anything ye need, ye let me know."

The strong burr of his voice would have given away his Scottish origins if his name had not, and Varina was reminded of the many Scots settled in the area. Then the contrast of Gordie's warm greeting with Andrew's impersonal one struck her, and remembering the contents of his letter to Uncle William, she wondered if Andrew had changed his mind about her coming.

Before she had time to further contemplate Andrew's cool welcome, Gordie had loaded her trunk and was ready to assist her onto the wide wagon bench. She looked about for Andrew and saw him already mounted on a gleaming chest-nut stallion that had been tied to the station hitching rail.

"I'll meet you at the house," Andrew called as he turned his horse, which trotted briskly toward the sound.

Varina heard Gordie sigh beside her and turned to see a worried frown on the man's weathered face.

"Dinna fret yourself about him, lass," he assured her. "He's got a lot on his mind. When you've been here awhile, you'll understand what I mean."

With that cryptic remark, Gordie clucked to his team again and the wagon rolled off down the main street that Andrew had taken. As they passed underneath the sturdy oaks that stood before the rough storefronts, people called and waved friendly greetings to Gordie, and the men tipped their hats to Varina. Then straight ahead of them Varina saw the sunlight dancing in explosions of color on the clear waters of the sound. Gordie explained that the flashes of silver that broke the water's surface so frequently were mullet.

"Sometimes the mullet are so thick that the housewives just wade into the shallows and catch them in their aprons."

Varina could not be certain if he was teasing, but she gave the matter little more thought as she turned in every direction to take in the sights of her new home. Stretching ahead into the waters of the sound was a long dock where, as Gordie explained, in years past steamboats and sailing vessels had loaded and unloaded cargoes, passengers, and mail.

"It's quieter now since the railroad came, but that water route used to be our most important link to the rest of the world. And that store there by the water's edge used to be a cotton gin, but a hurricane wrecked it; after that, folks gave up cotton and are growing oranges instead, a good cash crop at a penny apiece. Folks look to get rich with what they call Florida gold."

When they reached the water's edge, he turned the team north on a road that paralleled the shore. Overhead, the road was shaded by massive oak trees; to their left, a variety of seabirds, great blue herons, snowy egrets, and long-billed curlews walked awkwardly about on stiltlike legs, leaving delicate lacy tracks in the sand flats below the bluff. In the distance, about a mile or so away, shimmered a long green island that formed a barrier between the town and the Gulf of Mexico.

"Oh, Mr. Roth, it's beautiful and so wild!"

Varina inhaled the tangy salt air, her body tingling with the intoxicating sense of freedom that she felt in this strange new place.

"Aye, that it is, lass, but look to your right and you'll find yourself back in civilization."

Opposite the water on the bluff road were stately Victorian homes with wide verandas and gingerbread trim, manicured lawns and neatly clipped hedges and flower beds. Were it not for the delicate gray strands of Spanish moss that bearded the wind-gnarled oaks, Varina would have thought herself at home again in New Bern.

"Ye can thank the railroad for these, lass. It has brought craftsmen, builders, supplies, and fine furnishings. Many of these homes are owned by rich folk from the North and Midwest who come down for a few months a year to hunt and sail; others belong to year-round residents. Your Andrew and his Jamie live down at the end of this road—Victoria Drive, it's called, after the queen. But even the McLarens had to live in a rough grove house until the railroad was cut through. But now Fair Winds is a bonnie house."

"Do you live there, too?"

"Fiona and I live in the grove house on the edge of the plantation. Fiona is the housekeeper and I work in the stables and help Mr. McLaren with his plants. And when I have time, I give my brother, Duncan, a hand in his citrus groves. His property is just north of Andrew's."

By now they had passed the last of the elegant homes, and the clipped lawns gave way to a dense undergrowth of palmettos banked by tall pines whose needles carpeted the sandy track that wound along the top of the bluff at the water's edge.

"Does Mrs. Roth take care of Jamie?"

Gordie paused briefly, as though weighing his words before he spoke. "Aye, lass, she looks after the wee bairn as best she can while keeping house, too. He needs a lot of love, poor wee thing, and that Miss Vandemere—" He spat in disgust over the wagon's side.

"Miss Vandemere? Whom do you mean?"

"Miss Cordelia Vandemere." Gordie's mouth screwed up as if he'd just bitten into a piece of bad fruit. "She's Mrs. McLaren's sister from New York. Didna suppose you'd know she was here. She just appeared on the doorstep a week or so ago, trunks and all, announcing she'd come to stay."

Varina experienced a sinking feeling in the pit of her stomach, thinking that with Theodora's sister here, Andrew didn't need her now. Perhaps that accounted for his cool welcome.

If Cordelia was here to care for Jamie, Varina might have to return to New Bern, but the caress of the gentle breeze off the sound and the murmuring it made through the tall pines were like the music of the Lorelei begging her to stay. She was already enchanted by her new surroundings and hoped that she would not have to leave. Being the cheerful product of Mae's upbringing, however, she couldn't stay unhappy for long. She would make the most of her visit, whether long or short, and report to William as he had requested.

Varina's thoughts had distracted her so that she came upon Fair Winds unaware. The road had veered inland and a wide strip of lawn now stretched between them and the sound. Opposite the road, shaded by an ancient oak whose trunk was bigger than the large wheels of the wagon in which she rode, was Fair Winds. Varina caught her breath with delight. The spacious two-story house with its wide verandas on both floors was a tasteful array of wings and gables with large French windows and doors that overlooked the waterfront. The pale yellow clapboards and gleaming white woodwork were complemented by delicate blue blossoms of banks of plumbago. A wide curving walkway of bleached yellow bricks, edged by borders of liriope with pale lavender spikes of flowers, led to the front entrance where Andrew stood awaiting their arrival.

Gordie stopped the team, dismounted, and lifted Varina down to the walkway before climbing aboard once more.

"I'll carry your trunk up to your room, Miss Cameron."

He tipped his hat and smiled, the twinkle lighting again in his soft gray eyes, before driving the team around back to the stables. Watching him go, Varina felt that she had already made one friend in Dunedin.

As Andrew observed from the steps, she stood at the end of the walkway, turning in every direction to take in the beauty of Fair Winds. The wide expanse of clear aquamarine waters to the west, a wilderness of pines and palmettos to the north, and Andrew's gracious house to the east, had an air of serenity and quiet, broken only by the lap of waves upon the shore, the soft rustle of wind in the trees, and the melodic trills of mockingbirds.

She lacked the vanity or self-consciousness to be aware of the picture she presented as she turned from view to view, a slender girl in a trim navy suit, whose crisp white petticoats and shiny black boots peeked from beneath her skirt as she pirouetted on the lawn, her arms flung wide as if to embrace all that she saw. Her cheeks were pink with pleasure and her green eyes danced with excitement. Then she remembered Andrew and stopped short, gathering her composure, smoothing her skirts and adjusting her stylish navy hat before walking with ladylike dignity up the wide brick path.

Her enthusiasm, however, could not be contained, and when Andrew stepped down to assist her up the broad porch steps, it bubbled over.

"Oh, Andrew, how lucky you are to live in such a paradise!"

For a moment, the hard line of Andrew's handsome jaw softened and the look of his old self that she had glimpsed at the station touched his eyes.

"Do you really like it?" he asked as he tucked her arm through his and stood beside her, studying his domain as if seeing it for the first time through her eyes.

"How could anyone not?" Varina said, then wished she could take back the words as Andrew replied, his voice void of any emotion, but chilling in its tonelessness, "Theodora hated it here."

Again, his face closed over like a mask, and Varina felt his body tense beside her as the front door opened behind them and a woman appeared. She was tall and slender with a stiffness to her posture, a suggestion of her inner nature. Her face, with the ice-blue eyes of Theodora and its frame of red hair like spun gold, had all the beauty of a painting by the old Dutch masters, but a rigidness in her expression implied a lack of humor and flexibility. When she spoke, her words themselves were pleasant enough, but the whining nasal quality of her voice gave the impression of a spoiled child. She was dressed in a stylish gown of black bombazine trimmed in velvet, and Varina wondered if she was still in mourning for her sister.

"You must be Varina, Andrew's little niece, who's come to be Jamie's nursemaid."

She extended her hand with such condescension and regal formality that Varina had to suppress the urge to curtsy. Instead, she politely grasped the proffered hand, surprised to find it cold and clammy, even in the moderate warmth of the brilliant Florida morning.

"And you must be Cordelia, Jamie's aunt." Varina smiled, hoping to bend the stiffness of the older woman's manner, but Cordelia had already turned from Varina as if she were not there and was addressing Andrew.

"Now that you've welcomed your guest, Andrew dear, will you take me into town? There are a few things that I need and then perhaps we can have lunch at the Yacht Club Inn."

She smiled up at Andrew, tilting her head first in a most appealing attitude that showed her pretty features to advantage, then turned back to Varina.

"That will give you time to get settled in, won't it?"

Charlotte Douglas

The pseudo-smile that accompanied her words held a message behind it. Here was a woman used to having her way, and anyone who crossed her would be sure to regret it.

"Oh, please," Varina insisted, "don't change your plans on my account. Perhaps Mrs. Roth can show me my room and I can unpack, but I would like to meet Jamie before you go."

At the mention of his son's name, Andrew's face again softened and Varina saw once more the pain in his eyes that she had remembered from his visit to New Bern. Having come from a home filled with openness, love, and laughter, she found the reactions of both Cordelia and Andrew strange, and in trying to understand and interpret their behaviors, Varina felt as if she were struggling with a foreign language. William had been right. Something was very wrong here. A palpable unease hung in the air, unlike anything that Varina had ever experienced in her happy and secure upbringing.

But that feeling disappeared at the arrival of another woman, short and plump, with salt-and-pepper curls escaping a sensible crown of braids on the woman's head. Her blue eyes were merry in a face where lines and wrinkles had been patterned by decades of smiles and laughter. Her blue gingham dress, covered by a dazzling white starched pinafore, had its sleeves rolled to the elbow. With a dusting of flour on one cheek, the woman reminded Varina of Aunt Mae.

"Welcome to Fair Winds, miss." The woman curtsied. "I'm Fiona, and Gordie asked me to tell ye that he has taken your trunk to up to your room. I'll show ye there, if ye want to freshen up after your journey."

"Thank you, Fiona." The pleasantness of the woman's welcome was a gratifying change from Cordelia's coolness. "But I'd rather meet Jamie first." Varina turned to Andrew. "May I?"

Again the hardened mask dropped from his face, and Varina knew that nothing else she could have said would have pleased him more.

"Where is he, Fiona?"

"He's been helping me in the kitchen, sir," Fiona replied, and held open the wide front door for them to enter.

"I'll go up and get my hat and gloves, Andrew," Cordelia said, ignoring the others as they entered the spacious front parlor.

Varina surveyed the room, shocked by its gloomy and depressing contrast to the house's cheerful exterior. Even the air seemed different, for the musty room felt cold and damp after the warmth of outdoors. Her eyes took a while to adjust after the bright sunlight, but gradually she was able to see the dark wooden paneling, the heavy crimson draperies that, even when opened, blocked most of the outside light, and the massive ornately carved furniture, upholstered in shades of deep crimson and bilious jade.

The interior darkness and oppressive atmosphere were a jarring contradiction to the house's handsome and welcoming facade, reminding Varina of a delicate rosebud she had clipped one summer to await the glorious blossoming that it promised, only to find as the perfect petals unfolded a heart diseased and rotting.

That same sense of disease hovered here in the darkened parlor, where the only spot of light was a life-sized portrait of Theodora over the mantel, exactly as Varina had remembered her, cool and aloof in a magnificent white dress. The stark white of the portrait glowed eerily with a phosphorescent brightness in the dim room. Varina's attention was drawn to the only spatterings of color in the portrait, handpainted blue roses on a silk fan that Theodora grasped purposefully in her delicate childlike hands. The elegant fan, a coquettish weapon of feminine wiles with its carved ivory framework and watery blue silk tassels, was an unexpected intrusion of coloration unfurled against the unyielding paleness of her expensive gown. Her silver-blond hair and flawless complexion were also practically devoid of tint, and the coldness of her colorless eyes filled Varina with an overwhelming and inexplicable foreboding.

Fiona followed Varina's glance.

"That was Mrs. McLaren's wedding portrait," she explained, pulling at her apron and shifting her feet as if Varina's inspection of the picture somehow made her nervous.

"She was buried in that dress," Andrew added in a flat emotionless tone.

Once again, Varina was struck by the radical change in Andrew, almost as if the man were two different people, one of whom she thought she wasn't going to like much.

"Jamie's through here, miss."

Fiona, seemingly anxious to be out of the parlor and away from the cold, sad gaze of Theodora's portrait, led the way back through the entrance hall, then into a large dining room, gloomily paneled in the same dark wood as the other rooms. Then they passed through a butler's pantry, and finally into the kitchen, which, unlike the rest of the house, was a bright spacious room with two focal points, a large well-scrubbed wooden table and a tremendous wood stove of black cast iron, crouching hugely against one wall like some strange mythical beast.

The table was awash in the pale northern light of the late-morning sun that streamed through the tall uncurtained windows, forming a brilliant nimbus around the fair hair of the boy who sat there. The angelic child was so small for his age that Varina knew he had inherited his diminuitive physique from his mother. His features twisted in concentration as he assembled bits of pastry dough on a baking sheet to form the shapes of animals. He did not look up as they approached but kept his attention on his task.

"Jamie." Andrew spoke to him in a voice that had lost it tonelessness. It now held both love and an underlying poignancy. "This is Varina, Jamie. She's come to take care of you."

Still the small fellow kept his head of sandy curls bowed over his work, seemingly oblivious to the others. Andrew started to speak to him again, but Varina touched his arm to quiet him and went to the table, kneeling down to the boy's eye level. She experienced an overwhelming wave of relief that Andrew obviously did want her to care for Jamie, in spite of Cordelia's presence, and she vowed to herself that she would give the boy her best care and attention.

"What wonderful animal cookies you're making, Jamie," she said softly to the boy. "This one looks like an elephant and this one a lion."

Slowly, the boy lifted his face to hers, and her heart contracted with pain at the emptiness in the boy's large brown eyes. He looked like Harris had looked at that age, but a Harris with all the spirit drained from him. She tried again.

"I'm not sure what this one is. Can you tell me, Jamie?"

Behind her she heard Fiona gasp. Then Andrew spoke in the same toneless voice as before. "Jamie has not said one word nor made a sound since the night his mother died over a year ago."

Chapter Four

Dear God, thought Varina, *what have I gotten myself into?* She struggled to keep pity for Jamie from showing in her face. Instead, she placed her hand softly against his chubby cheek and smiled reassuringly into the lightless eyes.

"That's all right, Jamie, dear. We'll make up a sign language, like the Indians do, and it will be a great game."

He rewarded her with the barest flicker of expression that never reached his eyes before he returned his concentration to the pastry dough.

"I'll see my room now, if you please, Fiona," she requested as she stood by the table, her eyes still on the youngster.

She hoped she could deal with Jamie's problems with skills she had learned from

Aunt Mae. As for the other problems in the house, they seemed menacing and nebulous, but she'd have to put a name to them before she could expect solutions. Even then, all she might be able to do would be to report them to Uncle William, who had much more wisdom in these matters than she.

"There you are, Andrew." Cordelia stood at the kitchen door, surveying the group with impatience. "If we don't leave now, we'll be late for luncheon at the inn."

The whine in her voice reminded Varina of Theodora years before, and she fully expected Cordelia to stamp her foot petulantly as Theodora had, but Andrew was already moving toward the rear door, calling over his shoulder that he would bring the buggy around front and that Cordelia should meet him there. He exited without a word to Jamie or Varina, but no one else seemed to notice, so Varina accepted his behavior as typical.

Cordelia also disappeared without a word, and Varina saw a flash of disapproval pass over Fiona's face as she watched the woman go. Then her countenance quickly settled back into its pleasant lines.

No wonder Jamie is silent, Varina thought. *People in this household say very little in words, but volumes in other more subtle ways.*

She turned her attention back to Jamie.

"When you've finished with your animal cookies, perhaps you'll come up and help

60

me unpack. I've brought you some presents
from Aunt Mae and Uncle William and your
cousins in New Bern."

Jamie lifted his face and nodded absently,
then climbed down from his chair and went
to the sink where, standing on a low stool, he
painstakingly washed the flour from his small
pudgy hands. Then he wiped them dry on a
clean kitchen towel and once again on the
seat of his short trousers before reaching up
to take Fiona's hand. Still expressionless and
pathetically quiescent, he waited for Fiona
to lead the way. His quietness was a stark
contrast to the rambunctious playfulness of
Varina's young cousins, and her heart ached
for the solemn little boy.

"This way, miss."

Fiona went ahead down a long dim hallway
toward the front of the house and into the
second parlor where the family spent most
of their evenings. Varina followed Fiona and
Jamie up the stairs, stopping on the landing to
admire the view from the broad high windows.
Beneath her stretched a luxuriant green lawn
all the way to the water's edge, and she saw now
what she had not noticed before. At the end of
the brick walk that crossed the road and wound
among the pines and tall palms was a pier that
extended far out into the sound. Docked at its
end was a large sailboat, its sails now furled
and covered, its hatches battened down.

Reluctantly, Varina abandoned the pictur-
esque view from the landing and climbed the

last flight of stairs to the upper hallway. Fiona
had opened the first door into a large but
lightless bedroom above the main parlor, its
waterfront view and the sunlight blocked by
the thick branches of the ancient oak which
cast a pall over the front of the house.

"Mr. McLaren said this was the best room
for ye because it's next to the nursery. Mr.
McLaren's room is just across the hall, and
just past that is Miss Cordelia's."

With bustling efficiency, Fiona opened windows, drawers, and closets for Varina. Varina's
trunk stood where Gordie had deposited it at
the foot of the huge bed with its massive
cherry headboard carved with bows, ribbons,
and roses. The walls, like the rest of the
house, were darkly paneled.

Varina could feel the dark atmosphere of
the house closing in upon her, and she longed
for the bright airy rooms of the manse. Perhaps
the depressing surroundings were a possible
explanation for Jamie's silence. The dark and
oppressive environment was daunting for an
adult, much less a tiny boy.

Varina led Jamie to the bed and lifted him
onto it near the footboard so that he could
watch her unpack. She handed her clothes
to Fiona, who hung them in the cedar-lined
closet or folded them away in the deep
bureau drawers that smelled of lavender
and potpourri. When Varina reached the
bottom of the trunk, she lifted out several
parcels wrapped in brown paper tied with

string and placed them on the bed next to Jamie.

"Go ahead, open them," she encouraged him. "I've brought them all the way from North Carolina just for you."

For a few moments Jamie sat and studied the bundles as if he wasn't quite sure of what to do with them. Then slowly he reached for the biggest one and methodically began to unknot the string. Again Varina was reminded of Harris and Andy, who by now would have ripped the cords with their teeth if necessary and shredded the paper to confetti to get at the contents.

Jamie rolled the string into a compact ball which he set aside before carefully turning back the edges of brown paper. Slowly, he extracted the large stuffed bunny that Mae had lovingly constructed from a good section of a tattered old fur jacket. She had lined the bunny's long ears with pink velvet to match his nose and sewn on bright black buttons for eyes and a large white powderpuff for a tail. For several more long minutes, Jamie sat immobile, simply staring at the furry toy. Then impulsively he grabbed it and buried his face in the soft fur. The other packages were forgotten.

"Come now, laddie," Fiona said as she folded away the last of Varina's belongings. "I'll take ye down for some lunch while Miss Cameron changes out of her traveling clothes."

She picked him up and carried him in her arms toward the door as tenderly as if he were her own child.

"Then you'll have a nice nap while I serve Miss Cameron's lunch. Come down when you're ready, miss."

"Thank you, Fiona, and please call me Varina. I'm not used to formality. And will you have your lunch with me? That way you can tell me some of the things I'll need to know."

Varina nodded toward Jamie in Fiona's arms. Fiona's blue eyes glistened with sudden tears.

"Yes, Varina, I'd like that very much. Thank God you're here now. Ye have no idea what it means."

Embarrassed by her outburst, she turned and hurried down the stairs.

Varina washed the dust of travel from her face and hands, changed into a cool dress of sea-green calico with crisp white yoke and cuffs, and smoothed the tendrils of escaping curls back into place. As she pinned the ivory cameo set in gold that Mae had given her at the throat of her dress, she wished with all her heart that her aunt were there to give her advice. Something was happening at Fair Winds. She didn't need prescience or a gypsy fortune teller to know that. The undercurrents of something dark and evil hung in the air like the Spanish moss upon the trees. Andrew was a changed man, a sour unhappy man, who showed only momentary glimpses of his former self; poor Jamie had been struck speechless; and Cordelia's presence was both unexplained and somehow threatening.

She was aroused from her musings by the sound of Fiona tucking Jamie in for his nap in the room next door. Perhaps during lunch, Fiona could enlighten her.

"Fiona! Where are ye?"

The shout of a masculine voice shattered the quiet of Fair Winds, and Varina heard Fiona running quickly down the stairs toward the kitchen where the voice had originated. Varina followed close behind and entered the kitchen as Fiona was opening the door for a tall, rugged young man, red-bearded and gray-eyed like Gordie. At the sight of Varina, he snatched the battered wide-brimmed hat from his head and nodded politely.

"Varina," the housekeeper said, "this is my brother-in-law, Duncan Roth. He farms the groves north of here."

"Ma'am." The attractive stranger nodded again, the warmth in the friendly gray eyes so like his brother's that Varina felt as if she knew him already.

Duncan turned and picked up a large basket from the back porch and carried it into the kitchen.

"I've brought some early fruit, mostly the Sevilles that you wanted for marmalade, but they're some other oranges there, too. Good for juice."

"Thank ye, Duncan, you're a good lad."

Fiona beamed at her young brother-in-law, obviously fond of him and pleased with his gift. He turned to Varina and smiled with an open and friendly air that Varina found refreshing in the oppressive atmosphere of Fair Winds.

"So you're new to Florida?"

"I just arrived today, but I already love it. It's a beautiful place."

"Have ye never seen an orange grove then?"

"No, besides what I've seen from the train window, I haven't seen anything else except between here and the railroad station."

"Then may I show ye my groves someday?" A shy man, he struggled with conversation, but he was clearly proud of his land.

"Why, yes, I'd like that very much. And thank you for your invitation. You are very kind."

Varina was curious to see as much of Florida as she could, and she had the impression that Duncan Roth would be an excellent guide.

"That's settled then." He sighed with relief as if exhausted by so much conversation. "I'll send word by Fiona to set a time. Good day, Miss Cameron, Fiona."

With another self-conscious nod, he slipped quietly out the way he had come.

"Well I never!" Fiona exclaimed. "If I hadna seen it with my own eyes, I'd never believe it. Shy Duncan actually talking to a lady, much less inviting her on a tour of his land! You've caught his fancy, miss."

"Nonsense," Varina replied. "He was merely being hospitable. And I would like very much to see the orange groves."

"Aye, I'm sure ye will." Fiona's eyes were twinkling.

After lunch, as she sat at the large table in the bright kitchen enjoying a cup of tea, Varina decided the best way to approach Fiona was directly.

"How can I help here, Fiona? Both Jamie and Andrew seem so unhappy. They must miss Theodora very much."

Fiona, her back to Varina as she removed a steaming apple cobbler from the oven, made what sounded like a snort. After placing the dish on a counter by the window to cool, she returned to her seat at the table and took a sip of tea before answering, picking her words with care.

"Mrs. McLaren's death was a terrible shock, but the unhappiness here started long before she died. She was an unhappy person from the start. Her mother had died when she was a wee lass, leaving a grand fortune to Theodora and her sister, Cordelia. Then right after she came to Florida, her father died, and Cordelia stayed in their big house in New York City. I think Theodora always wished she was there with her.

"She hated this place, called it too wild and uncivilized, and she hated the work that Andrew loves and that takes so much of his time. And she drove him to work even harder, because—God forgive me, I know I shouldna speak ill of the dead—when he was at home all she did was nag at him to give up the plantation, to move back to New York. Ye see, because Mrs. McLaren had plenty of money of her own from her parents, she kept telling Andrew that he didna need to work."

Fiona poured them both more tea from a brown earthenware pot, laced hers liberally with milk and sugar, then let it cool as she continued her story.

"What Mrs. McLaren never saw—because she never took the time to look—is that Andrew McLaren needs to work with his plants like most men need to breathe. This plantation is life itself to him. Ask him to show it to ye. You'll see."

Fiona's cheerful features saddened as she stirred her tea and absent-mindedly added even more sugar.

"And as for the wee bairn . . . Ah, that's a tale that'll break your heart. Some women, the good Lord knows, are not meant to be mothers, and Theodora McLaren was one of them. From the moment Jamie was born, she wanted naught to do with him. I've raised the wee lad as if he were my own . . ."

Varina saw the tears well in Fiona's eyes and splash down in wet blotches on her starched white apron before the older woman regained her composure.

"That dear child saved my life. My own lad, Robbie, a fine young man of fifteen, was tall and comely, and good at his studies. He made his father and me proud. He died in the yellow fever epidemic here in 1888, just a year before Jamie was born. I almost went mad with grief and might very well have lost my mind except that the poor bairn whose mother would have naught to do with him needed me."

"Has Jamie always been quiet then?" Varina asked, thinking perhaps his mother's rejection had caused his reticence.

"Jamie is intelligent like his father. He learned quickly na to draw his mother's attention. He was like a wee mouse around her, but with his father and with Gordie and me, well, he was always a normal, boisterous boy."

"Until his mother died?"

"Aye, miss, until that awful night that—" Fiona stopped suddenly, rose from the table, and began clearing the luncheon dishes, her eyes avoiding Varina's.

"Uncle William said that Theodora died of yellow fever."

"Aye, the yellow fever," the housekeeper answered, but with a look of such pain on her kindly face that it made the words seem like hot coals on her tongue. Again Fiona

avoided Varina's eyes as she filled the dishpan with hot water from the stove and began
rattling flatware, scrubbing it fiercely.

Varina knew that the conversation was finished. She was sorry she had brought up
the painful memories of the death of Fiona's
son, but again something unsaid, unexplained
hung in the air. With exasperation, Varina
saw that for every answered question, she
was stumbling upon other mysteries.

She went to the housekeeper and placed
her arm around her plump shoulders.

"Thank you for a delicious lunch, Fiona.
I'll go up now to check on Jamie and perhaps take a nap myself. I didn't sleep well
on the train."

With a repentent look, Fiona turned from
her dishes, her manner open once more. "It's
glad I am that you're here, Varina. There's a
terrible sadness in this house. Perhaps you're
the one to chase it away."

After wiping her tearful eyes with a corner
of her apron, Fiona showed Varina the back
stairs that led from the kitchen to the upper
floor. Varina climbed them quietly, going past
the bedroom which must be Cordelia's, then
into the hall where the nursery and her room
were. The house was a warren of wings
connected by halls, built that way, Varina
assumed, so that all the rooms could have
as many windows and as much exposure to
the cooling effects of prevailing breezes as
possible. Becoming familiar with the twists

and turns of the dark-paneled hallways was going to take awhile.

She tiptoed into the nursery where Jamie slept soundly in his small bed, the fur rabbit clutched tightly to his chest. He was a beautiful child, perfectly formed, with silky blond curls and ruddy cheeks flushed with sleep. He slept peacefully and undisturbed until as Varina turned to leave, he whimpered, a pitiful heart-rending sound from a child who had been rejected by his mother in life and deserted by her in death. Varina returned to the bed, sat upon its edge, and stroked his golden curls, singing softly a lullaby that Aunt Mae had sung to all her children.

Suddenly she had the distinct feeling that there was someone else in the room, watching her, but when she turned to look, no one was there. She went to the door and looked into the hall, but still saw no one. But she realized that in the maze of halls and crannies on the upper floor one could come and go quickly unobserved—but why?

Weariness from her journey and from the perplexing situation in which she found herself overcame her, and she returned to her room to rest, hoping that a few hours of sleep would help her think more clearly.

Confusion and fatigue hung like chains upon her slender frame. Varina drew the heavy draperies to block out the feeble sunlight, turned back the hand-crocheted coverlet, and lay across the wide bed, inhaling the sharp scent of salt mixed with the resinous air of pines as she buried her face in the smooth sun-bleached linens. Exhausted from travel and excitement, she fell immediately into a deep sleep.

But her slumber was anything but restful, filled with nebulous dreams, dark and threatening, taking her anxiously through an unending labyrinth of dark-paneled hallways in which each door opened onto another maze of black passageways, where she was pursued by an eerie spectre in flowing white, who would stop just long enough to stamp a tiny foot and shake her pale curls before taking up the chase again. Finally, the last door that Varina opened led to a wide flight of stairs. As she began to climb, she looked up to see Andrew on the landing, his dark eyes burning into hers, drawing her nearer and nearer, as the white wraith grabbed at her shoulder, engulfing her in cobwebs, trying to pull her back.

Varina attempted to shake the hand that restrained her, but it held firm. She returned to consciousness with a jolt, aware that someone indeed had hold of her sleeve where her arm hung over the bed's edge. Her eyes flew open in alarm, and she found herself looking directly into another pair of eyes, brown and expressionless. With a start, she recognized Jamie, standing only a hand's breadth away from her face, tugging her sleeve to awaken her.

Gratefully shaking away the dregs of her nightmare, she gave him a smile which evoked no response and saw that he still clutched the fur rabbit to him. Then she remembered the parcels he had not opened.

"Have you had a lovely nap, too, dear?" she asked as she rose and stretched, pulling the coverlet back on the bed. "I'm glad you're well rested, because you have more presents to open."

She threw open the curtains, noting there were still a few hours of daylight left. Jamie watched her impassively as she removed a large bulky package from the bottom drawer of the bureau.

"Do you like boats?"

She found these one-sided conversations difficult and was pleased to see him turn and look toward the pier on the sound. Even that minor response was better than none.

"Your cousin, Andy, who is named after your father, loves boats. Every chance he gets, he goes rowing or sailing on the Trent and Neuse rivers near our home. And he made a very special present for me to bring to you."

She took Jamie by the hand, drawing him close to her as she sat in a low slipper chair by the French doors with the parcel in her lap. But before they could attend to unwrapping Andy's parcel, a splash of blue on the marble-topped table beside her chair caught her eye. Spread gracefully across the table top with its blue silk tassels dangling over the table's edge was the distinctive silk and ivory fan that Theodora had held in her wedding portrait. Varina was certain it had not been there when she went to sleep, and thought perhaps that Jamie had found it among his father's keepsakes and brought it to her. She picked it up and held it out to Jamie.

"Did you bring this to me?"

The child looked up at her with empty eyes, registering no response to her question or his mother's fan. Varina, stifling her rising frustration at her inability to communicate with her small charge, folded the fan carefully and laid it back on the table, recognizing it as an object of probable sentimental value that should be returned to Andrew. Then she handed Jamie the package that held Andy's gift.

The child unwrapped the package with painstaking slowness because he refused to relinquish the rabbit. Varina waited patiently as with his free hand he turned back the paper to reveal a sturdy wooden boat with a graceful keel and a canvas sail. A long cord, attached at the bow, was wound about a wooden spindle. He studied the craft with great seriousness, his brow wrinkled in thought as he turned the toy first one way and then another, observing every feature that Andy had added to make the craft authentic, including a tiny rudder and tiller.

While he was deep in his inspection of this new toy, Varina looked about the room and was struck again by the dreariness of the house, thinking that what Jamie needed was sunshine and fresh air.

Chapter Five

"Come," she said, grabbing up the boat and taking him by his free hand. "We're going sailing."

Downstairs, Varina sought out Fiona to tell her that she was taking Jamie with her. She found the housekeeper polishing furniture in the second parlor.

"I'm taking Jamie down to the pier to sail the boat Andy made for him."

Fiona's face reflected her affection for the little boy as she observed him with the cumbersome boat in his arms and the stuffed rabbit jammed beneath one armpit.

"Aye, being outdoors'll do ye good, lad. You're far too pale from staying cooped up with me in this big dark house."

Varina, with Jamie in tow, started for the front door, but as she passed the parlor, the sight of Theodora's portrait stopped her, and she returned to Fiona.

"Jamie brought his mother's fan, the one she's holding in her portrait, to my room, and I left it there. Perhaps you can see that it's put back where it belongs."

Fiona looked at her in disbelief. "That canna be. Ye must be mistaken." Varina was surprised to hear overtones of fear in Fiona's words.

"Don't worry. He didn't harm it. It looks exactly as it does in the portrait, which is why I recognized it."

The plump little woman sat suddenly on the piano bench, as her legs had given way. "Ye dinna understand. It *canna* be the same fan." She looked at Jamie, standing passively while his elders talked. "Get ye on outside, lad. Wait on the front steps for Varina."

She waved weakly at him with one hand while the other clutched her heart, then waited silently until she heard the front door close behind him. Her bright blue eyes were wide with fright when she looked back to Varina.

"It couldna be Theodora's fan. All of Mrs. McLaren's belongings, that fan included, were burned because of the yellow fever. I placed that fan on the fire myself and saw it turn to ash."

Varina felt a shiver of fear before her innate common sense took charge. "There's one way to know for sure. Come with me."

Taking Fiona by the hand as she had earlier grasped Jamie, Varina hurried up the front stairs to her room, pulling the older woman behind her.

"Here it—" She stopped short halfway across the room. "I don't understand." Varina looked pleadingly toward the housekeeper for an explanation. The surface of the marble-topped table by the slipper chair was bare, and Theodora's fan was nowhere in sight.

Fiona backed toward the door, appearing anxious to get away.

"There now, miss, 'tis the long journey catching up with ye. Weariness plays tricks on us all."

She fled from room, and Varina could hear the rapid cadence of her feet descending the stairs. Puzzled by the fan's disappearance, Varina gave the room a cursory search, but the fan was not there. Baffled, but certain there was a reasonable explanation, she pushed the missing fan from her mind, and hurried downstairs to Jamie and his new boat.

Varina and Jamie hurried as fast as his short legs allowed down the wide front steps, along the yellow brick walk, across the road, and onto the pier where the waters of high tide lapped only a foot below the planks beneath their feet.

Together they lay on their stomachs on the dock, slipped the tiny craft into the water, and watched it sail away with the current, slowly unwinding the restraining cord from its spindle. Varina studied the small face close to hers, seeing now and then a flicker of interest in the dull eyes, as Jamie followed the boat's voyage toward the shore. When the cord had played out, they wound the boat back in and began again.

Varina was so absorbed in watching her small charge that she had not heard anyone approach, but a vibration of the plank on which she lay alerted her. She turned to find her nose inches away from a pair of riding boots so highly polished that she could see her reflection in their shine. Looking up, she saw Andrew, regarding the scene before him, amusement tugging at the corner of his mouth.

When she started to rise from her precarious position over the edge of the dock, he reached to assist her, gently lifting her by the elbows as if she were no heavier than a flower. Her toe caught in the dock's rough planking and she stumbled. Instantly, his arms were about her to prevent her from pitching over the edge into the deep water, and his touch went through her like a shock. She looked up to see an unreadable expression on his face and was discomfitted by the intensity of her own reaction to his closeness.

Embarrassed at her clumsiness and confused by her surging emotions, she tore her glance away and began tucking up her hair where it had fallen about her face as she hung over the water.

"I see you've taken up yachting." Andrew nodded at the tiny boat Jamie was winding toward the dock. Again laughter pulled at the corners of his mouth, and this time Varina could not resist smiling in return.

"Andy sent it for Jamie. He carved it himself."

Andrew studied his son, who was methodically winding the cord about its spindle to pull the craft toward the dock; the fur rabbit was wedged tightly under one arm to free his hands. Again Varina could see the love and pain in Andrew's face, and this time he made no effort to hide them.

"I need your help, Varina."

Andrew turned to her with a look of such anguish that she wanted to throw her arms around him to smother his hurt. Instead, taking Jamie by the hand, Varina walked with Andrew to a rugged bench at the end of the dock where they could sit and talk, and at the same time, she could guard Jamie closely against falling into the water.

"Does he swim?"

Andrew shook his head.

"He should learn, living this close to the water. Perhaps I could teach him. Remember how Uncle William insisted that we all learn to swim before he would let us take the boat on the river?"

"Ah, William." Andrew sighed. "If only he were here. My brother is a very wise man, as I'm sure you're aware. His advice in this case"—he nodded toward Jamie—"would be very helpful."

"I agree. However, as 'this case' has ears, perhaps it's better discussed at another time."

"You're right, of course. He stays so quiet that I forget sometimes that he's not deaf, too. Perhaps tomorrow we can talk, after I've shown you the plantation. That is, if you'd care to see it."

"Yes, please. Uncle William has told me something of your work here, and I look forward to learning all that I can about it."

Andrew smiled another rare smile, gratified at Varina's interest.

"I haven't had a chance to thank you for coming," Andrew said. Inexplicably, a stony expression had suddenly replaced his smile. "I'm sure you left many friends and broken hearts behind for this wilderness."

"Many friends and a dear family, but no broken hearts. And I wouldn't have missed this for anything." She gazed across at the long green island that floated like a mirage on the horizon. "This is truly the most beautiful place I've ever seen."

Then she stammered, remembering the paucity of her traveling experiences. "Not that I've been to that many places," she admitted, "but I can't imagine anywhere on earth more lovely than this—clear, sparkling water, an abundance of flowers, lush trees, the changing colors of the sky—" She stopped. "You must think I'm silly."

"Not at all," Andrew said, his demeanor relaxing once more. He stretched his booted feet out before him and leaned back on the bench, locking his arms behind his head. The taut muscles of his legs and arms, thrown into sharp relief against his clothes, reminded Varina of pictures of Michaelangelo's *David*.

"There are many people who feel as you do, and their numbers are growing every day." He spoke with the pride of ownership, but as he continued, his voice was ripe with irony. "The secrets of its beauty and climate are out. A hundred years from now, this state will be overrun with people who have discovered our paradise and are hell bent on ruining it."

He smiled at her again and Varina felt happiness well from deep inside her. What woman could want any more than this, she wondered, a handsome man at her side and a darling child at her feet in the midst of a tropical paradise? Then she realized the foolishness of her thoughts. Neither Andrew nor Jamie was hers, nor was this her home. She could not allow herself to be seduced by circumstances. Her practical side reminded her that eventually she must return to New Bern.

Turning her face toward the island to hide her thoughts and telltale expressions from Andrew, she noticed a thin curl of smoke rising from the trees.

"Look." She pointed and Andrew's eyes followed her gesture.

"Another of the many who have fallen under Dunedin's spell," Andrew said.

"Do you mean someone actually *lives* there?"

"Yes, indeed. And how he came to be there is a fascinating story. Would you like to hear it?"

"Oh, yes," Varina insisted. She saw that Jamie had retrieved his boat from the water and now sat curled at his father's feet, listening intently.

Andrew was also aware of Jamie and adapted his narrative accordingly.

"Once upon a time," he began in the story-telling tradition, speaking directly to Jamie whose eyes were riveted on his father, "a young man named Henry Scharrer was sent by the government of Switzerland to the United States. The dairy farmers of Wisconsin were puzzled, because no matter how hard they tried, they couldn't make cheese that was as delicious as the farmers in Switzerland made. It was Henry's job to find out why. Henry studied the cows in Wisconsin—"

Andrew saw that Jamie's eyes, although still without expression, were fastened on him, so he continued to speak directly to the boy. "They have lots of cows in Wisconsin like our Bluebell, son—and Henry discovered that because the grass that the cows eat is different in Wisconsin from the grass in Switzerland, that naturally, the cheeses made from their milk would taste different."

Andrew shifted forward on the bench, resting his elbows on his knees, his hands clasped before him as he continued. "With that problem solved, young Henry decided he would like to see South America. So he came to Florida to make arrangements. He was taking a sailboat—probably very much like the one you have there—for a trial voyage when a summer thunderstorm came up."

Varina found herself caught up in Andrew's narrative and sat entranced, unaware that her cheeks were rosy from the sun and wind, tendrils of soft curls caressed her neck, and her green eyes danced like sunlight on the water. Andrew appeared distracted when he glanced toward Varina, but turned his gaze back toward the island and went on with his tale.

"The storm was a terrible one. Broad strokes of white-hot lightning split the skies, and the earth shook from the sound of thunder. The wind howled like a mad dog, blowing the boat off course—"

Andrew looked to see if his graphic description was having its desired effect and was pleased to see that Jamie had moved even closer, still absorbing every word.

"Henry knew that if he was to save himself and his boat, he must take shelter. Fortunately, he came upon a bayou, there." Andrew pointed to where the column of smoke still rose from amongst the trees. "And he sailed in for safety. When the storm had passed, Henry found the island so beautiful, he decided to stay. Now he makes a living as a fisherman. He wraps his catch in palm leaves and rows here to the mainland to sell his fish. We will probably have Henry's fish for dinner some night."

As the story ended, Jamie leaned against his father's leg, looking up into his face with an inscrutable expression. Varina felt that she would gladly give all she had just to see the little boy laugh. What was it that he kept locked away within himself? Would she be here long enough to find out? Or would Cordelia Vandemere consider her an intrusion in her sister's house and with her sister's son? Varina jumped, for as if her thoughts had conjured the red-headed woman, she heard Cordelia's voice behind them.

"There you are! Fiona asked me to find you. She says it's time for Jamie's supper."

Her whining voice grated on Varina's ears, but she ignored the irritation, turning instead to Jamie.

"Go with your Aunt Cordelia, child." She stood behind the boy and pushed him gently toward his aunt.

"Don't touch me with your dirty little hands!" Cordelia snapped at the boy as he reached out to her. "And keep that horrid animal away from me." She pulled back her skirts in distaste, leaving a bewildered Jamie standing alone, his hand outstretched.

Varina and Andrew started toward Jamie, but Varina reached him first, knelt beside the child, and embraced him.

"It's all right, Jamie. Aunt Cordelia doesn't know that your hands really aren't dirty or what a lovely animal your rabbit is."

She glared at the older woman over the boy's head, appalled that anyone could treat a child in such a thoughtless manner. Andrew strode off the pier, calling back to them that he would see them at dinner. Oblivious to her own cruelty, Cordelia turned and followed him. Varina hugged Jamie's unyielding little body to her, then took his hand.

"Let's go see what Fiona has fixed for your supper."

* * *

Later that evening, after Jamie had been put to bed, still hugging his rabbit, Andrew, Cordelia, and Varina assembled in the dining room. Andrew's demeanor was again unapproachable, and Varina was struck by the similarity between father and son. Whatever had happened had wounded them both, and neither showed any signs of healing.

Sitting on Andrew's right, Cordelia kept a running patter of small talk throughout the meal, primarily focusing on Dunedin's deficiencies. Occasionally, she would lean coquettishly toward Andrew, placing her hand lightly on his arm and batting her pale lashes at him.

"Do you know," Cordelia's high whining tones filled the room, "there isn't even a decent dress shop any closer than Tampa? Andrew, you simply must take me there to shop. All I can find here are farm implements." She wrinkled her nose as if the words smelled bad.

Andrew sighed, and Varina, feeling sorry for him, changed the subject. "Do you get a newspaper here, Andrew? Uncle William always encourages us to keep up with current events."

"Yes, the *West Hillsborough Times* is quite a good paper. You're welcome to read it."

Cordelia stifled a yawn. Ignoring his sister-in-law's blatant disinterest, Andrew continued, "You'll find distressing news coming from Cuba. The papers have only begun to write about what's happening there, but I've been aware of the situation for a long time. Dr. Rauol Garcia, a friend and fellow botanist, has a villa on Cuba's northwest coast, and he has kept me informed of the growing tension in his country."

Varina saw that Andrew now had Cordelia's full attention and thought it odd that she would be interested in Cuban botanists.

"Natives there are on the verge of rebellion against the cruelties and restrictions of the ruling Spaniards. Rauol fears that there will be some bloody confrontations, but is afraid that it may all end very quickly and with no better results than the Ten Years' War. The rebels have little in the way of firearms or ammunition, although they can fight valiantly with *machetes*, the long knives they use to cut sugar cane."

"What do the rebels hope to gain?" Varina asked.

"The same that they hoped to gain in the war they fought from '68 to '78, which unfortunately, they lost. They want to drive the Spanish out of Cuba. For years the Spanish have been bleeding Cubans dry with taxes that go back to Spain instead of being used for roads, schools, hospitals, and other badly needed improvements in Cuba. The Cubans also find their personal freedoms greatly restricted by their Spanish rulers."

"But do they have a chance against a great power like Spain?"

"Their cause seems hopeless, but already it is gaining support in the United States. After all, Cuba is only ninety miles from Key West, so it is a close neighbor. We can't turn a blind eye to what's happening there."

Varina realized that the Cuban rebellion was a topic to which Andrew had given much thought and had formed strong opinions.

"You don't think we would actually go to war, do you?" Varina experienced a cold fear at the thought of young men like Andy going off to fight in Cuba.

"Perhaps it won't come to that," Andrew reassured her.

"The charming man I met today after lunch in the card room at the club is from Cuba," Cordelia said. "A pity you didn't stay long enough to meet him, too, Andrew. But no matter. He's taken up residence at the inn, so he'll be here awhile. His name is Estaban Duarte."

Varina dropped her dessert spoon and it clattered on her plate. Her face lost its color, and in an instant, Andrew was out of his chair and by her side, chafing her wrists.

"What is it, Varina? You look as if you've seen a ghost."

Embarrassed, she withdrew her hands from Andrew's and carefully took a sip of water from the long-stemmed crystal goblet beside her plate.

"Forgive me, but I believe the excitement of my journey has caught up with me. If you'll excuse me, I think I will go up to bed."

She hurried gratefully from the room, relieved that the others could not see her shaking as she remembered Duarte's menacing glances and threats on the train. Now he was here, settled for a time in Dunedin. Grasping the polished banister of the staircase tightly in an attempt to calm her nerves, Varina tried to convince herself that it was unlikely that she would see Duarte here on Andrew's plantation, or that even if she did, that he was not likely to remember her, but her trembling continued.

As she climbed the stairs on unsteady feet to her room, a wavering light in the parlor caught her eye, and she stopped short, startled from her thoughts of Duarte by the unearthly glow of Theodora's portrait over the mantle, shimmering in the gloom as if it breathed. Her practical nature struggled to bring her racing heart under control and to assure herself that the animation of the portrait was no more than a trick of moonlight.

With more courage than she felt, she continued up the stairs without another glance toward the portrait. Stubbornly, she refused to think of Duarte or Theodora, but focused instead on Jamie and Andrew and the unhappiness that held them both in its grip.

Chapter Six

Varina awakened early the next day to the sound of a mockingbird creating its own small symphony in the spreading oak outside her window, and lay contentedly watching the pale gray light of dawn filtering into the room through the French doors. She had left them open and uncovered the night before to enjoy the novelty of falling asleep to the lullaby of lapping waves upon the shore beneath the bluff.

Propping the large feather pillows behind her head, she observed the progression of sunbeams across the Aubusson carpet as she reflected over her first day at Fair Winds. As Uncle William had feared, something was troubling Andrew. Even if Varina had not been forewarned, she would still have known that he seemed disturbed, not only by the absence of his former boyish enthusiasm, but also by his radical mood shifts in just the few short hours they had spent together. One moment he was open, friendly and charming, the Andrew of her girlhood memories, and then within a space of seconds, an almost tangible malady of spirit descended upon him, and he would withdraw into himself, allowing no one in and very little of himself out.

Perhaps concern for Jamie was a part of that, but it seemed incongruous that worry for his child would cause Andrew to shut himself away from everyone, especially his son. Varina had seen Andrew's love for Jamie during his storytelling the day before, but throughout the episode, she had felt Andrew struggling to be himself, preferring to stay behind the protective walls he had erected. What would cause a man to hide himself so? Had he loved Theodora so much that her death had devastated him to the point that he could no longer face life fully?

And Jamie. Why his unnatural silence, his own pitiful withdrawal into himself? According to both Andrew and Fiona, Jamie's silence had begun the night of Theodora's death, but Fiona insisted that Jamie had been virtually ignored by Theodora, so why would her dying affect him so drastically? Or was his behavior a purposeful imitation of his father's? Varina sighed.

There were too many unanswered questions hovering over this household, and they all led back somehow to Theodora, the spoiled petulant young woman, whose restless spirit even now seemed to haunt those who lived at Fair Winds. Some part of the puzzle was missing, and until she found what it was, Varina was afraid that she could be of little help to Jamie or his father.

As she thought of puzzles, she thought of Cordelia. Why was the woman here? And why now rather than immediately after Theodora's death? Varina had assumed that Cordelia had come to care for Jamie, but her treatment of the little boy yesterday on the dock indicated, at best, a lack of sensitivity to him, and at worst, an actual dislike of the child. As for her relationship with Andrew, last night at dinner Cordelia's manner toward Andrew could only be termed flirtatious. Varina sat upright at the thought that Cordelia might have come to take her sister's place at Andrew's side.

The thought of Cordelia as Andrew's wife distressed Varina, and with a sudden clarity of vision, Varina saw herself falling in love with Andrew McLaren. She remembered how his mouth had curved with amusement when he had found her face down on the docks yesterday, how his touch had seared through her when she stumbled against him, how the lines of his face had softened as he had observed his son, and how his strong gentle hands had chafed her wrists at dinner last night.

Was this what it was to be in love, a catalog of all the expressions, words, and actions to call up from memory and savor over and over again? Or was her preoccupation with Andrew merely a revival of her childhood memories?

You are being ridiculous! she scolded herself as she threw back the covers and climbed out of bed. The practical side of her nature that Aunt Mae had cultivated so carefully took control, telling her that she was enchanted by new surroundings and new experiences and by the mystery of Andrew. Once she acclimated herself and found a way to help heal the hurt that both Andrew and Jamie wore like a banner, the romance of the situation would fade.

Feeling more like her old self with romantic nonsense thrust aside, Varina bathed, dressed in a crisp white shirtwaist, her brown twill riding skirt and boots, and braided her thick hair, pinning it to the crown of her head. She caught sight of herself in the cheval glass and nodded with approval. She would not embarrass Andrew when they inspected his plantation today. She was not as elegant as Cordelia, but she would do.

After hastily making her bed, she grabbed her riding hat and gloves and slipped quietly down the front stairs. The tall case clock in the front parlor was chiming seven o'clock as she made her way to the kitchen. Fiona had been there well ahead of her. Varina could smell the savory odors of coffee brewing and bacon frying. Gordie had been seated at the table, awaiting breakfast, but he sprang to his feet as Varina entered.

"Don't get up on my account, Mr. Roth," she insisted. "I refuse to be treated as company. I'm here to help." She turned to Fiona. "Put me to work, please. My aunt would be horrified if she found I wasn't doing my part."

The kindly Scotswoman smiled, her face radiantly red from the heat of the woodstove where she stood over a cast-iron skillet. She nodded to the large table where a juicer, pitcher, and basket of oranges stood.

"If you've a mind, ye can squeeze the orange juice. There's a large knife—"

But Gordie had already found the knife and handed it to Varina. She selected an orange from the basket, admiring its golden color, placed it on the table, and sliced it expertly in half. The two halves fell apart, and Varina stared at them with a terrifying sense of unreality, a scream of horror freezing in her throat. Oozing from the center of each half were brilliant drops of blood. She let the knife in her hand fall to the table and felt the room begin to circle around her, growing darker.

Gordie's voice close by her ear and his strong arm about her, guiding her into a chair, helped to revive her.

"Good Lord, woman, are ye daft? Did ye na warn the lass? Na wonder she's taken such a turn."

He had snatched up a clean tea towel and was fanning Varina's face with it. Fiona was beside her with a steaming cup of coffee.

"Drink up, lass, it'll do ye good."

Varina took a long drink of the hot black brew and made a face, unused to coffee without sugar or cream. As soon as the room stopped spinning, she looked back to the orange on the table to be sure she had not been hallucinating. Gordie followed her glance, picked up the two halves, and held them for her inspection.

"They *are* bleeding," she muttered in amazement, looking incredulously to Gordie for an explanation.

"Na, na really. It only looks that way. This variety of orange has an inner pigmentation that looks like blood, but it's just its color—like a pink grapefruit. It's a delicious fruit for juicing, but it does give a body a start if she's seeing it for the first time. Dinna feel bad. I've seen grown men faint when they cut into one of these unaware."

Gordie handed her cream and sugar as he finished his lecture on citrus, then returned to his breakfast.

"I'm sorry I didna warn ye," Fiona said. "I'm so used to blood oranges now that I forget what it's like for someone slicing into one of them for the first time."

"I feel so foolish," Varina admitted. "I've never been one to faint at the sight of blood. It must have been the unexpectedness of it that affected me. You must admit, it *is* unlikely for an orange to bleed."

"You may see stranger things than that if you stay here long enough," Fiona remarked, but Varina had experienced enough unsettling for one morning, so she asked for no further explanation.

Gamely, she picked up the knife and shakily resumed the task of extracting juice from the oranges for breakfast, soon filling the pitcher with the golden liquid tinged with pink. As she was washing her sticky hands, a sleepy-eyed Jamie wandered into the kitchen in his nightshirt, and Varina took him back upstairs to dress.

"Bring him back to the kitchen for his breakfast. Miss Cordelia doesn't seem to care for his company at the table," Fiona instructed with a hint of acid in her voice.

When they returned to the kitchen with Jamie washed and dressed, Gordie had left, but Duncan Roth was waiting. In his arms he held the largest bouquet of flowers Vanessa had ever seen. Some of the blossoms she recognized, such as the delicate yellow and pink tea roses and the dazzling blue agapanthus, but there were varieties of day lilies, daisies, and other exotic blooms she had never seen before.

"These are for you, Miss Cameron," he said, thrusting them toward her. "I thought you might like some color in this dark house."

"Thank you. They are beautiful—and unusual." She buried her nose in the bouquet, breathing deeply the mixed perfume, then extended the flowers before her to admire their beauty. "What are these large peach-colored daisies?"

Duncan lost his shyness when discussing flowers. "Those are Transvaal daisies, all the way from South Africa. Andrew knows I like flowers, and when he gets new seeds or cuttings, he lets me have a few for my garden."

Fiona went into the butler's pantry and returned with a tall vase of cut crystal, filled it with water, and handed it to Varina.

"These will be lovely in my room." Varina smiled at Duncan. "And you're right—they will brighten it up."

She sliced the ends of the long stems, expertly arranging the flowers as Aunt Mae had instructed her. When she came to a particularly fragrant blossom, she held it out for Jamie to sniff, which he did with all the seriousness and deliberation of a connoisseur before returning to his oatmeal. As she worked, Duncan sat at the table, drinking a cup of coffee and watching her assemble the floral arrangement.

"You do that very well." He caught her eye with a look of approval.

"Thank you. I've had lots of experience with flowers. My Uncle William is a clergyman, so often Aunt Mae and I were responsible for arranging flowers in the church. It's something I learned early and have always enjoyed."

She tucked the last of the long-stemmed roses into the bouquet and stood back to admire her creation with satisfaction. The magnificent blooms created an elegant millefleurs arrangement, European-style.

Duncan drank the last of his coffee, then stood twisting his wide-brimmed hat in his big strong hands, reddened and freckled by sun and hard labor.

"I came to ask if you'd like to see my groves today." His words came out in small explosions, a self-conscious effort for the large gentle man.

"I would like that very much, but I have already promised Andrew that I would inspect his plantation with him this morning."

Illogical guilt swept over Varina at Duncan's look of disappointment.

"But I would enjoy seeing your groves tomorrow, if that's convenient," she added, happy to see him smile with pleasure at her answer.

"Aye, tomorrow it is then. Perhaps after lunch while the wee lad is napping?"

"After lunch will do nicely. And thank you again for these lovely flowers."

He nodded, crushed his hat upon his thick red hair, and was gone.

Fiona shook her head in amazement. "You've worked a miracle with that 'un," she clucked. "In all the time I've known Duncan Roth, he's never had the time of day for anything except his groves and flowers. You've turned his head, miss."

"I'm sure," Varina insisted, "that he's only being neighborly."

"Then why didna Cordelia Vandemere get flowers and an invitation last week when she arrived?"

Varina had no answer for that, so she picked up the heavy vase and started toward her room. The bouquet was so massive that she could not see and had to move up the stairs slowly, a step at a time. When she reached the landing, she found

Andrew standing there, waiting to descend.

"Very pretty," he said tonelessly, his face once more set in its rigid planes.

"Yes, and good morning to you, too, Andrew."

Varina gave him her brightest smile. She refused to let his moodiness infect her.

He seemed taken aback by her reply, then slowly the lines of his face softened. "You should always have flowers, Varina. Here, let me carry them."

He took the awkward burden from her hands and preceded her up the steps and into her room, where he placed the vase on the marble-topped table. The brilliant colors of the flowers glowed like flames in the gloomy room. Andrew looked about.

"Do you have everything you need? I have trusted Fiona to take care of things."

"Fiona has been wonderful, and the room is perfect, except—"

Varina bit back the words she had been about to say. Growing up in the manse, she had become used to speaking her mind. She would wait for another time to talk to Andrew about making the rooms brighter for Jamie's sake.

"The room is perfect."

"I see you're dressed for riding this morning. Are you sure you are recovered from your journey enough to tour Fair Winds with me?"

Andrew stood with his back to her, gazing out the French doors across the sound, so she could not read his face. Did he regret his invitation of the day before? Even if he did, Varina needed to have him to herself so that she could discuss Jamie with him.

"I slept wonderfully well, and I'm anxious to see all that you've been doing here. The little bit I learned from Uncle William sounds fascinating. And we do need to talk about Jamie," she added honestly.

Andrew turned and offered her his arm. "Then may I take you down to breakfast? We'll start our inspection as soon as we've eaten."

Varina linked her arm in his and together they went down to breakfast, neither noticing a dim figure in the hall's recessed alcove who watched with a malevolent smile as they descended the stairs.

Chapter
Seven

After breakfast Varina and Andrew stood on the back veranda surveying a part of Fair Winds that she had not yet seen. In a wide grassy area Adirondack chairs and low tables were shaded by oaks and low sheltering branches of camphor trees. Through this lawn ran a wide yellow brick path that branched in one direction to the fenced kitchen garden, heavy now with the crop of fall vegetables, and in the other toward the stables and other outbuildings. Beyond these lay the road to Andrew's plantation, acre upon acre of experimental plants as well as specimens of native flora.

The morning was still young. Trees, shrubbery, and buildings alike sparkled with rainbows of color as sunlight struck their overlay of heavy dew. The quietness, the peacefulness of the setting was as Varina had always imagined Eden. And no sooner had she thought of that garden than the image of the serpent also entered her mind, and she wondered what evil dwelled in this place, a subtle presence whose hurtful influence could be seen in both Jamie and Andrew. Shivering at her thoughts, she saw Andrew ahead of her, striding toward the stables, and she rushed to catch up.

"Good morning again," Gordie greeted her as he led out a docile bay mare, already saddled, for her tour of Fair Winds. "It's good to see the color back in your cheeks."

She placed one booted foot in the laced fingers that he offered, and he lifted her up toward the stirrup.

"I hope any other surprises today are more pleasant ones." Varina smiled down at the rugged little Scot, feeling he was the one real friend she had in this strange new world. Then settling in the saddle, she took the reins he handed up, and nudging the gentle bay with her knees, followed Andrew on his chestnut stallion from the stables.

"Andrew's plants will be a very pleasant experience, I'm sure, lass," Gordie called after her.

The sandy road that led into the plantation was wide enough for two to ride abreast, and for a while they walked the horses in silence, listening to the birdcalls, the jingle of horses' tackle, and the ubiquitous soughing of wind in the branches overhead. The path itself, thick with pine needles, was dappled with shadows as the rising sun pierced the foliage above.

Andrew reined in his horse and sat quietly, motioning for Varina to do the same. Her stillness was soon rewarded as several young white-tailed deer crossed the path ahead on their way to the hammock to drink fresh water from the creek.

"Has Cordelia already seen the plantation?" Varina asked when the deer had disappeared.

"I invited her to come with us this morning, but she says she hates the out-of-doors and has no desire to see my bunch of sticks and twigs, as she calls them. I forget that not everyone is as interested in my work as I am."

"She is denying herself a great deal." Varina shifted in the saddle, surveying her surroundings with interest and delight.

"This is the section of the land that I've kept in its natural state," Andrew explained. "All the trees, shrubs, and flowers that you see here are Florida natives. That wild magnolia, for example, and this stand of maples whose leaves won't change for another month, dropping just in time for new ones to bud out. And, of course, there are the ever present palmettos. When we cleared for the plantation, we first had to burn them off, then dig the roots out one by one. Even so, it's a constant battle to keep them from reclaiming the land."

Varina felt as if she were the first human to enter this natural glade.

"It's an enchanting place. It reminds me of the

'forest primeval' in Longfellow's *Evangeline*.

"Yes, this is all much as it has been since the beginning of time. But don't be fooled. Emerson said, 'Nature never wears a mean appearance.' But nature also, underneath all that beauty, can be very deadly."

"Deadly? How?" Varina was unwilling that anything spoil this tropical Eden.

"As perfect a paradise as all this seems"—he waved his arm to encompass Fair Winds—"you must remember that there are always dangers lurking. Poisonous snakes, spiders, and scorpions, for instance, and stinging nettles that produce nasty welts, and plants and berries that can kill if you eat them, not to mention the clouds of mosquitoes eager to devour you with needlelike bites."

Andrew stopped for a moment as if distracted by his thoughts, and Varina thought of Theodora and Robbie Roth, both dead from fever. No wonder Andrew was preoccupied with danger.

"And that's only the beginning," he continued. "There are undertows and strong currents in the sea, storms with incredible lightning and killing winds—"

"Stop, please, I concede." Varina laughed nervously. "It is too pretty a morning for such a dreadful litany of disasters. If I promise to be careful, may we discuss less gloomy topics?"

"I'm sorry." Andrew appeared slightly embarrassed by his monologue. "But I can't say that I didn't mean to frighten you, because that was my purpose exactly, to frighten you enough that you will be very careful here."

Andrew's eyes burned with a fierceness Varina had not seen before, and she felt again the lurking evil, the unnamed danger that hovered over Fair Winds, and fear traced a cold finger down her spine.

"You must watch where you step. Check the weather when you go out. Shake your shoes for spiders and scorpions before you put them on. All these little precautions and more must become habit if you are to survive here. This is a magnificent land, with beauty unlike any you will ever see, but you must remember that things are not always as they appear. Will you promise me that you will be careful?"

Varina remembered the blood oranges and the mysterious appearance and disappearance of Theodora's ivory fan, which she had forgotten until now in all the excitement of her new surroundings, and acknowledged that often things were not as they seemed. Was she seeing reality where Andrew and Jamie were concerned, or would she have to look through the mists of illusion to find the answers to her puzzle? She came out of her reverie to find Andrew awaiting her reply.

"Yes I promise," she answered, humbled by his concern for her well-being.

They rounded a bend in the path and there before them were the heavy wooden gates to Andrew's plantation set in a wall of building material which Varina had never seen before.

As they drew closer, she could see that the pink tinge of the mortar came from thousands of tiny shells that had been mixed in the sand used for its construction.

"Those are coquina shells," Andrew informed her. "The shells give the mortar strength. And their inhabitants make a very good soup—very handy creatures."

The wall, so tall that they could not see over it as they sat on horseback, stretched away from either side of the gate as far as Varina could see. Tumbling over it in a profusion of verdant foliage and magenta blossoms were vines of bougainvillaea.

"The Gates of Paradise," Varina quoted. "Where's the angel with the flaming sword?"

Andrew didn't hear her question, for he had dismounted and was unlocking the padlock on the heavy gates and pushing them back on well-oiled hinges.

"Why the walls, Andrew? Do you have a problem with thieves?" Varina asked as she walked her horse through the open portal.

"No, not thieves. It's hogs that are a problem."

"Hogs? Wild ones?"

"Only in the sense that they run wild. Dunedin is still an unincorporated town, so there are no statutes requiring owners to keep their hogs penned. As a result, many of the animals root about in other people's gardens, cause a great deal of destruction, and generally make a nuisance of themselves."

By now Andrew had the gates secured behind them. He tethered the horses, and they turned to walk the wide paths of the plantation.

Varina had never seen such beauty. Andrew had formed the beds in curves and clusters so the plants were arranged, not in rectangular beds as in commercial production or more formal gardens, but like a gracious English garden. Paths wound among beds of flowers and shrubs banked in ascending height at the feet of various tree specimens.

The first beds were masses of deep lavender Madagascar periwinkles, plumbago, and wax myrtles. Next were Transvaal daisies in red, yellow, and orange, planted about shrubs of ixora, "flame-of-the-wood," with deep red-orange clusters of blooms. These were grouped about a tree fragrant with blossoms that Andrew identified as loquat, which bore summer fruit much like an apricot.

Andrew proudly named each flower, shrub, and tree and gave their origins. The exuberant young man who had held his brother and his family spellbound with his adventures had returned, and Varina was poignantly aware of how much she had missed him.

As they walked along the paths beneath the brilliant azure of the cloudless autumn sky, Varina was spellbound, not only by Andrew, but also by the exotic beauty that surrounded her. Here were borders of colorful kalanchoe, hibiscus with delicate blossoms from shades of white and yellow to deepest red and pale pink.

Wedelia with dense glossy leaves and delicate yellow daisies and shrubs of allamanda with saffron trumpet flowers grew about the base of Jerusalem Thorn, a tree of dainty yellow blossoms, feathery foliage, and vicious spines.

Andrew pointed out varieties of palm trees—Senegal date, cabbage, Washington, and others whose names were too numerous for Varina to remember, as well as sea grapes with large flat rounded leaves, multicolored crotons, oleander, beds of amaryllis and wandering jew. Along one wall, espaliered vines of pyracantha, their berries now ripe and red, attracted hungry cardinals and mockingbirds.

"These take my breath away. How did you manage to collect them all?"

"We botanists have a horticultural exchange program, a network of scientists all over the world who exchange both knowledge and plants with one another. Many of these were sent to me by colleagues. Others, like this Moreton Bay fig from Australia, were given to me by Thomas Edison, the inventor. He has quite a botanical collection of his own in Fort Myers, about a hundred and fifty miles south of us. I visit there from time to time on my way into the Everglades to look for new specimens."

"Thomas Edison—the one who invented the light bulb and phonograph—grows plants?"

"Yes, the very one. Horticulture holds a fascination for him. And no wonder. Look at this tree that I grew from a seedling he sent me. Its Latin name is *hura crepitans* and it's from South

America, but it's more commonly known as the 'dynamite tree.' "

"How did it get an outlandish name like that?" Varina examined its bark which was completely covered with sharp thorns.

"When its tomato-like fruit is ripe, it explodes violently, showering seeds as far as four hundred feet."

Varina regarded the tree with respect; then the colors of another caught her attention.

"And this tree. It looks like a mimosa, but those salmon-colored seed pods are something I've never seen before. What is it?"

"You should have seen it a few weeks ago. Before those rosy panacles formed, the tree was a mass of bright yellow flowers whose tiny petals shower to form a colorful carpet, and so its name, golden rain tree."

"A poetic name, but it fits." Varina hardly knew where to turn or what to ask next. Her eye was caught by a strange plant with fleshy stems like thick sausages with clusters of leaves at the stem ends. "What is this?"

"That is a plant whose flowers are as magnificently scented as its branches are ugly. It's a frangipani, a native of the Caribbean, one that Rauol Garcia sent to me from Cuba."

Andrew was the most happy and relaxed that Varina had seen him since her arrival. His love of the plants that he grew and tended was evident not only in his voice but also in the gentle way that he handled each leaf or flower, carefully extracting weeds from the beds that they passed or trimming back dead blossoms.

They spent most of the morning ambling along the pathways with Varina asking questions and Andrew supplying answers, enjoying his apt and interested pupil.

He pointed out the plants and trees with commercial value: cinnamon, bananas, camphor, mangoes, guavas, an orchid from which vanilla could be extracted, tea and coffee plants, bamboo, bay, and rubber trees. But most of his plants were ornamental in nature, grown only for their aesthetic value, some for their spectacular flowers, such as the purple jacaranda and scarlet royal poinciana, while others, like the gardenia and frangipani, were valued for their fragrance.

"These rather pedestrian bushes will be flamboyant in about four weeks." Andrew indicated a bank of plants located on a sunny expanse of the plantation wall. "They are poinsettias and the bracts at the end of each stem will redden into magnificent blooms around Christmastime. This plant was first brought to this country from Mexico by a South Carolinian named Poinsett, and the plant now bears his name."

Varina was delighted. She had always enjoyed gardening with Aunt Mae, but a garden of this scope was a wonder to behold, a stimulation to her senses and her inquisitive mind.

"How lucky you are to have this as your work, surrounded everyday by all this beauty. I would think you must be the happiest man—"

Too late Varina halted her words, remembering that Andrew was far from being a happy man. Afraid to look at him for fear that his stony expression had returned, she turned instead to another question.

"What is that?" She pointed to a long low building, its roof a thatch of dried palm fronds.

"That," Andrew explained, "is our potting shed, where we start seeds that we've been sent, and pot cuttings and do air layering for propagation. Some of the seeds and seedlings are sold, others we plant here."

They were walking closer to the shed now, a building open on all sides, containing long tables, bins of potting soil, mulch, and compost. Almost half of the building was stacked high with logs.

"Those logs," Andrew explained, "are something that I hope I do not have to use." His expression had turned grim.

"Why? What would you use them for, except firewood?"

"That's it—firewood. Although we live in a semitropical climate here, occasionally Mother Nature gives us the unpleasant and unexpected surprise of incredibly cold temperatures. Many of my plants cannot survive below forty degrees. Without some protection, most of them will die if the temperatures dip below freezing."

"Just one night of cold could erase over seven years of work?"

Andrew nodded. "Those logs are my insurance policy. If the temperatures drop too low,

113

then we'll come out here and begin stacking logs for bonfires. And if the horrible moment occurs when it looks as if a freeze is on its way, then we'll light the fires and keep them burning until the weather warms or we run out of logs—and we'll pray a lot."

Varina pictured the plantation with its paths filled with roaring fires burning through the night, a transition from paradise to inferno.

"Duncan Roth will be in even worse shape than I if a freeze comes," Andrew was saying. "He has hundreds of acres in grove and it would be impossible to protect so large an area."

The distress on her face was apparent, and Andrew attempted to reassure her. "Don't worry. For as long as I've been here, we've never had a bad problem with the weather. As I said, the logs are like an insurance policy—one which I don't plan to cash in."

By now the sun was high overhead, and Varina could hear the creakings and jinglings of an approaching wagon. Through the wide plantation gates rode Gordie with Jamie perched beside him on the wide wagon bench. With one hand Jamie clasped Aunt Mae's furry rabbit to his small chest; with the other, he clung to the wagon bench.

"Fiona sent ye a picnic," Gordie called to them as they approached the wagon. "She knew once ye started talking about plants, ye'd be here awhile."

He lifted a large hamper from the wagon bed as Andrew helped Jamie from the wagon.

The boy, smartly dressed in short pants and a middy sailor blouse, showed no expression, no welcome or even recognition of his father, no interest in his surroundings. Docilely, he held his father's hand, waiting to be told what to do.

Gordie leaned toward Varina as he placed the hamper before her. "That Miss Cordelia"— he made the name sound like an obscenity— "doesna like the bairn underfoot, so I brought him along," he whispered.

"What's that?" Andrew asked.

"I was asking the lass if the plants were as good as I promised," Gordie replied without missing a beat in the conversation, but without looking at his master either. He returned to the wagon for a large tartan blanket.

"Where would ye like this?"

"Over in the shade of the golden rain tree on that bit of lawn would do fine," Andrew instructed him.

Gordie spread the plaid robe on the shaded grass and carried the hamper to it. "Unless there's aught for me to do, I'll go back to the house. I'll come for the lad after lunch."

"Thanks," Andrew called after him. "And thank Fiona, too."

Andrew reclined on the tartan, propped on his elbow, with Jamie sitting cross-legged beside him, while Varina knelt beside the large hamper and removed the picnic lunch. The open air and exercise had given both adults an appetite, and Jamie, as always, obediently ate whatever was placed before him. There were great crusty pieces of fried chicken, still warm from the skillet, huge garden-fresh, acid-sweet tomatoes, crisp pickles, and hunks of spicy gingerbread, accompanied by flasks of cold tea and one of milk for Jamie.

As they ate, Varina pointed out a grotesque vine, a gray-green, ropelike cactus, growing profusely up one of the cabbage palms.

"Everything here is either utilitarian or ornamental," Varina remarked, "but that is one of the ugliest plants I've ever seen. What is its purpose?"

"That's a cereus, also from Mexico. It may seem unsightly to you now, but come nightfall in June, for a period of a few hours each night, the vine produces enormous exotic white flowers the size of dinner plates that glow like the moon. Then at daybreak they drop to the ground and are gone."

The reference to moonlight reminded Varina of Theodora's portrait the night before, and the hideous vine, night-blooming bearer of great beauty, was another reminder of illusions and deceptive appearances. Here she sat with Andrew and Jamie, leisurely enjoying an *al fresco* meal, a tranquil scene of domesticity to the casual observer. But again this, too, was an illusion, for Jamie could not or would not speak, Andrew was lost once more in his dark thoughts, and Varina, neither wife nor mother, but a country cousin from the Carolinas, had no help for either.

But she had no time to dwell on the dilemma,

as Gordie soon came to return Jamie to Fiona for his nap and to gather the remains of the picnic, and Andrew and Varina set out to inspect the remainder of the plantation.

Passing a stand of weeping figs, Varina saw a patch of ground the size of an average room enclosed by a stockade fence of three-foot pickets. Inside the fence the ground was carefully raked and bare with signs of recent burning. Had there been a monument or tombstone, the area would have resembled a funeral plot. Andrew walked past without glancing at it, but Varina held back, fascinated by the barrenness of the patch in the midst of such fecundity.

"Wait," she called. "What is this?"

He turned, and when he saw the barren plot, his face darkened, his body tensed, and his breathing sounded labored, as if he could not get enough air. His reaction terrified Varina, who had never witnessed such contolled anxiety. When he spoke, the quietness of his words was a terrifying contrast to the magnitude of his suppressed agitation.

"*That* is an experiment that failed, and I will say no more about it."

He turned, striding away, unable to hide his inner turmoil created by whatever memories the spot had evoked, leaving her standing alone on the path, staring at the scorched earth.

Chapter Eight

Varina watched Andrew's retreating back, then hurried down the path after him, her usual self-confidence badly shaken. She was dealing with a situation that she did not understand. Andrew's behavior was foreign to her, and she was unsure of how to respond to it. She was frightened by it and afraid to aggravate it, knowing that if she alienated him, she would have no chance of understanding him, and at this moment Varina wanted more than anything to understand the hurting, handsome man who strode away from her.

"Andrew, please wait," she called, running after him up the path. Her foot hit an uneven spot and her ankle twisted, pitching her forward with a thud and a cry of surprise.

Andrew turned to find her sprawled face down in the sand and mulch.

"Varina!" He returned to her, looking remorseful and reaching to help her to her feet.

She stood tentatively at first on the twisted ankle. Then finding it sound, she gave her attention to retrieving her hat, which had flown away as she fell, and removed bits of mulch from her hair and clothing.

"I must look like a scarecrow." She laughed as she pulled wisps of straw from her sleeve.

Andrew had gone back up the path to the large water barrels that stood ready for thirsty plants, dipped an oversize handkerchief in the nearest one, and returned, wringing the excess moisture from the linen square.

"Are you sure you're not hurt?" He held her chin gently between his thumb and forefinger, cleaning the dirt from her face as he would a child's.

"Only my dignity," she assured him, because, in truth, the sandy soil had cushioned her fall and all she had suffered, besides having the breath knocked from her, was surprise. She was glad, however, that the diversion had cleared away his agitation.

"Perhaps now is a good time for us to talk about Jamie," she suggested, satisfied that she had harvested as much of the debris as possible from her clothing and hair.

Andrew nodded and returned to the golden rain tree. He gathered up the tartan robe that Gordie had left behind and took it to the potting shed, where, shaded from the early-afternoon sun, he arranged bales of mulching straw and covered them with the blanket, making a chair for Varina. He motioned for her to sit and pulled another bale across from her for himself.

"Where should we begin?" he asked.

Varina resisted the impulse to plunge ahead and took a moment to marshal her thoughts. Andrew, now apparently at ease once more, waited for her to speak.

"Fiona tells me that Jamie was very much a normal little boy until the night his mother died. Perhaps that's an appropriate starting place?"

Andrew nodded, but Varina could tell it was difficult for him to speak of that night. When he finally did, his voice was low and he seemed to have difficulty choosing what he wanted to say.

"I had been away on one of my visits to Edison and the Everglades, and the night I returned was the night that Theodora died. It was late and we—Gordie, Fiona, and I—assumed that Jamie was in bed. Of course, our attention was diverted elsewhere, so it was not until later that we realized he wasn't there."

Andrew sat dejectedly, his eyes fastened on pieces of straw that he braided unthinkingly as he spoke. "When we realized that there was nothing more that could be done for

121

Theodora, I went in to check on Jamie, but he wasn't in his room. We searched the house for him, calling and shouting, but he didn't answer."

Andrew paused, emotions scudding like storm clouds across his face as he remembered.

"By then we were all very worried. Fiona was almost hysterical, afraid that he had wandered into the woods, or worse still, fallen off the dock. Gordie was about to go into town to gather men for a search party when Fiona heard a noise in the dining room. She noticed a door to the sideboard ajar and, opening it, she found Jamie, wedged in among the damask cloths and napkins. His face was streaked as if he had been crying earlier, but when we found him, he was totally unresponsive, emotionless—and mute."

Varina pictured the little boy, cramped and still for hours in the sideboard in the dark, and her eyes filled with tears for his suffering.

"At first, it was as if he were sleepwalking. His eyes were open, but he did not respond to anything or anyone. Gordie had a horse already saddled, so he rode for the doctor. When Dr. Thompson arrived, he checked Jamie over thoroughly and could find nothing physically wrong with him, but he described his mental state as catatonic, probably induced by a severe shock."

"The shock of losing his mother?"

"That's what he said, and we didn't correct him. You see, at that time, Jamie didn't know that Theodora was gone."

Varina's intellect struggled with this new puzzle.

"Perhaps Jamie had yellow fever, too, and it affected his mind?" she suggested.

"No." Andrew shook his head, worry for his son weighing visibly on his shoulders. "Jamie didn't have any fever. He's hardly ever been ill—except for occasional sniffles—in his life."

Once again more answers brought more puzzles, Varina thought.

"What happened after that?"

"For weeks, Jamie, unless Fiona or I was with him, would find a corner in which to hide and would sit for hours, staring into space. I slept in his room on a cot so he wouldn't be alone or frightened at night. This went on for months."

Andrew stood, threw down the braided straw, and began to pace about the potting shed.

"Gradually, he began to get a little better. Oh, he's not spoken or made a sound since that night, but he had begun to respond a bit, to look at us when we speak, to follow directions, to show interest in some tasks or toys. But a week ago he regressed, became less responsive, lost what little facial expression he had begun to show."

A week ago. That was when Cordelia had arrived, Varina thought.

As if Andrew had read her mind, he added, "That was about the time Cordelia came. She arrived on our doorstep, along with a cartload of trunks and hatboxes, looking as lost and forlorn as Jamie. She said she could no longer stand living in her large house in New York City with only the servants for company, so she had come here to be with what little family she had left. As for what her presence means to Jamie, all I can think is that she reminds him of his mother and that has in some way affected him."

He stopped pacing and looked down at Varina.

"Even before her arrival, weeks ago, I wrote to William asking if I could send Jamie to him. William's house was always a safe haven for me after our parents died, its atmosphere warm and loving and secure. I thought that if I could send Jamie into such a home, that it would make him better."

"But Uncle William thought otherwise."

"Yes, as I've said before, my brother is a very wise man. Even without knowing all the circumstances, he believed that taking Jamie from me and from his home would be a traumatic experience. In restrospect, I think he is probably right. So he sent me you instead. And now"—he looked at her with pleading in his brown eyes—"you must help me make Jamie well again."

Varina thought of how Hercules must have felt when he was assigned his labors. How does one make a little boy well if the cause of his problem is unknown? Only Jamie knew what had happened that night, and it was locked within him until he decided to speak and tell his story.

She looked at Andrew in despair.

"I'm not sure I even know where to begin."

"But you already have," he encouraged her. "You have treated Jamie as if he is a normal little boy, which I'm sure is exactly what he needs—that, and love. God knows I love him, but it is difficult for me to show him. I suppose the men in our family have never been very demonstrative. But you, you can give him the mothering he needs."

Andrew made it sound easy, but Varina was not so sure that love alone would effect a cure. Fiona had given a great deal of love to the boy, but still he appeared untouched.

Again it was as if Andrew read her mind. "I know that Fiona loves him as her own, but with her duties of housekeeping and cooking for all of us, she hasn't the time to spend with him that he needs. If you would be willing to spend that time with him, to make an atmosphere here at Fair Winds as much like your own home as possible, I would be eternally grateful."

Varina looked up at the tall capable man beside her, who at this moment reminded her of his forlorn little son, and wished she could take him in her arms to ease his sorrows. Andrew wanted her to create a home like hers in New Bern, but that home had evolved over the years through the love of Uncle William and Aunt Mae for each other and their children. Such a place could not be concocted from thin air, no matter how much she loved Jamie.

Andrew had taken her silence for reluctance, for he continued his plea. "Anything you need that you think will help Jamie, you have only to ask for. No cost is too great, no change is too drastic. I want my son back."

For a few seconds, Varina feared that Andrew would break down and weep, but he quickly regained his composure, settling once more on the bale across from her and taking her slender hands in his.

"Please say you will try."

"Of course I'll try," she exclaimed. "It's just that I can't make any promises other than to do the best I can."

A wave of unreadable emotion washed across the strong planes of Andrew's face, illuminating his eyes. He gently squeezed her hands.

"My gratitude is inadequate, but you have it nonetheless. Now"—he cleared his throat self-consciously—"what do you suggest we do as first steps?"

Varina's mind churned with ideas, but her practical nature recommended caution.

"The most important thing is for me to get to know Jamie, to spend as much time as I can with him," she suggested.

She paused, not knowing how to broach the next topic without causing offense, but thinking it important, she plunged on. "I hope you are not offended by what I have to say, but I believe there is something that can be done to improve the atmosphere of Fair Winds."

"Anything. You have only to ask it."

126

"My first impression of Fair Winds—indoors, that is—was that it is rather dark and foreboding. These qualities can be very frightening to a small child."

She watched Andrew carefully for his reaction and saw him nod thoughtfully.

"I agree. I remember the brightness and airiness of the manse whenever I visited there—very different from the way things are at Fair Winds. But the house is as Theodora wanted it. The interior is as much like her family home in New York as she could make it."

"Then perhaps you'd rather leave it—"

"No!" Andrew's reply was almost vehement. "You're absolutely right. Make up a list of what you want done, and Gordie and I will see to it. Anything else?"

"Just one thing. Do you suppose it would be all right for Jamie to have his meals with us, or breakfast and luncheon at least? I know Cordelia is uncomfortable—"

"Damn Cordelia's comfort! The boy will dine with his family. If she doesn't like it, she can take her meals in her room."

Andrew's annoyance with Cordelia's treatment of Jamie was obvious, but Varina's relief at his acceptance of this idea was counterbalanced by her dread of Cordelia's reaction.

"Thank you. That's all that I can think of for now, but I will make a list about the house."

Andrew stood, drawing her to him, and as he embraced her gently, she felt his breath against her hair as he spoke.

127

"You are the one to be thanked, Varina. You are an answer to my prayers."

He stepped away from her, holding her at arm's length, and plumbing the depths of her eyes with his own. When he released her, she felt suddenly bereft.

"Now I must return you to Jamie and myself to my work," he announced as he folded the tartan.

"This is a difficult place to leave," Varina admitted, surveying again the magnificence of Andrew's gardens as they passed through to their horses.

"Paradise lost," Andrew quipped, "but easily regained. You can come here whenever you wish."

He locked the heavy gates behind them, and as they rode away, Varina forgot the barren plot and Andrew's turmoil, remembering instead his pleas for his son and the warmth of his arms around her.

They gathered in the second parlor for coffee after dinner that evening. Even with the light from several lamps, the room was dark and uninviting with its heavy drapery and furnishings in dismal colors. Varina watched Andrew studying it, perhaps seeing it through her eyes.

Cordelia sat before a tapestry frame, embroidering a garish arrangement of flowers in crewel work. Andrew sat with the day's paper and mail. Varina tried the upright piano, finding it out of tune but adequate, and began to play a piece from Bach's *Well-tempered Clavier*.

Cordelia finally protested. "Don't you know anything livelier than that? It sounds so stuffy."

"Sorry." Varina smiled. "Being raised as a minister's daughter, my repertoire is mainly hymns and Bach."

She thought for a minute, considered an upbeat version of "Swanee River," then closed the lid instead. She had the impression that nothing she played would suit Cordelia, so she settled in a chair by a good light and picked up a section of Andrew's paper.

"This should cheer you, Cordelia," Andrew announced, looking up from the thick letter he had just opened. "How would you both like to accompany me to Tampa week after next? We could stay at the Tampa Bay Hotel, you can shop, and I can spend time with my good friend, Rauol Garcia, who will be visiting friends in Ybor City."

"How wonderful!" Cordelia was delighted. "A chance to get away from country living."

"Don't get your hopes too high," Andrew warned. "Tampa is a bigger place than Dunedin by far, but nothing like the northern cities to which you are accustomed. However, there are a few very good dress shops." He paused to be sure he had Varina's attention. "And fabric and furniture stores as well."

"Yes, I'd like to go very much," Varina declared. "I'm sure there's much I can accomplish with such a trip."

"That's settled then. I'll stop at the station tomorrow and telegraph our reservations."

"Is there an orchestra at the hotel?" Cordelia inquired. "I'd love for you to take me dancing, Andrew."

Varina saw Cordelia batting her pale eyelashes at him again. Whatever was the woman up to? If she was after Andrew's heart, she would get there faster by better treatment of his son. Surely even Cordelia could see that?

Tonight, however, perhaps because for the first time in months he felt hopeful about his son, Andrew was in a congenial mood and returned Cordelia's request with gallantry.

"I think that some elegant dining followed by dancing would do us all good."

Cordelia shot Varina a look that said her anticipation of such enjoyment was tempered by the necessity of Varina's presence, but Varina refused to enter into competition with her, returning to her paper and the world news.

Soon Varina found herself muffling a yawn with the back of her hand and experienced a sudden weariness, not surprising when she considered how she had spent her day. In addition to her tour with Andrew, she had played with Jamie when he awoke from his nap, going once again to the dock to sail his toy boat. She had sat with him in the kitchen while he ate his early supper of mashed potatoes and new peas with Fiona's hot scones dripping with butter, still uncommunicative but cooperative.

Then she had taken him upstairs for his bath, helped him into his linen nightshirt, soft from many washings, and tucked him into his narrow bed, sitting next to him and singing "Sweet and Low" until he had fallen asleep. She had had to rush to bathe and dress for dinner and had arrived breathless and just in time as Andrew was seating Cordelia at the dining table, but the look of approval he had given her was an ample reward for her troubles.

But now the day's activities had taken their toll. She arose, folded away Andrew's paper, and said good night to her companions.

Once in her own room, after donning her nightdress, she threw back the heavy draperies and opened the doors onto the wide veranda. The wind, which had shifted to the west, filled her gown like a sail and lifted her hair away from her face. The strong breeze was laden with moisture, and on the northwest horizon, she glimpsed flashes of lightning as a storm, harbinger of a cold front, approached. Tomorrow would be cooler, a pleasant time for visiting Duncan's groves. And tomorrow morning would be a good time to write to Uncle William. Now, at least, she could tell him of their plans for Jamie. Tomorrow she must also begin making shopping lists for their trip to Tampa, and lists of other chores and projects to make the house brighter and more cheerful. And lists of activities for a small mute boy. She was going to be very busy, but she liked having tasks to accomplish. And she would be helping Andrew, and she liked that even more.

Taking an extra blanket from the cedar chest and placing it at the foot of her bed, Varina said her prayers, climbed between the soft sheets, and fell immediately asleep.

An explosion of thunder awakened her hours later and she could hear the torrential drumming of rain on the roof and the running rivers of water in the downspouts as she turned in bed to go back to sleep. At that instant, another flash of lightning illuminated the room, and Varina blinked in astonishment.

There, just within the open veranda doors, stood Theodora, the glowing white folds of her wedding dress whipping in the wind of the storm, her face and pale hair obscured by bridal veils. Varina, thinking that she must surely be having a dream brought on by the shimmering portrait in the parlor, sat up in bed. The concussive noise of violent thunder brought her fully awake.

At that moment, Theodora, clearly visible in another blaze of lightning, slowly lifted her arm, pointing to Varina with a slender white finger. Varina stared in fascinated horror at the ivory fan, dangling from the spectre's wrist by its blue silk cords as it twisted and turned in the wind.

"Murder," Theodora moaned eerily, her voice easily heard above the rain. Again the thunder crashed violently, and the gossamer fabric of her gown swirled about her in the gale that gusted through the open doors.

At that moment, Varina did what any rational, clear-thinking person would do. She dove beneath the blankets of her bed, pulling them tightly over her head and struggling to deal with the phantom she had seen. When her heart had slowed its ferocious pounding and she had reminded herself that sometimes things are not what they appear, she bravely threw the covers back, ready to tackle the ghost if necessary. But when she looked to the veranda doors, Theodora was gone.

Chapter Nine

Varina awoke at her usual hour, after a long harrowing night, of which she had spent very little sleeping. When she had emerged from the covers to find that Theodora's ghost had disappeared, she had gone immediately to the open doors. The floor and carpets were wet where the rain had been blown in by the storm, and the veranda was deep in water as well. She had closed and locked the doors against the continuing storm, thinking that if Theodora in fact, was a spirit and not a dream, locks would be of little use.

Then she had thought of Jamie, sleeping in the next room. Had he been frightened by the storm, or worse, the dreadful spectre that Varina had witnessed? Wrapping herself in a warm robe, she had raced down the corridor and into his room. Jamie slept soundly with Furry Rabbit tucked beneath his chin. She pulled the covers up about him, adding an extra blanket, then slipped from the room.

As she stood in the hallway, she remembered Andrew's comment on Cordelia's likeness to Theodora. Suspiciously, she groped her way through the inky blackness of the hallway to Cordelia's room and slowly cracked open the door just enough to view Cordelia's sleeping form. The wide upper veranda did not extend to Cordelia's room, so there was no way that Cordelia could have gone from Varina's veranda doors back to her own room without crossing through Varina's room itself. There had been no time for that to occur without Varina's knowledge, nor had there been any water tracked across the room.

Quietly, Varina had returned to her own room, where she sat until the storm abated, puzzling over her mysterious visitor. Had the gloomy atmosphere of Fair Winds and the unhappiness of its residents caused her imagination to produce such visions—first a disappearing fan, and now Theodora herself? Or had she simply dreamed it? Or had she really seen a ghost? And if it was a ghost, why was Theodora's spirit so uneasy that it could not rest? And what did it mean by the word "murder"? Was that a threat? Thoughts darted and hovered in her mind like hummingbirds until finally, physically and emotionally exhausted, she had fallen into a sound sleep.

This morning, with the limpid rays of dawn casting feeble puddles of light on the dark carpet, Varina was no less confused. She did not believe in ghosts, but she came from a part of the country steeped in the folklore of such occurrences. Unwillingly, the stories and legends from her childhood of strange mountain lights, headless railway men, and ghosts of residents of the Lost Colony surged through her mind. She sat shivering in the wide bed, chilled by the knowledge that she had seen Theodora with her own eyes in the very gown Andrew had said she was buried in, the wedding dress she wore in the parlor portrait, holding the ivory fan Fiona claimed to have seen consumed by fire.

Should she tell anyone? Surely not Andrew. He already had far too much worry about Jamie's well-being without this. Besides, might he believe that she was just a hysterical female over-reacting to a strange environment? No, she decided finally, the entire episode was best forgotten.

Suddenly Varina found herself shivering as much from cold as from fear. The temperature had dropped so drastically during the night that she could see her breath in little puffs before her when she exhaled. Pulling on her robe and slippers, she knelt before the fireplace, striking a match to the wood and kindling already laid there. Fiona found her on her knees on the hearth.

"Oh dear, I dinna know ye would be up and about so early or I would have come up sooner

137

to light this myself. I've already started the one in the nursery."

She bustled about the room, throwing open curtains and making the bed. "Did ye sleep well?"

Varina, who had begun brushing the tangles from her thick brown curls, stopped short, eying Fiona sharply.

"Yes. Shouldn't I have?"

Fiona spoke as she continued her chores. "I was afraid all the booming and crashing would have kept ye awake. The thunderstorms here are like a mighty battle."

"Yes, the storm did awaken me, but once I closed the doors and windows, it didn't bother me again."

Varina wound her long tresses into a coil at the back of her neck and skewered them with silver hairpins, leaving the slender column of her neck exposed to the room's cold drafts.

"Andrew's plants!" In that instant she had remembered the danger to the plantation. "How cold is it, Fiona?"

"Dinna fret. The plants are fine. It is na so cold as that. It only seems that way because yesterday was so warm. Now get ye dressed. I have hot coffee in the kitchen."

With a bob of the salt-and-pepper curls that framed her cheery face, the older woman left the room.

Selecting a soft wool dress the color of cinnamon, Varina hastily donned her clothes. The blazing fire was beginning to chase the chill

138

from the room, but not knowing if the rest of the house was as warm, she also took a shawl of cream-colored cashmere and knotted it about her shoulders.

After checking on Jamie, who was still soundly sleeping, she quietly descended the back stairs, purposely avoiding the parlor with its portrait of Theodora. Fiona, already engaged in her day's baking, greeted her with a smile.

"Sit ye doon, lass, and I'll pour ye some coffee. Gordie has already had his breakfast and gone."

She set the cup and saucer before Varina and returned to kneading bread dough.

"What plans have ye for today?" she asked as she skillfully turned the dough, expertly kneading and folding it before placing it in pans to rise near the warmth of the stove.

Varina's nerves, frayed by the inexplicable event of the previous night, slowly knitted in the warm and familiar atmosphere of the kitchen. She sipped the delicious coffee, inhaling its full aroma and the pungent smell of yeast and wood smoke. Surrounded by the practical implements and activities of everyday life, she found that the phantom of the night before seemed less real than ever.

"This afternoon while Jamie's napping, I'm to go with Duncan to see his groves. But first, I've lists to make, and perhaps you can help me. Andrew has told me that I am to make any changes in the house that I think will benefit Jamie."

"Praise God from whom all blessings flow!" Fiona exclaimed. "Just let me know what ye want me doing and I'll see to it. The same for Gordie. We're both that anxious to see the wee bairn himself again. And there's pencil and paper there in the table drawer, if you've a mind to start your list now."

Varina rummaged in the drawer, a catch-all place with bits of twine, garden shears, nails, and a hammer, finally finding a pencil and pad.

"There now"—she settled back to her place at the table as Fiona refilled her cup—"I'm ready to begin."

Across the top of the first sheet, she wrote in her neat but elegant script, "Activities for Jamie." Then her mind went blank, overwhelmed at the idea of finding things for the silent little boy to do. She turned to Fiona for help.

"What can I do to occupy and entertain a five-year-old who doesn't speak?" she asked in frustration.

Fiona looked up from the biscuit dough she was mixing for Andrew's breakfast, her ruddy face wrinkled in concentration.

"What did your young cousins do when they were that age?" she asked.

"But they could talk . . . No, you're absolutely right, Fiona. In fact, you're brilliant!" Varina laughed. "Andrew said that we should treat Jamie like any normal boy, so naturally his activities should be the same as those of a boy his age. Now let me think."

She tapped the pencil against her chin, searching back in her memory to the days when Andy and Harris were only five. Even if the weather was warm, the waters here were too cold now to teach Jamie to swim, but he could begin to ride. Perhaps Andrew could find a pony for him.

"Do you think Gordie would have time to give Jamie riding lessons?"

"Na only that, lass, but we still have the pony cart that Robbie used. A wash and a coat of paint would fix it up nicely."

Fiona had turned the biscuit dough onto a floured board and was now rolling it out with little pats and thuds. Varina was reminded of the first time she had seen Jamie, when he had sat at this table assembling animals from pastry scraps, something Varina had done herself as a child, except instead of animals, Varina had made her alphabet as Aunt Mae had taught her the letters.

"Does Dunedin have a school?"

"Aye, just last September Elizabeth Baird started a school here. She's a fine teacher and the children love her, and the school is only about a mile inland, on the road to Jerry Lake."

She stopped, her floured biscuit cutter suspended in midair, her blue eyes wide with amazement.

"You're na thinking of sending the wee lad to school, are ye?"

Varina smiled. "That's exactly what I'm thinking." She added "school" to the list, just below "riding lessons."

"Don't worry. I'll meet Elizabeth Baird and talk with her first. She must be willing to encourage the children to be kind to Jamie and not to tease him for his silence. But you have said yourself how bright he is, so there is no reason that he shouldn't begin to learn. And he would have the added benefit of being around other children, which might help to draw him out of his shell."

Varina tore the top list from the pad. Before she completed it, she would go to the nursery and take an inventory of the toys there. Jamie should have building blocks and toy soldiers and jigsaw puzzles. These were play activities that he could enjoy, even without speaking. If he didn't have these toys, she would buy them on their trip to Tampa.

From the corner of her eye, Varina glimpsed a white-clothed figure descending the back stairs. The memory of last night caused her heart to pound in her throat, even after seeing that it was only Jamie, rubbing sleep from his eyes with one fist and clutching Furry Rabbit with the other. She gathered the small figure in her arms and kissed his chubby cheek, marveling at the silky smoothness of his skin.

"Good morning, my favorite boy," she said as she hugged him once more before releasing him, realizing with a start how strongly he had worked his way into her affections. She loved her cousins, Andy, Molly, Margaret, and Harris, but they were no longer children. Jamie touched her heart as if he were her own child.

"Come." She took him by the hand after Fiona had greeted him. "We'll go up and get you dressed. You'll be having breakfast with your father this morning."

As she dressed him in short pants with warm woolen stockings and a soft sweater over his sailor shirt, she looked about the nursery, its dark, dreary paneling and heavy curtains the same as the rest of the house.

This is where we'll start redecorating, she thought. *A nursery should be full of light and air and cheerfulness.*

Lacing Jamie's sturdy boots, she mentally began a list of things to be done to make his room more pleasant. When he was dressed, they went down to breakfast together, finding Andrew and Cordelia already at the table.

Andrew looked up from his steaming biscuit, dripping with butter and orange blossom honey, to greet them before popping the tempting morsel into his mouth. He looked rested this morning, better than Varina had seen him since her arrival, and she was glad that she had not bothered him with what must have been her nightmares of Theodora.

As Varina pulled the youth chair out of the butler's pantry and hoisted Jamie into it, Cordelia nodded to them with a thin-lipped expression that could have charitably been called a smile but appeared more like a grimace.

The sun threw the brilliance of its morning rays through the windows of the dining room, catching Cordelia in its path, and her red hair shone like burnished copper, contrasting sharply with her black mourning clothes. Again, Varina was reminded of a painting by Vermeer. The woman was beautiful, but she was certainly hard to like.

Suddenly, Varina heard Aunt Mae's voice, as if she were whispering in her ear, admonishing her as she had time and again during her childhood: "Always remember that many times the people who need friends most are the very ones who are the most difficult to love."

As Varina slipped into her own chair, she was stricken by a case of conscience. Of course Cordelia needed friends. She was miles away from her own home, her parents and her sister were dead, and at Fair Winds was the only family she had left. Andrew had shown great generosity and kindness in providing a place for her. Varina berated herself for her previous suspicion of Cordelia's motives. The lonely woman belonged, and if her behavior had been unpleasant, her unhappiness was ample reason for it. Varina promised herself that she would be more considerate of Cordelia.

"Good morning, Cordelia," she spoke to her warmly, immediately making good her intentions. "I hope you rested well last night. Did the storm keep you awake?"

"No, not at all. I can sleep through almost anything." She smiled a wan smile at Varina, which quickly dissolved at the sight of Jamie, seriously if not neatly absorbed in consuming his oatmeal.

To distract her from Jamie's less than pristine table manners, Varina continued as she helped herself to biscuits. "Do you have plans for the morning? Perhaps there is something we could do together."

Andrew looked up from his breakfast. "That's a good idea. I have a great deal of work to do today, so if you can entertain yourselves, all the better."

"I will be writing letters in my room this morning," Cordelia announced coolly, pointedly ignoring Varina's offer. "And for luncheon I have an engagement with the Ridenour sisters at the Yacht Club Inn. We'll be playing cards afterwards, so I'll be gone all afternoon. May I take the buggy, Andrew?"

"Of course, Cordelia." He turned to Varina, who noticed for the first time the way his eyes crinkled pleasantly at the corners when he smiled. "Well, what about you? Do you have plans as well?"

Varina told him that she would spend the morning writing letters home and that Duncan Roth would be showing her his groves in the afternoon while Jamie napped. He was strangely silent for a moment, retreating back into his brooding mood. Then he took a last sip of coffee, placed his napkin on the table, and rose.

"Then if you will both excuse me, I've work to do. I'll take lunch at the plantation, so I will see

145

you at dinner." Tousling Jamie's hair affectionately, he strode from the room, and Varina felt strangely as if the sunlight had faded.

Daffy girl, she scolded herself. *First you dream of ghosts, and now you're off in the clouds over Andrew's smile. You'd better get hold of your common sense if you're to be useful around here.*

As soon as Andrew left, Cordelia immediately arose and headed for the stairs, her breakfast barely touched. Varina sighed. So much for Jamie having meals with his family. The two finished their breakfast in silence.

Chapter Ten

With her letter to Uncle William on its way with Gordie to be posted and Jamie settled for his nap, Varina sat in the kitchen with Fiona, awaiting Duncan's arrival. She marveled at the older woman's energy and efficiency as she handled the multitude of tasks necessary to keep their large household running smoothly. Today she was making marmalade from the tart Seville oranges that Duncan had brought, and the kitchen air was redolent with the smell of sliced peel and bubbling sugary fruit.

Varina looked up at the sound of footsteps on the back veranda and saw Duncan approaching. He was a large man, but he moved his long well-muscled limbs with unexpected gracefulness. At the sight of Varina, he smiled a slow, steady grin that moved from his generous mouth to his soft gray eyes. Although he wore the rough clothes of a farmer, he wore them with a dignity and bearing that indicated he was not born to a life of hard labor. In addition to his inherent shyness, there was also a suggestion in his manner of the training of a gentleman.

He greeted Fiona and held the door open for Varina.

"I'm glad to see ye havna changed your mind," he stated forthrightly as they walked toward the stable. There by Duncan's own mount was the gentle bay, which Duncan had already saddled for her.

"I never even considered it," Varina replied truthfully, feeling very comfortable in the presence of the gentle grove owner. "I want to learn all that you can teach me about the citrus business, especially since it is so important to so many people here."

"Aye, that it is," Duncan agreed. "It's become practically the basis of our entire economy. Once oranges could be enjoyed only by the very wealthy. Now with the expansion of groves both here and in California, we may soon find them as common to the average person's table as the apple is."

They had started off from the stables in the opposite direction of the plantation, traveling first behind the kitchen garden, then onto a well-traveled path that led to a small low house situated beneath the low branches of a camphor tree. Duncan indicated it with a nod as they passed.

"The wee house there is where the McLarens lived before Fair Winds was built. Now Gordie and Fiona live there."

They continued on through a pine hammock before breaking out onto rolling cultivated land, filled with row upon row of small trees heavy with golden fruit as far as Varina could see.

"These are the navels. They're an early crop," Duncan explained. "The valencias, over in the next block, will ripen after Christmas."

"But the trees are so small," Varina observed, looking into the topmost branches from her horseback perch.

"We grow them that way." Duncan grinned. "These are all budded trees. That means that they are grafted onto root stock, usually rough lemon or sour orange, rather than grown from seeds."

"Why do you do that?"

Duncan eased back in the saddle, tipped his wide-brimmed hat so that the sun shone full upon his face, and happily launched into his lecture.

"Trees grown from seedlings sometimes take as many as fifteen years before they begin to bear fruit. In addition, the trees are covered with thorns, which dinna make the pickers too happy. The trees from seedlings also grow very tall and scraggly, again a problem for harvesting. And the crowning reason is that the fruit itself doesna taste as good when it comes from seedling trees."

He slid from his horse and lifted Varina down

so that she could inspect the trees more closely.

"These trees were grafted onto rough lemon root and started bearing fruit within five years. Also, as you can see"—he pushed the nearest branches back in illustration—"they have practically na thorns and are compact and low to the ground, which makes picking the fruit much easier."

With a practiced twist of his wrist, he plucked a large navel from one of the highest branches.

"Fruit growing high on the tree is the sweetest," he explained as he opened his knife and sliced the plump orange in two, offering half to Varina while biting into the other half himself.

To Varina it tasted wonderful, juicy and sweet, but Duncan shook his head.

"We'll need a few more nights of cold weather to sweeten these as they should be. Citrus growing is a game of chance. Ye need rain and sun and enough cold to sweeten the fruit, but na so much it freezes the crop or kills the trees."

Varina finished the fruit and wiped her hands on the large bandanna Duncan offered her before remounting and continuing their tour. They saw blocks of grapefruit, oranges, and tangerines, rank and file of glistening jade leaves studded with golden orbs marching across the gray sandy soil. Duncan's enthusiasm for his work shone on his face as he explained the workings and schedule of his grove.

When they had come full circle, they followed the path along the creek to a cleared area where another small and tidy grove house stood amidst beds of fall flowers. Thick Virginia creeper, its green leaves tinged with scarlet, climbed among the rocks of the chimney along the north side of the house. Outbuildings to the back held cultivation equipment and stables, and built along the south wall of the barn was a greenhouse almost as large as the barn itself.

When Duncan led Varina into the greenhouse, she soon forgot him in her admiration of the exotic orchids, bromeliads, and the profusion of delicate blossoms of cold-tender plants that filled the glass-enclosed space. Because the day had warmed, Duncan had propped open sections of the glass roof and a cool gentle breeze rustled the foliage and blossoms.

Varina went from flower to flower, admiring each delicate and flamboyant display, inhaling the melange of scents from the peppery fragrance of carnations to the cloying perfume of gardenias.

"Come," Duncan called to her when she had seen all that she wanted, "I'll fix ye some tea. Ye must be thirsty after all that grove dust."

They returned to the grove house and Duncan held open the door for her. The building consisted of two rooms, the first a combination kitchen-and-living area, and the second a bedroom, both spartan and practical in furnishings and immaculately clean. Duncan filled a kettle and placed it on the squat black woodstove.

"Perhaps ye'd like to sit on the porch in the fresh air," he suggested with a stammer, and

Varina saw his embarrassment at the impropri-
ety of an unchaperoned female in his bachelor
home.

"I'd like that. And you can tell me how you
came to America."

As they settled in wooden rocking chairs on
either side of a small tea table, Varina felt a
growing fondness for Duncan. Unlike Andrew,
there were no secrets here. Duncan was as open
and unsecretive as Andrew was mysterious, and
Varina found the change refreshing. She did not
have to be on the alert for swift changes in mood
or to struggle to understand the undercurrents
of things unsaid.

"Our father, Gordie's and mine, was a solici-
tor in Edinburgh, but he died when I was quite
young. We were raised by relatives, but Father
had left us enough inheritance that we could
both attend university. Gordie first and then I
several years later studied agriculture."

Now Varina understood Duncan better,
knowing why he seemed more than just
a farmer. He was the educated son of a
gentleman.

"But how did you come to Florida?"

"Well, ye might say that Gordie came first, and
the long way round." Duncan laughed. "While
I was still a lad, he and Fiona set out for Iowa.
They had purchased land there and were going
to be potato farmers. They endured two of the
most horrible winters they had ever seen before
they finally admitted that Iowa wasna the place
for them. Gordie swore that he never wanted to

see snow again. That's when they moved here and Gordie started these groves. When I graduated from university, I came to help him."

"Why does he work for Andrew rather than run his own groves?"

"When his lad, Robbie, died, the heart went out of Gordie. He had been building up the groves for his son. With him gone, he lost interest. And about that time, Andrew's grove house came empty and he needed help, so Fiona and Gordie both went to work for him. It's been good for them. Jamie has given Fiona someone to mother, and Gordie doesna have to spend all his days in a grove he knows his son will never carry on."

Varina's face showed the sadness she felt at Fiona and Gordie's loss, and Duncan looked uncomfortable that he had made her unhappy.

"When you've finished your tea, I have a surprise for ye in the barn," he promised.

Varina, her curiosity piqued, swallowed the last of her tea and set the cup aside.

"Let's go. I love surprises."

They walked the neatly raked path between the flower beds, then crossed the sandy expanse of yard in front of the barn, whose wide double doors were closed and barred. Duncan lifted the bar and set it aside, keeping his weight against the door to hold it closed. Varina thought she heard a sound, but could not recognize it.

"Stand back and stand very still," he warned, a hint of laughter in his voice. With a fluid motion, he threw the door open wide and a small blur

153

of gray fur raced out and circled Varina's feet, yapping happily. It stopped for a moment, sat back on its small haunches, and tilted its head up at Varina, inspecting her with bright black button eyes. Then it stood and wagged its tail so vigorously that its entire body moved.

"A puppy!" Varina dropped to her knees, gathering the small dog in her arms. It immediately began to lick her face with its rough pink tongue. Its soft fur smelled of fresh hay as she cuddled the small animal.

"Aye, and not just any puppy. He's a purebred cairn terrier from Scotland. I bought him from a farmer east of here who raises them because they're so good at chasing vermin. But they're good with children, too, so when this one has learned all his manners, I'll be giving him to Jamie."

"Oh, what a wonderful idea! How soon do you think that will be?"

"I'd think by Christmas I'll have him trained so he willna cause Fiona grief."

"What a perfect Christmas present for Jamie." She buried her face again in the puppy's soft fur before putting him down. "Does he have a name?"

"Well, I had named him Robert Bruce, but it's a bit pretentious for such a wee dog, so I call him R. B."

"R. B. Arby, that's a perfect name. Oh, Jamie is going to love him. I already do."

Varina watched the pup, who had found a short stick and was attempting to coax Duncan into playing with him by butting his head against the man's boots. Duncan took the stick and tossed it, and Arby was off in a gray blur to retrieve it.

Varina laughed at the antics of the small terrier, enjoying for the first time since her arrival at Fair Winds a respite from the puzzles and problems there. But her respite was short-lived as Duncan took her arm, and with Arby trotting at their heels, they walked back to the porch.

"I must talk with ye about Fair Winds, Varina," Duncan said as they settled again in the wooden rockers with Arby at their feet, panting after his exertion. Duncan's face was grim and Varina was sorry that all the joy seemed to have gone out of the day.

"I know I have no right to interfere, and I willna blame ye if ye tell me to mind my own business, but I think ye should be warned."

Varina looked into the intelligent gray eyes of the handsome man across from her and knew he would not speak unless he felt compelled to do so.

"Please tell me what you can, Duncan. There are so many things at Fair Winds that I don't understand. If you can help me, I'd be very grateful."

"I dinna know if I can explain anything. There is so much I dinna understand myself. All I know is that there is something terribly wrong there. Wrong enough to make my own brother lie to me."

"I can't imagine Gordie being untruthful."

"Nor could I, lass, but there were many strange things that happened there over a year ago. Strange enough to make me fear that you might be in some danger even now."

"What things?"

"It all goes back to the day Theodora died. Andrew was due to return from one of his trips to the Everglades. I had stopped in at Fair Winds that afternoon, and Fiona was all aflutter. She said that Theodora was in one of her 'rare moods,' which is what Fiona used to call it when Mrs. McLaren's temper got the better of her. She hated it when Andrew went off and left her, and Fiona said Theodora had been pacing the parlor floor and muttering to herself the better part of the afternoon. I saw her myself when she came to the kitchen and scolded Fiona for na serving her tea on time. She had a tongue like a scythe, that 'un did."

"But I thought she was ill with yellow fever."

"She was right as rain when I saw her at four o'clock that afternoon," Duncan insisted. "And she was well enough when Fiona and Gordie left Jamie with her when they went to prayer meeting that night. But by the time they returned home, Andrew was there and Theodora was dead. Dr. Thompson was called and the funeral was held the next day. The doctor and Gordie and Fiona insist that she died of yellow fever, but they're na telling the truth, and they know that I know that they're na telling the truth, but they're too loyal to Andrew to go against his story."

"But if she didn't die of yellow fever, how *did* she die?"

Varina had turned pale at the knowledge that Theodora had not died of fever. "Murder," her ghost had moaned, but Varina pushed the image from her mind.

"Only Andrew, Fiona, and Gordie, Dr. Thompson—and Jamie—know, if anyone. And none of them is talking. So you see why you must take care, Varina. God only knows what the truth is, and it canna be good. Why else would they be so secretive about it?"

Varina felt the thoughts colliding in her mind as she tried to sort through what all of this meant. Again it seemed the more she learned, the less she knew. Duncan leaned toward her and covered her small hand with his large sun-burned one.

"If ye need me, Varina, let me know. Ye know how to find me now. And I'll help ye all I can."

Varina felt torn between gratitude toward Duncan for both his information and offer to help and feelings of disloyalty to Andrew. She wanted to write to Uncle William for advice, but how could she tell him that his own brother had lied about how his wife had died? And if the yellow fever was a lie, what was the truth? Fatigue swept over her as she struggled with this new dilemma.

"Thank you for your warning, Duncan." She stood, pulled on her riding gloves, and gave Arby a farewell pat. "And for showing me all your wonderful groves and flowers. But I must get back to Fair Winds. Jamie will be up from his nap by now and Fiona will need my help."

She had said good-bye to Duncan at the boundary of Fair Winds and walked her horse home, mulling over the new information she had received. As she unsaddled the bay and rubbed her down, she thought of various ways that she might approach Andrew or Fiona to find out the truth, but rejected them all. She was so preoccupied with her thoughts that she barely noticed Andrew's stallion standing at the stable entrance, saddled, with its reins dragging in the sand.

When she entered the kitchen, it was crowded with people. Andrew sat in a chair by the table, his white shirt soaked with blood which ran from a ragged tear across his left cheek. A small thin man in a rumpled black suit hovered over him, mopping the blood from his face and rinsing out the cloths in a basin. Fiona stood nearby, wringing her apron in her hands, and Gordie paced behind the doctor as he worked. None of them paid any attention to her.

"It's only a flesh wound," the doctor was saying. "I don't think stitches will be needed. I'll fix a plaster that should take care of it."

"Damned hunters," Andrew said, "It must have been a stray shot. There wasn't anyone in sight."

"Stop talking or you'll start the bleeding all over again," the doctor ordered. "I'm going to plaster this, then give you something for the pain and to make you sleep. I want you to rest so the wound will heal quicker."

Varina watched helplessly, knowing that she could do nothing but stay out of the way. She saw that, except for the lurid gash across his cheek, Andrew's face was as white as death, and she was frightened for his life, in spite of the doctor's assurances. If the situation scared her as much as it did, how must Jamie feel? She looked about the room, but did not see him.

"Where's Jamie?" Varina asked, and Fiona started, so intent upon Andrew that she had been unaware that Varina had entered the room.

"He's still asleep," Fiona said distractedly, her eyes returning to Andrew and the doctor.

Varina rushed up the back stairs to the nursery, but Jamie was not in his room. She searched the upstairs rooms quickly, but he was not to be found. Then she remembered. She passed Andrew and the doctor coming up as she ran down the back stairs, but Andrew was already groggy from the medicine the doctor had given him, and the doctor was too burdened with his patient to pay any attention to her.

Running into the dining room, she saw the sideboard door slightly ajar. Curled inside was Jamie, his eyes wide with fear, fiercely clutching Furry Rabbit. Gently, she lifted the small boy from his cramped hiding place among the table linens, cradling him in her arms and whispering in his ear.

"Everything's all right, my favorite boy. Your father's gone up to take a nap, and when he wakes up, he will be all better," she assured him, sounding more positive than she felt. "Now, let's you and I go into the kitchen for some milk and cookies."

As she carried him through the butler's pantry, she could hear Gordie talking to Fiona.

"Hunters, my eye! There was only one shot, the one that hit him. And if whoever it was wasna such a lousy marksman, Andrew would be dead now."

Chapter Eleven

Varina sat cross-legged in the middle of the bed, her flannel nightgown tucked over her bare toes for warmth. Gingerly, she massaged her temples with her fingertips in the vain hope that physical manipulation might somehow put her tumbled thoughts in order. The day's events had raised even more questions, and her brain reeled as she attempted to sort out the answers.

When she had returned to the kitchen with Jamie, Gordie had already gone back to his work, and Fiona had cleared away the basin and bloody cloths. All that remained to indicate that something was amiss was Fiona's nervousness. The normally placid demeanor of the house-keeper had disappeared, and in its place was a bundle of nerves as agitated as drops of water on a hot griddle.

"I'm sure that Andrew is going to be fine. You must try not to worry. Let's have ourselves a cup of tea while Jamie has his cookies," Varina had suggested, hoping to restore calm to the older woman's jangled emotions.

Preparing tea had worked to some extent. The routineness of familiar tasks had a tranquilizing effect, and soon Fiona was sitting with them as Varina shared her delight over Duncan's groves and flowers, while avoiding the topic she wanted most to discuss, the puzzling circumstances of Theodora's death.

"Aye," Fiona remarked with a hint of pride, "Duncan is a fine young man, and he knows his business. But I worry about him all alone up there in his lonely wee house. He needs a good wife to look after him." She looked at Varina to make sure her comments had registered. But Varina would not be led.

"I'm sure you're right, and I'm sure there are any number of girls in Dunedin who would jump at the chance to share his life. Now, young man"—she handed Jamie his napkin—"wipe that moustache of milk away and we'll go for a walk before dinner."

She had taken Jamie up the path toward the plantation where they found the whitetail following their usual path to the creek, and they had watched the animals in silence. Jamie, as usual, had not spoken, but his mouth had formed an amazed *O* as he observed the graceful creatures, and Varina took even that minimal response as a hopeful sign.

Later, after his supper and bath, she had taken him in to say good night to Andrew, who had grinned sleepily from his bed at his small son before falling asleep once more. When Jamie was tucked snugly in his own bed, convinced that his father was all right and with the reassuring presence of Furry Rabbit clasped to his chest, Varina had descended to the kitchen to confront Fiona.

"I heard what Gordie said about someone trying to kill Andrew. Who would want to do such a thing and why?"

Once more the uncharacteristic evasiveness returned to the older woman's face as the nervousness returned to her movements.

"Ye mustna pay any mind to what Gordie says, lass," Fiona insisted, hiding her face in the oven as she basted a roast she was preparing for dinner. "I'm sure it was hunters, a stray shot. Why, I had a bullet go through that very window a couple years ago." She pointed over the sink. "And found out later it was Gus Granville after wild boar. He missed his target and the bullet traveled over a mile to end up in my kitchen."

Avoiding Varina's eyes, she had moved briskly about the large kitchen, seemingly engrossed in preparations for their meal.

Varina had seen that she would get no cooperation from Fiona, so she had let the matter drop. She had endured an uncomfortably quiet dinner with only herself and Cordelia in the dismal dining room, barely managing to squelch her irritation at the older woman's lack of concern over Andrew's wound.

"It's the price he pays for living in this God-forsaken wilderness," Codelia whined. "If he had moved back to New York as my sister had wished, perhaps he would be safer." She picked at her food distastefully, eating hardly anything at all before excusing herself.

Varina had finished Fiona's delicious dinner alone. Now she sat in her room, trying to make sense of so many senseless things that had happened since her arrival at Fair Winds.

Was she herself becoming so jittery that she was reading into events significance that was not there? Was Andrew's wounding an accident, or was it another of those things that were not what they seemed—in fact, an attempt on Andrew's life? But if someone had tried to kill him, who was it and why? And if she had not died of yellow fever, what had been the cause of Theodora's death? Duncan Roth appeared to be one of the most scrupulously honest men Varina had ever met. If he said Theodora's death was not from fever, then it must be true. Or was Duncan, too, a deception?

Varina sat enwrapped in speculations, all leading down trails to nowhere, until finally, frustrated and exhausted by the day's puzzles, she climbed between the smooth linen sheets and fell asleep.

Her sleep was deep and undisturbed by restless spirits, and as she opened her eyes the next morning, she felt refreshed after a night's respite

Darkness at Fair Winds

from questions unanswered. But as she came fully awake, she saw from the corner of her eye a monstrous black form crouched upon her pillow. With a strangled scream, she threw back the covers and leapt as far from the bed as possible and stood shivering in the morning air from fright and from cold.

A few moments later, Fiona found her backed against the French doors, her eyes fastened on a gigantic black spider the size of a man's hand that sat unmoving upon her pillow.

"I heard ye cry out. Are ye all right?" Fiona's eyes followed Varina's pointing finger. "A banana spider! Na wonder ye screamed. 'Tis enough to give anyone a start, great hairy monster that it is."

Fiona moved to shoo the creature away. "We dinna like to kill these. They're harmless and they eat other bugs—a friendly spider, if na so pretty."

The spider, however, did not move, in spite of Fiona's waves and flutters.

"Ah, I should have warned ye about these sooner. You've killed it already. Well, na harm. I'll dispose of it. And ye should get on something warm. You'll catch your death of a chill standing there in your nightie." Fiona lit the fire, then lifted the spider, pillow and all, and carried it from the room.

Varina wrapped herself in a blanket from the bed, then collapsed in the slipper chair, staring at the object she had held hidden in her hand. Before Fiona's arrival, Varina had inspected

165

the spider herself and found it skewered to the pillow with one of her own silver hairpins. Unlike Theodora's ghost, there was no question about the reality of this incident. The spider had been purposely placed on her pillow by someone who had entered her room as she slept. But who? Andrew had been too weak and drugged to move from his bed. Cordelia with her fastidious ways would have found the creature too repugnant to touch. Jamie? Varina refused even to consider that any ill intentions lay beneath the malady of spirit the small boy suffered. Could it have been Fiona or Gordie? They were close-mouthed about happenings at Fair Winds, but that did not make them capable of such maliciousness. Theodora?

Varina shivered violently, although the fire's blazing warmth now filled the room. The light from the fireplace threw wavering shadows in the dim light of dawn, and tentacles of darkness reached out toward her from the black recessed corners. Someone had entered her room as she slept and left her a gruesome message. Was the spider impaled on her pillow a warning for her to leave Fair Winds? Or worse still, was it a threat of what might happen to her if she stayed? The malevolent presence that she had felt upon her arrival now pressed heavily upon her and she felt suffocated by fear.

She ached for the safety and comfort of the manse, homesickness welling in her until she felt weak with longing for those she loved. Going home was the answer. There in the security of

Aunt Mae's kitchen and Uncle William's wisdom, there would be no threats, no haunted spirits, no answerless puzzles.

Neither would there be poor mute Jamie for her to love and encourage, nor Andrew, whose hurt somehow seemed as deep and tragic as his son's. And if she returned home, what would she tell her family—that she had been frightened away by rumors, dreams, and a dead spider? That she was a coward who ran home with her tail between her legs after only three days?

Varina stood and threw off the blanket with a determined gesture. Bright rays of morning light burst through the south windows, dissolving the shadows, and with them her fears and doubts. She had a responsibility here for a little boy who needed her, and it would take more than nebulous threats to keep her from it. A sense of purpose filled the void left by fear. She dressed hurriedly in her riding clothes. Today she would visit Elizabeth Baird and enroll Jamie in school.

Later, after a strained breakfast with Jamie and an equally uncommunicative Cordelia, Varina walked to the stables. Fiona had agreed to let Jamie help her bake sugar cookies while Varina visited the teacher. Gordie greeted her cheerfully and saddled the bay while giving her directions to the schoolhouse.

As she traveled south on the bluff road toward town, Varina marveled that only a few days ago she had ridden up this road for the first time. So much had happened in that short space of days that she felt she had been here a lifetime, and her thoughts again tumbled over one another as she tried to make sense of all that she had seen and heard. Gradually, however, the rocking gait of her horse, the gentle lapping of the outgoing tide, and the soft onshore breeze soothed her tormented reasonings, and she relaxed and enjoyed the beauty around her.

Although Fair Winds occupied lonely acres at the northern end of the bluff road, only a mile or two away were signs of an active community. Maids pegged linens onto laundry lines in the back yards of the stately homes along the waterfront, small children romped on the neat lawns, and occasionally Varina glimpsed groups of women enjoying their morning coffee on the wide verandas that overlooked the sound.

When she reached the west end of Main Street, dozens of people milled about on the city dock as a large paddle steamer unloaded passengers and cargo. Varina felt comforted by the presence of others, recognizing for the first time how isolated she had felt since her arrival. Surrounded by the normal activities of the town, Varina found that her fears and doubts about Fair Winds seemed somewhat foolish. By the time she had turned east up Main Street, she felt embarrassed that she had worried so over events that seemed less urgent in the strong light of the Florida sun.

Except for the ruggedness of its roads and buildings, Dunedin's business section was much like New Bern's. Women with shopping baskets over their arms walked along the boardwalk, and a group of rough-looking men, gathered in the stable yard, threw appreciative glances at Varina as she passed. But she paid them little mind, for her attention had been captured by the belfry of a church south of Main Street. She turned her horse down a residential street past the railroad station and headed toward the spire that towered over the trees.

At the end of the block and surrounded by a picket fence stood a small but elegant little church, its stained-glass window gleaming in the sun. Once again homesickness assailed her as she was reminded of New Bern Church and Uncle William. If only he were here to counsel her, perhaps she would not feel so inadequate at dealing with the strange and often frightening circumstances at Fair Winds. Lost in thought, she almost missed the small sign identifying the building as First Presbyterian Church and the pastor as Archibald Baird. The name reminded her of her errand, and she turned back to Main Street, promising herself that she would come to worship on Sunday and bring Jamie with her.

The road to Jerry Lake was dusty and deserted. In the quiet of the late November morning, Varina could hear a multitude of bird calls. Stopping to listen more closely, she became aware of sounds behind her on the track, but when she turned to see, there was nothing there, only the rattle of palmetto fronds as the wind passed over them. She continued on her way, but with a pounding heart, for the rustling sounds seemed to follow her, just behind and parallel to the road she traveled. The skin between her shoulder blades itched, as if someone were watching her back. The bay picked up her nervousness and fought against the bit so that for a few terrifying seconds she was afraid the horse would bolt. But Varina's relief when she heard the shouts of children transferred to the animal, and it was once more docile as she rode into the dusty schoolyard.

A group of about twenty children of assorted ages, sizes, and degrees of cleanliness were engaged in a rowdy game of baseball during the morning recess. On the front steps of the rustic board and batten building stood the teacher, overseeing her charges. Varina tied the bay out of harm's way and walked around the edge of the yard, avoiding the outfielders, to reach the schoolhouse.

Elizabeth Baird came down the steps to greet her and was unlike anything Varina had expected. A tiny, elegant woman of about thirty, Elizabeth was remarkably beautiful. Her black hair, upswept into a soft style that framed her flawless complexion, accented her startling wide eyes of deep lavender. Her clothes, a dove-gray skirt and white shirtwaist with silk violets at the throat, were as immaculate as if she stood in her own parlor instead of the dusty playground deep in the pines and palmettos. Her only jewelry was a delicate watch dangling from a tiny gold bow pinned to her breast. Such physical perfection would have been daunting had she not smiled in welcome, an expression of such warmth and good humor that Varina was immediately at ease.

"You must be Varina Cameron." Elizabeth extended her hand in welcome and laughed at Varina's startled expression. "You mustn't be surprised that I know you. My father is the minister here, and therefore I know everything that goes on—and that is rumored to go on—in Dunedin. But I don't need to explain that to you, for I understand you were raised in a manse yourself."

"Yes, I know what you mean." Varina found herself smiling back at the friendly teacher. "Miss Baird—"

"Please, call me Beth, because I want us to be friends. Come inside so we can talk away from this noisy gang."

Inside, the schoolroom was as neat as Beth herself, free of dust and sand, the desks and floor polished with lemon oil and the windows filled with plants and flowers. Along the walls hung colorful maps, pictures of the presidents, and samples of student writing and artwork. The high ceiling, open-beamed, and the many tall windows insured ample fresh air and light for the students. Both cheerful and stimulating, the room was exactly the kind of atmosphere that Varina wanted for Jamie.

"How can I help you, Varina?" Beth pulled a chair next to her desk and they were both seated. Varina noted that although they were

171

in the corner of the schoolroom farthest from the noise, Beth had positioned herself to have a clear view of her charges on the playground.

"It's about my cousin, Jamie McLaren. He's only five, but he's very bright, and I'd like for him to start school."

Beth was still for a moment. When she spoke, she went directly to the point. "Jamie doesn't speak, does he?"

"No, he hasn't spoken since his mother died. But I'm hoping with the right care and attention that he will speak again. That's one of the reasons I want him in school. Perhaps if he's around other children, he can be drawn out of himself and be a normal little boy again."

Varina's eyes filled with tears as she thought of poor Jamie and how different he was from the noisy children just outside the window. "I know how cruel children can be, especially toward anyone who is the least bit different from them. But I also know how important it is for Jamie to be with friends his own age. You work with these children everyday, Miss Baird—Beth. What do you think?"

"I haven't seen Jamie for almost two years, and he was only a toddler then, and it was before his silence began. I would hesitate to make a recommendation without meeting with him first. Besides, if we do decide school is a good idea, Jamie may be less frightened if he knows me. Tomorrow is Saturday. Why don't you and Mr. McLaren and Jamie have dinner with us after church on Sunday? If we decide Jamie is to start school, he can begin on Monday."

Varina thought of Andrew, lying heavily sedated so his facial wound might heal.

"Mr. McLaren has been . . . ill and may not be able to come, but Jamie and I will be there."

Suddenly Beth rose and moved to the window, motioning for Varina to join her.

"Marjorie will be there, too. Jamie should have at least one friend here, and he could not have a better friend or guide than she is."

The pretty teacher pointed to the child who stood behind the makeshift homeplate, serving as umpire for the rowdy game. Although Marjorie was only a few years Jamie's senior, even the oldest children treated her with respect. She was not an attractive child, stockily built, with long limp hair and round wire-rimmed spectacles with lenses like bottle bottoms, but she had an air of authority that went unquestioned on the playground.

"Marjorie is my Solomon and my peacemaker. She despises cruelty and injustice and will not tolerate either. The other children know that she is fair, and they seek out and respect her opinions. If Marjorie is Jamie's friend, none will dare tease him for his silence, or they will have Marjorie to contend with."

For the first time since meeting Jamie, Varina felt that she was making progress toward helping him. Here were others who would treat him as a normal boy and perhaps help release him from his prison of silence. Marjorie had noticed the two women looking her way and waved and smiled, looking pretty in spite of her glasses. Varina hoped she would be Jamie's friend.

"Thank you, Beth. You've been very encouraging. In a case like Jamie's, it's difficult to know the proper path to take. I'll be happy to have your advice on the matter."

"And I look forward to seeing you both on Sunday."

Beth picked up a brass hand bell from her desk and walked with Varina to the steps of the schoolhouse. Varina watched her closely, impressed by her competence and the efficiency with which she ran her school. She longed for a friend in whom she could confide and turn to for advice. Perhaps Beth Baird would be that friend.

As Varina rode away, the sound of the brass bell and the laughter of children as they lined up to continue their lessons rang through the woods. No sooner, however, had the sounds of the schoolhouse disappeared than Varina again heard inexplicable rustlings in the underbrush along the trail, and her nervousness returned. She pushed the bay into a gallop, eager to leave the woods, but as she approached the eastern edge of town, she slowed the horse, feeling foolish at her fears. But at that moment her forebodings were fulfilled when a man on a huge black stallion rode onto the track ahead of her, blocking her path. Estaban Duarte tipped his hat and smiled the sinister smile that she remembered from the train.

"So, *Senorita* Cameron, we meet again. Did I not say so?"

Varina tried to edge her horse by him, but he maneuvered the stallion to prevent her passing.

"You persist in placing yourself in dangerous circumstances." His words were conciliatory, but she thought his tone was ridiculing. "A woman alone on these deserted roads is at great risk. You should have an escort when you ride. I, of course, would be happy to provide such a service."

Terror and anger welling inside, Varina gripped her riding crop, ready to defend herself. But with the lightning reflexes of a jungle cat, Duarte stretched out his powerful arm and grasped the crop, holding it fast, until Varina was forced to release it or be dragged from her horse.

"Yes, this is a very dangerous place," Duarte continued, the softness of his tone making his words sound even more ominous. "If I were you, *senorita*, I would go home to my family where no harm can reach. And I would go today."

"Why do you threaten me? What have I done to offend you that you should treat me in such a manner?" Varina's voice cracked with emotion.

Duarte smiled slowly, smacking the palm of his gloved hand with Varina's riding crop and shaking his head in mock despair.

"You misunderstand me, my dear *Senorita* Cameron. I have only your best interest at heart. That is why I insist that Dunedin is not the place for you. If you believe I wish you ill, you are mistaken."

He handed the crop back to her, tipped his hat with an elegant flourish, then wheeled his horse and galloped toward town, leaving Varina shaking so violently that her knees could barely hold her in the saddle. Were Duarte's threats another illusion, or did he really know some reason that she was in danger here? Did he have information that made him truly concerned for her welfare, or was he actually what he seemed, a dangerous and unscrupulous man who wished her harm?

She wanted to tell Andrew, to ask for his advice and protection, but with the thought of him lying weak and helpless, his face slashed by the bullet from an unknown rifleman, she knew she could not cause him any more distress.

As she rode trembling back into town, fear rode with her, pushing aside the satisfaction she had gained from her meeting with Elizabeth Baird.

Chapter Twelve

Varina rode along Main Street, so preoccupied with Duarte's threats that she did not hear Duncan calling her name. Not until he stepped into the street and grabbed the bridle of her horse was she jolted back to the present.

"Are ye all right, lass? Ye look as if you've seen a ghost."

The handsome young Scot smiled up at her, and Varina welcomed his friendly face with a feeling of relief. Perhaps Duncan could help her sort out what to do about Duarte and his threats.

"I've been at the schoolhouse to talk with Beth Baird about enrolling Jamie in her school." Varina accepted Duncan's assistance in dismounting and led the bay off the street to where his wagon stood.

"And I've just finished loading my supplies. Why dinna we tie your horse behind the wagon and ye can ride back to Fair Winds with me?"

Varina gave her approval. Not only did she want to talk with Duncan, but she would feel less anxious if he was with her. After her encounter with Duarte, she felt frightened of her own shadow, a strange and uncomfortable feeling, one at odds with her accustomed self-assurance. She climbed gratefully onto the wagon seat.

"Miss Baird's school has a fine reputation. Being there might be good for the wee lad," Duncan commented as he headed the team toward the waterfront. "And Miss Baird is a bonnie woman—"

He broke off self-consciously as if he had said too much, and Varina noted with interest that the big man was actually blushing beneath the wide brim of his hat. Then the sound of a horse approaching rapidly behind them made her turn in alarm, and only when a local farmer had passed in a dust cloud did she realize that she had been holding her breath in fear.

"What is it? You've seemed distracted by something since I first saw ye in town. There's naught amiss at Fair Winds is there?"

Varina restrained herself from laughing hysterically, thinking there was nothing else amiss other than someone trying to kill Andrew, Theodora's ghost wandering the halls, and someone leaving dead spiders on her pillow. But she knew how mad she would sound to the practical Duncan. She could hardly accept any of it herself. Breathing deeply to calm her skittishness, she related to him her meeting with Duarte on Jerry Lake Road. But even as she told him, she was aware how innocuous the event seemed in the telling and began to wonder herself why she had allowed it to scare her so.

"He didna actually threaten ye then, or harm ye in any way?" Duncan insisted.

"Well, no. He said that it was dangerous for me to travel alone, that the wilderness around Dunedin was not safe for a solitary woman, and that I would be better off going home at once."

"I canna argue with a word of that. The man seems to have your interest at heart. Consider this. He may be one of those unfortunate people who project a fierce image that belies what is underneath." Duncan's brow wrinkled as he struggled to find the words he wanted. "It's hard to explain what I mean. Perhaps if ye knew Kate Johnson, you'd understand."

"Kate Johnson?"

"Aye, Captain Kate had a sloop that used to run regularly between here and Cedar Key, and even though she's a woman, she was one of the best captains around. I arrived here on her sloop, and I can still see her signaling our arrival with mighty blasts on a conch shell. Now she's retired and lives quietly in her log house, but ye can still see her striding the streets in her black skirt and bonnet. There are those who call her the witch of Dunedin because of her strange appearance and manner, but there's not a kinder soul alive. Perhaps this Estaban

Duarte is like Kate. Threatening on the outside, but well-intended on the inside."

Now Varina was thoroughly confused. Was she so befuddled by the unexplainable events at Fair Winds that she had misinterpreted all that Duarte had said? Her head began to ache again with unanswered questions and ambiguous interpretations of all that had happened. By the time they arrived at Fair Winds, her head was pounding fiercely and she was grateful for Duncan's offer to stable her horse.

"Come over and visit Arby when you've time. It will be helpful for him to know someone in the household he's to live in, and it's na that long until Christmas." Duncan smiled and touched his hat brim in salute as they parted.

She found Fiona and Jamie in the kitchen, baking the last of the batches of sugar cookies. Fiona had the kettle on, and Varina welcomed a cup of tea to ease her headache. As she sipped the liquid and nibbled warm cookies, she told Fiona of her meeting with Beth Baird and the invitation to Sunday dinner.

"Elizabeth Baird is a fine young woman," Fiona agreed. "At one time we thought our Duncan . . . Well, never mind that. She's been taking care of the Reverend Baird and the manse ever since they came here years ago."

Fiona's blue eyes glowed with the satisfaction of relaying a good morsel of gossip.

"People thought she would live out her days as an old maid taking care of her father until last year. Then a wealthy widow, Mrs. Henrietta

Freedman, came to spend the winter months at the Yacht Club Inn. She attended church regularly, and by spring, to everyone's amazement, she had married Mr. Baird, and her only ten years older than Elizabeth herself! Why, her daughter, Marjorie, is only seven, young enough for Beth to be her mother."

"Yes, Beth pointed out Marjorie to me." Varina nodded, understanding now how Beth could be sure that Marjorie would be at Sunday dinner. "She also promised me that Marjorie will be Jamie's special friend."

Fiona poured more milk into Jamie's glass and moved the plate of cookies within his reach. The small boy ate silently, and Varina couldn't tell if he paid attention to anything that was said.

"Oh, there was some that wagged their tongues and called it a scandal when Henrietta married the minister, what with her husband na yet dead a year, but for anyone with eyes in his head, it's plain to see she's made the good man happy, and she's the soul of kindness herself, never putting on airs like some ministers' wives I've known. Anyway, perhaps Elizabeth can find a husband and a home of her own, now that her father's well cared for."

"As beautiful as she is, I'm surprised the men aren't lined up at her door." Varina turned her attention to Jamie. "You're going to like Miss Baird," she assured him as she described the school and the children she had seen on her morning visit. His round brown eyes were fixed on her, but he gave no reaction to what she said. Varina sighed and changed the subject.

"How is Andrew this morning?"

A worried frown creased Fiona's brow. "The doctor was here right after ye left and gave him another dose of laudanum. He said the quieter he keeps, the sooner the cheek will heal, but I dinna hold with drugging a man like that, and I told Doc Thompson so. He agreed and asked if I knew any better way of keeping him still, and I had to say I didna."

"The rest should do him good," Varina insisted. "He lost a great deal of blood, so he must regain his strength as well as allow his cheek to knit. Come, Jamie, we'll go up and see how he is so Fiona can fix lunch."

"Miss Cordelia won't be here for lunch—"

"Don't tell me." Varina smiled. "She's having lunch at the inn with the Ridenour sisters."

"How did you know?"

"A lucky guess—or my Scottish sixth sense. She doesn't seem to be very happy here, does she?"

Fiona scrubbed away at the cookie sheets in the dishpan. "Ah, she's a mystery, that 'un. She doesna like it here, but she's here to stay."

Varina felt a twinge of guilt at how little effort she had made to carry through on her intention to be kinder to Cordelia and spend more time with her.

"Dinna ye be frettin' yourself over that 'un. She's like her sister with her sister's strange ways." Fiona stopped rattling her pans and turned to Varina to make her point. "There's na understanding women like that, so ye can save yourself a bundle of sorrow by na trying."

Varina wanted to ask her more about Theodora, but Fiona returned to her dishwashing, the stiffness of her back rebuffing any questions.

Varina took Jamie by the hand and led him up the back stairs and through the maze of murky hallways to Andrew's room, where the door stood open. Suddenly the eerie forebodings that had previously tormented her returned, and she felt a strange reluctance to enter the room, but her reluctance at frightening Jamie was greater, so she straightened her shoulders and went in.

The room, like all the others in the house, was dark and dreary, but even worse, it reeked with the stale medicinal smell of the sickroom. Varina sat Jamie in a chair by the bed while she threw back the heavy velvet draperies and opened the French doors. Pale sunlight and a warm sea breeze, fresh with salt, filled the room, dispelling the musty atmosphere and Varina's apprehensions with it.

Andrew slept his drugged sleep, his face as white as the sun-bleached linens on which he lay, all color drained from his former tanned complexion so that even the white plaster on his left cheek appeared darker than his skin. With his hair tousled from sleep and his face relaxed from its usual stern lines, he once again resembled the boyish Andrew of Varina's youth, and she felt a stab of pity that life had treated him so harshly, erasing the joy and exuberance that had once consumed him.

Oh, Andrew, she thought with a sigh, *I loved the man you once were, but the man you are now is a stranger to me, and a stranger with many faces, at that.*

She saw that Jamie had scrambled onto his knees in the chair to get a better view of his father in the high bed.

"See, Jamie," she reassured the small boy, "your father is sleeping peacefully and his cheek is healing nicely underneath the patch the doctor made for it."

She smoothed the pillows and bed linens and was turning to leave when Andrew opened his eyes and looked directly into hers.

"Varina, thank God you're here," he spoke in the barest whisper, his words slurred by the drug's effect. "Please tell Theodora to go away and let me sleep."

She felt the hair rise on the back of her neck at his words, and she wheeled to look behind her across the empty room. When she turned back to Andrew, his eyes were closed and he was asleep again. Varina's heart was beating in her throat, and for a moment she could not speak. Making a heroic effort to gather her wits to keep from scaring Jamie, she smiled encouragingly at the child and finally found her voice.

"You see, he's dreaming. Let's tiptoe out so we don't awaken him."

On legs that threatened to fold beneath her, Varina hurried from the room, nudging Jamie before her in a swift retreat to the security of Fiona's kitchen.

When Sunday arrived, Andrew remained weak and unsteady, but Varina doubted that he would have accompanied them to church in any event. He had left his bed that morning and was ensconced on the sofa in the second parlor, propped up with pillows and tucked about with a tartan blanket, a pot of tea and a stack of newspapers within his reach.

"I haven't been to church in over a year and don't intend to go now, even if I were strong as an ox." Andrew attempted to bellow, but he hadn't the strength; however, his expression of defiance at the mention of church conveyed his displeasure more than adequately.

"But you have no objection to my taking Jamie there or to the manse afterwards for dinner?" Varina was losing patience with Andrew's moodiness, and he looked surprised at the sharpness in her voice.

"Of course not," he answered a bit more reasonably. "Besides, I like the thought of Jamie's attending school, and Miss Baird's idea of meeting him and assessing the situation first seems very practical."

He seemed more approachable now, and with Jamie waiting in the kitchen with Fiona, Varina gathered her courage and ventured into dangerous straits.

"Andrew, do you remember Friday morning when Jamie and I came to your room?"

185

"What about it?" His tone had grown cold again, and Varina, reluctant to continue, but not knowing how to avoid it, hurtled ahead.

"You asked me to tell Theodora to go away and let you sleep. Whatever did you mean by that?"

By now Varina's hands were shaking at the audacity of her question. As she waited for Andrew's answer, she saw again the phenomenon she had witnessed many times since her arrival. The lines and planes of Andrew's face hardened and shifted, and his body assumed a rigidity that suggested tension in every muscle, almost as if another being had claimed his body as its own. His eyes narrowed to catlike slits, hypnotizing her with their feline expression.

"I have no idea what you're talking about."

Then almost immediately Andrew was himself again, so quickly changed that Varina knew she must have only imagined that he had been different.

"It's just as I thought," she replied, thinking quickly of a way to extricate herself from this awkward topic as she pulled on her Sunday gloves and adjusted her hat. "You must have been talking in your sleep. I must go now or we'll be late, but I'll let you know what Miss Baird thinks about school for Jamie when I return."

Later, however, as she sat in the quiet sanctuary of the church, she was no longer certain. Ever since she had come to Fair Winds, she had felt as if she were swinging on an emotional trapeze, vacillating from certainty to doubt, from confidence to fear, with no respite from the dizzying ride. She had been carefully schooled by her uncle in reason and logic, but the problems she had encountered in Dunedin defied both.

Growing up in the manse with Aunt Mae and Uncle William, carefully schooled as well in the Bible and theology, Varina had never doubted the existence of evil, of the powers of darkness that lay in wait for the unvigilant, but she had always felt safe from them, sheltered by the love and faith of her adoptive parents. Here she missed the comforting buffer they had always afforded her.

" ' . . . let us therefore cast off the works of darkness, and let us put on the armor of light.' "

Mr. Baird's reading of the familiar text broke into her thoughts, almost as if he had known what they were. He stood tall and majestic behind the pulpit with the light from the stained-glass chrysanthemum window casting a golden nimbus about his mane of white hair. Varina tried to concentrate on his scholarly sermon, but her mind kept returning to the phrase "works of darkness." Was that the presence she felt at Fair Winds? And if it was, how could she cast it out?

She realized that the rest of the congregation had risen for the final hymn, and she fumbled in her hymnal to find the page, but even the words of "A Mighty Fortress" brought her more unease than comfort. When she sang of "the prince of

187

darkness grim," Estaban Duarte's image filled her mind. With relief she heard Mr. Baird pronounce the benediction, and she took Jamie's hand and moved into the aisle.

The church was crowded that morning, and many spoke friendly greetings to Varina and Jamie, but others looked at them warily, as if not knowing how they should be treated. Then the crowd of people suddenly parted to allow a fair-haired, middle-aged woman, fashionably dressed in cornflower-blue that matched her eyes, to pass through.

"You must be Varina and Jamie." She smiled a warm, sincere smile, only slightly marred by the imperfection of her overbite. "I'm Henrietta Baird." She grasped Varina's hand, then bent and offered her hand, gloved in blue suede, to Jamie. Solemnly, the boy shook hands with her, then continued to hold onto her, as if protected by her presence.

Beth joined them then, along with Marjorie. As the three women walked together toward the manse next door, Marjorie and Jamie trailed behind, and Varina caught bits of Marjorie's one-sided conversation.

"It's all right if you don't talk. Really it is. Most people talk too much anyway." She had picked up a stick and was pulling it across the pickets of the church fence as they passed. "Here, you try. It makes a lovely racket." She pressed the stick into Jamie's hand, and agreeably he clattered it along the boards as they walked.

Darkness at Fair Winds

Varina relaxed, knowing that with Marjorie, Jamie was going to be fine. She turned her attention to Beth and Henrietta, walking companionably arm in arm next to her.

"I'm very lucky to have Henrietta," Beth was explaining. "When she married Papa, I got not only a new mother but a wonderful friend as well."

Varina was overcome with a poignant homesickness, seeing how content the two seemed to be with their lives. She had been away from home less than a week, and she wondered now why she had ever wanted to leave.

As they entered the manse, a melange of delicious odors greeted them, and by the time they had removed their coats and hats, the housekeeper had dinner on the table. Mr. Baird arrived, and the family and guests sat down together.

Dinner was a satisfying feast of baked grouper, new peas, sweet-potato souffle, and a four-layer chocolate cake with rich icing and whipped fresh cream. The table conversation was much as Varina remembered it had been at home: who was in church, who wasn't, and any other news of the parish and its members.

"Henrietta"—Mr. Baird's affection for his bride could be heard in his inflection—"tell Varina about your latest civic venture."

Henrietta laughed, a pleasant sound, like water bubbling over rocks, and launched into her narrative.

"The city leaders had decided that the trees around the railroad station should be cleared away. They wanted the approach to Dunedin to seem more open and commercial, less pastoral and provincial. Their desires were understandable, but the trees they were planning to destroy were ancient and venerable oaks."

Henrietta was an animated conversationalist, her face reflecting a range of expressions and her gestures vivid and lively as she spoke.

"Several of the women of the town, myself included, believed that cutting those magnificent trees would be an irreplaceable loss to the community, so we petitioned the council to reconsider. Our petition, however, was ignored. Well, you know what has no fury like women scorned. The signers of the petition met here, and we decided to take action."

Skillfully building the suspense of her story, Henrietta took a slow sip from her water goblet.

"Before daybreak on the morning the trees were to be cut, we ladies assembled at the railroad station, and, with the assistance of several ladders we had brought with us, we climbed into the trees. When the men arrived with their saws and axes, we told them that we would not budge, that if they wished to destroy those splendid oaks, they would have to bring us down with them."

Mr. Baird's eyes never left his wife. Although he had heard the story before, his enjoyment of its retelling was evident.

"We stayed in the trees until sundown. The men, of course, had long since given up and gone about their other chores, but we were afraid they would return if we left. That night, feeling that we had made our point and saved the trees, we returned to our homes triumphant, feeling very satisfied with ourselves."

"That's a marvelous example of how people can make a difference by becoming involved," Varina said.

"If only it were." Henrietta shook her head. "But the next morning just before daybreak, the men returned with their saws and cut down the trees. So much for militant females!" Her bubbling laugh sounded again, and this time her husband laughed, too.

Varina found that just watching the couple so obviously in love made her feel good inside, and she felt very much at home in their company.

After dinner, the grown-ups retired to the parlor for coffee, while Marjorie and Jamie, with admonitions to stay close by, went outdoors to play.

"Well, Varina," Beth observed, "I believe, with Marjorie's help, that Jamie will fit in quite well at school. Why don't you bring him tomorrow morning?"

Before Varina could reply, Henrietta, in her endearing fluttering way, broke in, "What a darling boy he is! It's such a shame his mother's murder has had such a tragic effect upon him."

A dead quiet descended on the parlor before all three Bairds began to speak at once.

"Henrietta, you mustn't—" began Beth.

"Please forgive my wife, Miss Cameron. She is new to our community and has Jamie's mother confused with—" Mr. Baird attempted to cover his wife's *faux pas*.

And Henrietta, large tears forming in her deep blue eyes, declared, "Oh my, I've put my foot in it this time, haven't I?"

The entire scene had such a sense of comedy to it that Varina, nerves already stretched to the breaking point, began to laugh, a bit hysterically at first, but as the laughter released her tension, she found she couldn't stop.

Soon, in spite of themselves, the Bairds joined her, and Henrietta was so obviously relieved that she had given no offense that Varina did not have the heart to reveal that her words had conjured frightful memories of Theodora's ghost and its eerie declaration.

Chapter Thirteen

As Varina bid good-bye to Mr. and Mrs. Baird, Henrietta embraced her.

"It has been a delight to meet you, my dear, and to know that Beth has such a friend. You must consider the manse your home away from home and come here often." She smiled so genuinely that her protruding front teeth seemed an asset, a charming addition to her comely face.

Reverend Baird's farewell was also a warm one.

"I have spent many pleasant hours with your Uncle William when we were both delegates to the General Assembly. He is a gentleman and scholar who holds my respect and admiration. Please call on me if I can help you in any way, child. I know how unsettling a strange household and new surroundings can be, and you must come to me if you have any difficulty."

Varina thanked him, smiling to herself at how like Uncle William he was in his love of words and the generous use of them.

Beth and Marjorie walked with Varina and Jamie to their carriage.

"Remember to bring your lunch in a pail tomorrow, Jamie, and a slate, if you have one," Marjorie reminded him.

Jamie nodded, then turned to Beth, slowly extending his small hand in farewell. Beth knelt beside the tiny boy as she took his hand.

"We're going to have a wonderful time at school, Jamie. I'm going to teach you your alphabet and how to read and how to write your name, and you're going to meet lots of other children who will be your playmates."

Varina admired the manner in which Beth addressed Jamie, treating him as she would any child, careful that no hint of pity or condescension showed in her tone or movements. Jamie nodded somberly in response, and as Varina lifted him into the carriage, she felt his arms tighten about her neck in a fleeting embrace. As they drove away from the manse, Jamie turned in his seat, watching Beth and Marjorie until they were no longer in sight, then continuing to watch the road behind him as if in hopes they would reappear.

Varina reported these hopeful signs to Andrew when she returned. The sedating effects of the drugs he had been given were finally waning, and he was up and dressed, much like his former self, except for his unusual pallor and the plaster on his cheek.

"I feel like such a fool." He cracked his knuckles in exasperation. "Perhaps being around other children is what Jamie has needed all along, and I've been so protective of him, so afraid he'd be made fun of, that I've kept him from the very ones who might help him most."

"Don't be so hard on yourself. Jamie did very well with Marjorie, who is an exceptional child, but how well he'll handle a schoolroom full of children only time will tell."

Varina knew she was warning herself as well as Andrew that their plan might still fail.

Cordelia, who had been working at the embroidery frame during this conversation, jabbed her needle into the canvas and surprised them both by expressing an opinion on a subject for which she had formerly shown little interest.

"I think you both spoil him too much. Of course he doesn't speak! The clever child has found that his silence garners all the attention he requires. Give him the back of a hairbrush and send him to bed without supper. Then you'll see how much noise he can make."

"You can't be serious," Varina sputtered, while Andrew looked at Cordelia incredulously.

The older woman, the picture of domesticity with her red-gold hair bent over her sewing, stabbed the canvas again. Then she lifted her head and smiled demurely at her companions. "It's only a theory," she insisted. "And isn't everything you've discussed for him up to now just that?"

Alarmed at Andrew's rising anger, visible in the veins standing out on his neck, Varina swiftly changed the subject. "That reminds me, Andrew. When we go to Tampa next week, will we be taking Jamie with us, or will he stay here with Fiona and Gordie so that he can attend school?"

"Let's see how well he settles in with Miss Baird and her charges before we make that decision. We can decide at the last minute if need be. Our reservations at the Tampa Bay Hotel are confirmed, and Rauol will be arriving soon in Ybor City. We can all be certain to enjoy ourselves."

With Cordelia's calloused opinion on childrearing forgotten in the anticipation of their upcoming excursion, Andrew returned to his newspaper.

During the following tranquil days, Varina began to wonder if her fears and questions had truly been the result of settling into a new environment as Reverend Baird had suggested. Even the fright she had experienced at Mrs. Baird's mention of murder had quickly subsided, her good common sense telling her that such a family, plainly with malice toward none, would not have laughed at rumors with substance. For the first time since her arrival, she began to feel like her normal self, no longer plagued by shifts in moods or fears and doubts, and beginning to enjoy herself immensely. While Jamie was at school, she completed her lists for shopping in Tampa, took long walks among the flowers of Andrew's gardens, and spent many happy hours playing with Arby, who would run and romp at her heels until exhausted, then curl up contentedly in her lap and sleep, while she shared a cup of tea with Duncan.

The afternoons and early evenings she spent with Jamie, sailing his boat from the dock, walking the paths where the deer crossed, and reading aloud her favorite stories before tucking her small charge in for the night. Evenings with Andrew and Cordelia were pleasant and relaxing, as Andrew read his newspapers and worked on his correspondence, and the two women read or sewed or took turns playing the piano. The pace and rhythm of her life had become comfortable and satisfying again, unbeset by rumors or restless spirits.

Jamie seemed to be adjusting well to school. Each morning after breakfast with his shiny new lunchpail packed with delectable goodies by Fiona and Robbie Roth's slate tucked under his arm, Jamie rode off to school in the wagon with Gordie. And each afternoon at three, Gordie brought him back, his lunchpail emptied and his slate filled with the day's lesson. He was still quiet, but he appeared to be more interested in what was happening around him. Varina and Andrew watched him closely, anxious that his school experiences be productive ones, and equally concerned that he not be harmed in any way. They tried also to be patient. The boy had been silent for a long time; talking again might take a while.

Another bright spot in the household was the change in Cordelia. Varina pondered over the reasons for Cordelia's growing interest in the other family members and her kinder treatment of them. Perhaps Cordelia, like Varina herself, was finally becoming acclimated to her new surroundings. Even the high-pitched whine of her voice had modulated to a more pleasant level, an indication of less tension perhaps. Both women were looking forward to their trip to Tampa the following week, so the formerly dreary dinner conversations were now alive with discussions of what they would see and do in what Andrew called the "Cigar City," a reference to the famous Cuban cigars that were handrolled in the factories there.

That Thursday evening as Fiona cleared away the dessert dishes, Andrew invited the two women to accompany him on a picnic the following day at Jerry Lake.

"I want to inspect some grove property that I'm thinking of purchasing. I need the land to raise some of the hybrid citrus strains I've developed. I thought we could drop Jamie off at school on our way, drive about the acreage, and then enjoy a picnic on the lakeshore."

"Sorry, Andrew, but you know how I feel about the great outdoors," Cordelia replied. "I much prefer the confines of the cardroom at the inn."

"Count me in, please," Varina answered. "I want to see as much of the country as I can."

"A picnic for two it is then," Andrew agreed. "And we will make it up to you next week, Cordelia, with more civilized entertainment in Tampa."

Cordelia smiled, an expression that for once went beyond her lips, extending to the vivid blue of her eyes, and Varina was struck anew by the woman's extraordinary beauty. If Theodora had looked like that, Varina thought, no wonder Andrew loved her.

A mild breeze, warm with the smell of pines, wafted out of the east the morning of their picnic, and as the threesome started out in the carriage toward school, Andrew checked the sky.

"See"—he pointed out to Jamie—"those high thick fleecy clouds, like cotton batting? That's called a mackerel sky, because the wavy clouds are like the markings on the fish."

Jamie leaned his head back over the seat as far as he could for a view of the clouds, until Varina, afraid that he would topple backwards out of the carriage, grabbed him about the knees and held tight.

"And the most important thing about such a sky," Andrew continued, encouraged by Jamie's interest, "is that it's a sign that the weather is about to change. Within the next twenty-four hours, the wind should shift to the north, and the temperatures will drop."

Jamie kept his awkward position, studying the clouds, until they entered the woods of Jerry Lake Road. Then he began to gather his belongings for school. When the carriage pulled into the schoolyard and stopped, Jamie hopped out without a backward glance and raced toward the group of children where he had spied Marjorie.

Beth Baird came forward to meet them, moving effortlessly through the heaving throngs of children on the playground.

"Good morning, Varina, Mr. McLaren." Unlike the stereotypical schoolmarm, Beth was elegant and lovely in a dress the color of her amethyst eyes. "I'm happy to see you are recovered, Mr. McLaren. I've been wanting to give you a report on Jamie."

"And I'm anxious to hear."

"Jamie is adjusting well to the routine of the classroom. He still does not speak, of course, but he is definitely a bright child who is very much aware of all that is going on around him. He is learning to write his alphabet and his numbers already."

"And how are the other children treating his silence?"

"When I introduced Jamie to the class, I told them that although he knows how to speak, for now he chooses not to. So far, there have been no problems, but, believe me, I will tolerate no teasing, and Marjorie will handle any in the schoolyard. Those two have become fast friends.

They need no words to communicate."

The three adults watched the small girl and boy sitting silently, observing the chaos of children playing before them.

"It's time for school to begin, so you must excuse me. I'll keep you informed, especially if there's any change."

"Thank you." Andrew stepped back into the carriage and picked up the reins. "You can send a message to me by Gordie Roth if need be."

Beth said good-bye, then rang the bell to line up her pupils for their opening exercises. Varina watched as Jamie took his place behind Marjorie without being told. She sat back in the carriage seat with a sense of satisfaction as they drove out of the schoolyard.

"I have the most hopeful feeling that Jamie is going to be talking soon."

Andrew, looking very pleased himself, put the horses to a trot. "Yes, I must admit that sending the boy to school seems to have been a very good idea—so far. But I can't allow myself to become too hopeful. It would make my disappointment all the worse if he doesn't improve."

The road made a right angle turn up a gently sloping hill. On their right were orange groves, but the land on their left was uncultivated and thick with pines, oaks, palmettos, and climbing vines that partially obscured many of the trees.

Andrew turned the carriage between two massive stone pillars, and there, nestled incongruously in the tangled wilderness, was the carefully tended lawn of a cemetery, its headstones and markers scattered beneath the moss-bearded oaks. Varina wondered if Theodora was buried here.

"Originally the center of the community was here," Andrew explained, "even the church, until the elders recognized that the population living closer to St. Joseph Sound was growing faster than the number of farmers and growers here and around Beckett Lake."

He brought the horses to a standstill and pointed east through the thicket that bordered the cemetery. "Just through there you can see Jerry Lake. The property I want borders the lake for quite a distance. Would you like a close-up view?"

With Varina's consent, Andrew moved the team slowly down the narrow trail that wound through the underbrush to the lakefront where a rowboat was secured to the pilings of a rugged dock that stretched several yards into the lake.

Once they were aboard, Andrew allowed the boat to drift along the shoreline as he inspected the slope and drainage of the property. Varina, enchanted by the primeval quiet of the scene, watched a group of red-beaked gallinules swim for shelter among the cattails. Further along the shore where wax myrtles bent toward the water, a gray anhinga clutched a branch that almost swept the glassy surface of the lake and spread its massive wings to dry in the warm sunlight.

"Look, Andrew." She pointed to the lake's surface a few feet in front of them. "What are those small bumps in the water between us and the shore?"

"We're being observed. Those 'bumps,' as you call them, are the eyes of an alligator. You can measure his size by computing the distance between his eyes. That one, I'd say, is over six feet long, and he's probably contemplating a gallinule entree for lunch."

Varina shuddered at the thought of the powerful reptile swimming only a few yards away, its tiny eyes breaking through the surface like the tip of a deadly iceberg.

"Don't worry. They rarely attack humans. Smaller prey is more to their appetite."

Andrew pulled at the oars, moving the boat toward the middle of the broad lake, then let it drift on the still waters. Varina, adjusting her straw boater to keep the sun from her face, could see the tallest of the cemetery monuments on the crest of the hill. She didn't want to think about death today. Instead, she looked at the man only a few feet away, and wondered about him as she had done so many times before.

Andrew had removed his jacket and rolled up his shirtsleeves, and now sat relaxed, soaking up the sunshine and looking as if troubles had never touched him. She felt an irrepressible desire to know all she could about him.

"What was it like growing up with Uncle William?"

"William is fifteen years older than I, so he was already in college by the time I was old enough to remember. Then he was off to seminary in

Richmond, and after that he married Mae and went to Memphis for his first church assignment. Most of my relationship with my brother was through our letters until after our parents died. After that I stayed with William and Mae whenever I wasn't on an expedition. They always made me feel that their home was mine; too, a haven I could return to whenever the glitter of travel began to tarnish."

The expression in his eyes was soft and warm as he remembered. "William and Mae always accepted me for myself and never tried to change me. They welcomed me when I arrived, treating me as a member of their wonderful family, and were sad when I departed, but they never attempted to tell me how I should live my life. They simply loved me for myself."

A gentle breeze ruffled Andrew's fine dark hair, and the healing scab on his left cheek stood out in stark relief against the pallor of his face. Varina thought of the multitude of experiences that Andrew had compressed into a relatively short lifetime: the formative years of his childhood spent in the midst of a bloody civil war; a youth lived in the deprivation of Reconstruction; a young adulthood filled with global travels; and finally maturity with the wrenching loss of a beautiful young wife and the pain of a son who would not speak. The reasons for Andrew's complexity of personality were understandable, but Andrew himself remained an enigma. Varina sighed, finding herself plagued by puzzles once more.

"Is all this boring you?"

Varina, her reveries broken, started guiltily.

"No, this could never be boring. There is too much to observe and learn. And yet it is all so soothing, too, and tranquil—"

The quiet was broken by the scream of a gallinule and the thrashing of water as the gator snapped his prey between his powerful jaws and plunged beneath the water's surface. The anhinga cried in alarm and beat the air with its wide wings as it flew away.

"So much for tranquillity." Andrew smiled a twisted smile. "It must be time for lunch."

Later, when Fiona's picnic lunch had been satisfactorily consumed, and they sat on a tartan spread beneath an ancient cypress tree in the cemetery, Andrew lay back with his arms folded behind his head and studied his young companion.

"What about you, Varina? I've been so preoccupied with Jamie and how you might help him that I've never thought to ask what plans you have for your future. With Jamie making such fine progress, I expect it won't be long before you'll be wanting to return home."

Varina, engrossed in removing sprays of beggar weed from the hem of her skirt, was glad Andrew couldn't see her face, because she knew that it reflected her dismay at the thought of leaving Jamie—and his father. She tried to make her voice sound lighthearted and channeled her thoughts in a happier direction.

"Uncle William and Aunt Mae have taught me to live for each day, *carpe diem,* and that's pretty much what I do. Oh, don't misunderstand. Uncle William saw to it that I am as well-educated as most men are, although I have no desire for a career. I've always thought that someday I'd marry and have a family—" She broke off in confusion, for her mention of marriage had tracked her thoughts back to Andrew. She assumed her casual tone again as she continued, "But the right person hasn't come along yet."

"And how will you know he's the right person?"

Andrew's question caught her by surprise, and she looked up to see his deep brown eyes studying her closely. Just in time she bit back the words that had sprung automatically to her lips, that the person she would want to spend the rest of her life with would be just like him. Instead, she shrugged, still attempting to appear nonchalant.

"I suppose he'll be someone like—" She groped awkwardly for an answer, any answer but the truth. "Like Uncle William," she lied.

Andrew, for the first time since her arrival, threw back his head and laughed a hearty resounding laugh that came from deep within him, a laugh of such intensity that tears gathered in his eyes and rolled down his cheeks. His laughter was so infectious that Varina joined him, until a stitch in her side caused her to gasp for breath.

Still chuckling, Andrew checked his pocket watch, then began gathering their belongings so they would be on time to pick up Jamie after school. When he had stowed the picnic basket and tartan in the carriage, he turned abruptly and walked across the lawn, stopping before a monument of the whitest marble Varina had ever seen. For several minutes he stood unmoving, every muscle rigid, as he stared at the marker. Varina stood behind him and read the words carved in the immaculate stone:

Theodora Vandemere McLaren
1865-1893
non semper ea sunt quae videntur

Things are not always what they appear to be, Varina translated to herself with a start. How many times had she said these very words to herself since her arrival here? And why were they engraved on Theodora's headstone?

Andrew said nothing and Varina was reluctant to ask him now. The man who stood before the grave of his wife was not the man she had spent her day with. His shoulders were braced as if he bore the weight of the world on them, and if he relaxed, his world would crumble around him. The malady of spirit had gripped him once more. Varina laid her hand gently upon his arm.

"Jamie will be waiting."

Once more she observed the metamorphosis occur as Andrew returned to himself. He placed his hand over hers and together they walked to the carriage. As they rode between the monuments and tombstones, Varina felt a smothering wave of guilt at experiencing such happiness with Andrew in the place where his wife was buried.

Later that evening as she sat in the nursery reading Jamie a bedtime story, she wondered why Andrew bore such a terrible weight from Theodora's death. The burden seemed greater, different somehow, from the painful but uncomplicated bereavement of a spouse. Did he feel guilty that he had not taken her back to New York so that she would not have died of—what? Her thoughts took her again in frustrating and dangerous directions, because she did not know how Theodora had died. Perhaps if she were here long enough to gain Andrew's trust, he might tell her the truth. Until then, she must try not to think of it. She laughed at the conundrum she had created for herself. All that was necessary to make a thought churn endlessly in her mind was to order herself not to think it.

She leaned over and kissed Jamie's plump cheek, fresh with the smell of soap, and quietly extinguished the lamp. Exhausted from his day at school, the little boy had fallen asleep before Varina had finished his story. He lay now, his golden curls spread on the pillow and Furry Rabbit clasped against his chest, cherubic and serene in his slumber. Varina's heart ached with a love that could not be greater if he were her own child.

She moved silently to her own room to find the book she wanted, looking forward to a few hours of solitary pleasure. Fiona and Gordie had long ago retired to their home for the night, and Andrew had gone to a meeting of the Citrus Growers Association at Library Hall, dropping Cordelia at the inn for an evening with the Ridenour sisters on the way.

Book in hand, Varina started down the front stairs toward the parlor when her attention was caught by the fog thickening against the landing window. Duncan had warned her about the treacherous sea fog, caused by the difference in temperatures between the air and water, but she had not observed it until tonight. The view from the window was almost obscured, but the heavy sea mist flowed on the wind currents, billowing in eddies and streams across the front lawn, and parting briefly, giving Varina a momentary view of the water's edge.

The sight exposed by the rift in the mist brought Varina to a halt. She stood as if frozen, dropping her book on the stairway and feeling the blood pound in her head like surges of ice water. There at the water's edge, seemingly suspended in the shrouds of mist, was Theodora, her wedding gown and veils almost indistinguishable from the fog that swirled about her.

Panic clawed at Varina's throat as she fought the impulse to scream and flee. Her hands gripped the windowsill as her eyes remained fastened on the spot where Theodora disappeared and reappeared in the fog. Lightheadedness caused by her hyperventilating made Varina fear that she would faint and plummet down the stairway until the thought of Jamie cleared her mind. She must see to it that Theodora did not frighten the boy. She would beg her to leave before she could do him more harm. Perhaps if she tried to speak with her, Varina could find out what the woman's restless spirit wanted and banish it forever. Before her resolve could melt away, Varina charged down the stairway and out the front door, determined to confront Theodora.

As she rushed onto the path that led across to the dock, she could no longer see the white spectre. The cloying fog filled her eyes and nostrils and dampened her clothes and hair, molding them to her body as she moved closer to the waterfront. Still there was no sign of Theodora. Varina stopped to listen, marveling at the muffling effect of the fog, fearing that she had gone deaf, until a thud at the end of the dock caught her attention and she moved toward the sound. As she stepped onto the dock, she thought she saw Theodora at its end, but the fog by now was so thick that she could not be sure.

Rashly moving onto the dock, determined somehow to put this ghost to rest, Varina slipped on the wet planking and would have pitched headfirst into the waters of the sound had there not been a piling there to stop her. More cautiously now, with her bravado gone and terror building again within her, she moved toward the end of the dock where Andrew's sailboat was moored. Briefly, the fog cleared, and Varina found herself alone on the dock with no sign of Theodora.

Then, seized by the horrifying thought that this had been a ploy to lure her away from Jamie, Varina turned back toward the house, prepared to run the length of the wet dock to return to the helpless boy. She gathered her skirts up to her knees, but before she could take the first step, she heard a noise on the boat. She was turning to look behind her when the blow fell, sending her flying off the dock and into blackness.

Chapter Fourteen

Varina swam against the smothering darkness, fighting her way back to semiconsciousness to find herself sprawled face down on wet boards amidst nets and lines that reeked of fish. Someone was pushing heavily upon her back and muttering in what sounded like German. In that instant, she knew she was going to be dreadfully sick. Pulling herself shakily to her knees, she lunged toward the side of the boat. Strong hands grasped and held her fast as she emptied her stomach of the salty seawater she had swallowed in copious quantity.

"Careful, girl. I fished you out once. Don't make me have to do it again." The heavily accented voice was kind, and the arms were gentle that caught her as she slipped back into darkness.

She was roused to consciousness a second time by a blast of sound. Lifting the heavy weight of her eyelids, she looked up through a curtain of sodden curls from where she lay in the bottom of a rowboat. Seated above her was a middle-aged man, slight but muscularly built, with a balding head and a thick blond beard and moustache. His bright blue eyes were magnified by the powerful lenses of his wire-rimmed spectacles, and his cheeks expanded like bellows as he blew on a large shell, sending a melancholy wail out into the fog. The noise intensified the pain that radiated from the back of her head, and she moaned softly.

"Hold on, girl. We're almost there," she heard the gentle voice assure her. Then the boat brushed against the pilings of a pier, and Varina watched as the man tied the boat fast, then reached into the bottom of the boat to lift her to the dock. When he had scrambled onto the dock himself, he took off his heavy oilskin coat and wrapped her in it.

"We have to get you inside. You're turning blue." He spoke compassionately, but Varina could barely hear him over her clattering teeth, which were rattling like castanets from the chill emanating from the center of her body. Gathering her again in his strong arms, the stranger carried her up the walk toward Fair Winds. As they approached the front door, Gordie and Fiona threw it open, illuminating Varina and her rescuer in the rectangle of light that spilled out from the hallway.

"We heard your signal . . . Good God!" Gordie stopped short as he recognized Varina in the man's arms.

"Bring her in, Henry," Fiona called. "Gordie, show him to her room and start the fire there. I'll bring extra blankets and get her out of those wet clothes."

Later, after Fiona had taken her soaked garments away and dressed her in a warm flannel gown, Varina sat propped up by pillows in the large poster bed, sipping a toddy of whiskey, honey, and lemon juice that Fiona had heated with a hot poker from the fireplace. Gordie and Henry had gone off to inspect the dock, searching for the assailant who had struck Varina across the back of her head, sending her into the water.

"Why ever did ye go out in that soup in the first place, lass?" Fiona asked as she rubbed Varina's wet curls with a towel. "Ye can get so disoriented in that mist that ye'd be lost till it cleared, and sometimes that takes days."

Her tone was stern but her expression was benevolent as she took the empty mug from Varina's shaking hands.

"I thought I saw someone at the waterfront. I . . ." Varina's voice trailed off weakly. She could not bring herself to say what she had seen. Fiona already thought her daft enough for going out in such weather. Talk of ghosts would make the woman believe her insane indeed.

"Well, God was looking after ye tonight, that's for certain. Only Henry Scharrer could have found ye in such a fog. With all his years of living on the island, he knows these waters like the hairs on the back of his hand."

"I'm sorry to be so much bother." Badly shaken as she realized how close she had come to drowning, Varina could barely speak, and she fought against the desire to weep.

Gordie entered the room, going directly to the fireplace to dry the dampness from his clothes. "Henry's gone home. He was anxious for his wife. Doesna like to leave her alone long, her being in the family way."

Steam had begun to rise from his wet clothing and he gratefully accepted the toddy Fiona had prepared for him.

"Henry said he was headed home when he heard a cry and then a splash, as if someone had fallen overboard. When he found ye and dragged ye out of the water, ye were unconscious and had swallowed a lot of water."

Gordie took a long drink of the potent brew. "Before Henry left, we searched the area as much as possible in this weather. And we found who knocked ye off yon pier."

Varina's head snapped up so sharply at Gordie's words that she rapped her already bruised crown painfully against the headboard.

"Who?" she winced.

" 'Twere na person, lass." Gordie smiled at her. "So ye can put your mind at ease about anyone wishing ye harm. The boom on the sailboat had come untied and was swinging free. What with the tide running high, the boom and its tackle would have been at about the height of your head."

Varina lay back and closed her eyes, trying to picture the boat as she had seen it through the fog, but her thoughts were clouded by the pain in her head. Had she imagined everything, including Theodora, in the swirling mist? Had her fall from the dock been a freak accident rather than a premeditated attack? She struggled to remember what she had been thinking before she was hit.

"Jamie! Is he safe?"

"Sleeping like an angel through all this hubbub, so dinna fret ye about the lad." Fiona placed more logs on the fire and settled into the rocking chair by the hearth. "Get ye home to bed, Gordie. I'll stay the night with Varina."

"Good night to ye then." Gordie's gray eyes smiled down at her, and his cheeks and nose glowed red from the cold and the toddy, like an image of Saint Nicholas. "I'm glad ye were na drowned. You're a good lass to have about."

"Get on!" Again Fiona's tone was stern, but her face was alight with love for the little man as she watched him scurry from the room.

The persistent throbbing of the back of her head awakened her, and when she opened her eyes, Varina saw that daylight filled the room. She lay quietly, hoping to still the pounding in her brain, but her eyes scanned the room nervously, reflecting her fear of being alone. At the window, framed in the noonday sunshine, was Cordelia, standing so motionless that she scarcely seemed to breathe. The fine bones of her patrician profile and her fiery hair were illuminated by the light that poured through the window in such unprecedented profusion that Varina felt disoriented, much as she had in last night's fog.

Memories of last night made her head ache worse as she grappled with the ambiguities of those events. She had been thoroughly convinced that she had seen Theodora before she ran from the house, but now in the cold and rational light of day, her former certainty seemed somewhat ridiculous. She had almost gotten herself killed by her foolishness, and she flushed with shame at the trouble she had caused.

Then another recollection—or was it a dream?— bubbled into her consciousness, a vision of Andrew, his face anxious and drawn, sitting by her bed, holding her small hand in his as the fire burned low in the grate. Dream or not, the image comforted her, and she clung to it, pushing thoughts of fog and icy waters away.

"Silly man," Cordelia spoke in a low voice to herself. "There won't be any tree left at the rate he's hacking away at it." She turned at the sound of Varina's stirring and moved to plump the pillows behind her as Varina sat up cautiously, each movement sending tiny slivers of pain through her head.

"So you're finally awake. How are you feeling?" Cordelia, her black taffeta skirts rustling as she moved, smoothed the bedclothes, then pulled the bell that signaled the kitchen.

"Beastly," Varina replied, "but no more than I deserve for acting so foolishly."

"We're all very relieved at your incredible good fortune. If Henry Scharrer had not been passing by—and I understand only he would venture onto the water in such weather—you would now be the late Miss Cameron."

Varina again was assaulted by guilt and confusion, but her thoughts were interrupted by noises outside the window, and she looked to Cordelia, puzzlement visible on her face.

"It's only Gordie," Cordelia explained. "He's been pruning and sawing at that tree for hours. He's already filled the wagon with the Spanish moss he's removed, and now he's thinning out the branches to let more light into the house."

Now Varina understood why the room was brighter than before. Andrew and Gordie were wasting no time in getting started on the lists of chores she had made for them, all intended to improve the atmosphere of the house for Jamie.

"Where is Jamie?" Her fear that someone might harm him, as irrational as it now seemed, returned.

"He's been off to school for hours now. It's practically noon. I've rung for Fiona. She said to let her know when you were awake and she would bring your breakfast."

Cordelia settled in the slipper chair and picked up her handwork which lay on the table. Varina watched the nimble movements of her long slender fingers as she crocheted intricate patterns of lace. The soothing monotony of the repetitious motions of Cordelia's hands had almost lulled her back to sleep when Fiona bustled into the room with a breakfast tray.

"Ye still look a bit peaked, lass," she clucked as she placed the tray across Varina's lap. "Ye best stay abed today."

Varina felt too weak to argue as she sipped hot tea and nibbled the toast. She had no appetite, and her head was spinning as much from unanswered questions as from the blow she had received.

"Please take the tray away." She thanked the kindly housekeeper before she lay back amongst her pillows. Her last sight before drifting off into unconsciousness once more was of Cordelia, sitting in the beam of sunlight that poured in the window, working complex designs into the fragile lace.

When she awoke again, the pain in her head had subsided, and she could tell from the angle of the sunlight through the French doors that it was late afternoon. As she sat up in bed, she started when she saw that Jamie sat propped against the footboard, watching her intently.

"Hello, my favorite boy." She opened her arms to him, and he hastened to her, twining his chubby arms around her neck and burying his face in her hair. "You mustn't worry about me," she assured him. "I really am all right."

Drawing back, the little boy scrutinized her carefully, making his own assessment of her well-being. Seemingly satisfied that she was indeed in no danger, he clambered down from the high bed and went off toward his room.

Fiona stood aside in the doorway to let him pass.

"You've got visitors," she announced. "News travels fast in this tiny town, and I'm sure we have our Gordie to thank for it. Mrs. Baird and Elizabeth are here to see ye, if ye feel up to it."

Varina felt remarkably recovered, the only ill effect from her mishap the tender spot on the back of her head that caused her to flinch as she brushed her hair. Drawing on a beribboned bed jacket, she instructed Fiona to send the Bairds up.

Henrietta swept into the room in a flourish, the ostrich plumes of her elegant hat bobbing and weaving as she came forward to greet Varina, kissing her warmly on the cheek and pressing a handpainted tin box into her hands.

"We were so distressed to hear of your accident that we had to come immediately to see for ourselves that you are unhurt." Settling gracefully into the slipper chair, her eloquent hands fluttering as she spoke, she smiled fondly at Varina. "However, you look absolutely blooming, and I am glad to see it."

Beth also greeted Varina with a kiss, tapping the tin box that Henrietta had given her.

"Cookies," she explained. "Henrietta's favorite remedy for whatever ails you."

Varina was touched that the two women had come to see her. Their presence brought home once more the isolation she had felt since coming to Fair Winds. As she listened to Beth's news of the school and Henrietta's plans for the Christmas dance at Library Hall, her accident of the previous evening seemed less and less real.

"You must help us decorate the hall for the dance, Varina," Henrietta insisted, "and Jamie, too. Marjorie will enjoy his company."

Before Varina could reply, Fiona bustled in, carrying a gargantuan bouquet of roses and lilies, their sweet scent filling the room.

"Duncan brought you these," she explained as she placed them in a large vase on the bureau. "I dinna have the knack for fixing these, but this will keep them fresh until ye feel like doing them yourself."

"Is Duncan here?" Beth asked, failing utterly at appearing nonchalant.

"Aye, he's having a cup o' tea in the kitchen." Fiona gave the blossoms a last adjustment. "Is there anything else ye need, lass?" she asked Varina.

Again Varina was cut off before she could reply.

"I'll come down with you, Fiona, if you don't mind. I'd like to ask Duncan to get a Christmas tree for the schoolroom. And I'll see you in church Sunday, Varina." With a preoccupied wave, Beth followed Fiona from the room.

"Mark my words," Henrietta said, looking extremely pleased with herself, "there'll be a wedding at our house before next summer."

Events were unfolding too rapidly for Varina, and it took a moment for her to understand the significance of Henrietta's words.

"You mean Beth—and Duncan? That's wonderful news! They do seem suited to one another, now that I think about it."

Henrietta nodded in agreement, the royal blue plumes of her hat punctuating her assent. "I understand they've been friends for a long time, but Beth always felt such a duty to her father and his church that she wouldn't think of marriage. But now"—the minister's wife giggled delightfully—"Beth can leave her father to me and have her own life. Isn't it marvelous?"

Varina felt her affection for Henrietta increasing with each minute she spent with the woman who was so unassuming and so genuinely fond of people that she virtually emanated good will.

Suddenly, however, Henrietta's manner changed as she rose and crossed the room, checking the hallway before closing the door noiselessly. She moved swiftly toward the bed, sitting on its edge and taking Varina's hands in her own.

"Now you must tell me exactly what happened last night."

Varina could not bring herself to tell even the lovable Henrietta about Theodora, but neither could she lie, so she decided on a middle ground.

"I thought I saw a woman at the waterfront, and thinking she was lost in the fog, I went down to check. When I ventured onto the dock, the boom of Andrew's sailboat had come untied, and swung in the wind, catching me on the back of the head and knocking me into the water. Henry Scharrer came along and fished me out. It's as simple as that."

It sounded so plausible as she told it, that Varina was beginning to believe that version herself, so Henrietta's next question caught her offguard.

"And where was Andrew McLaren all this time?"

"He was at the Citrus Growers Association meeting. Why do you ask?"

Distress was etched across Henrietta charming face. "There was no meeting of the Growers Association last night, Varina."

"Oh." Varina, unable to say more, sat looking blankly at the woman before her.

"Promise me, my girl, that you will be very, very careful, and that you will come to us if you need help. I am not one for rumor-mongering, but there have been strange tales circulating about this house and this family. There may be no truth in any of them, but something is definitely amiss here, and you must be cautious."

Then her serious demeanor shifted to her former warm smile, and Henrietta bid Varina good-bye until Sunday.

Lying back on the pillows, Varina wrestled with a new puzzle. Why had Andrew lied about his whereabouts last night, and if he had not been at the meeting, where had he been?

Chapter Fifteen

Feeling fully recovered, with the exception of a tender spot on the back of her head, Varina went down with Jamie for breakfast the next morning to find Andrew and Cordelia already at their places. Cordelia greeted them both with unaccustomed friendliness, and Andrew was uncharacteristically solicitous of Varina's well-being, insisting that she be seated while he served her breakfast from the buffet on the sideboard.

Both seemed so calm and reassuring that once again Varina chastised herself for her former apprehensions. That Andrew had not been at the growers' meeting did not necessarily mean that he had been involved in anything improper, including her own accident, but only that he did not think his whereabouts that evening were anyone else's concern.

"We leave Monday morning for Tampa as planned," he announced, "the earlier the better. And you, my boy, will stay with Gordie and Fiona while we are gone so you will not miss your lessons with Miss Baird."

Andrew spooned marmalade generously onto his toast as he spoke. "Gordie is going to paint the nursery while you're staying with him, and Varina will have some surprises for you when we return." He turned to Varina. "And there might be a surprise or two for you, as well."

"I don't know if I'm up to many more surprises," Varina admitted, unconsciously touching her tender scalp.

As she finished her breakfast, Andrew scanned the front page of the newspaper by his plate, shaking his head despairingly.

"The news from Cuba isn't good. The continued Spanish repression of the natives is deplorable. I'll be glad to see Rauol and get a firsthand account of what is really happening there."

Cordelia rose from the table. "Politics may fascinate you, my dear Andrew, but I, for one, am looking forward to shopping again. I've decided it's time to put aside mourning for my sister, so I will need a complete new wardrobe. That will keep me busy the entire time we are in Tampa, I should think."

"If it makes you happy, then it will be three days well spent." Laughing at his own pun, he patted Jamie's head as he left room with a lightness to his step and as carefree an expression as Varina had seen since her arrival.

The day of their journey was clear and fine, the Florida sky a spacious expanse of cloudless blue filled only with the mild caresses of a south breeze and the scent of pines and loquat blossoms. The two women stood restlessly, anxious to be off, as Gordie and Andrew secured their luggage in the carriage.

"We'll only be there three days, Cordelia. You've packed enough luggage for a fortnight." Andrew puffed as he struggled to wedge a hatbox beneath the seat.

Varina turned to Jamie, who stood waiting with Fiona until Gordie could drive him to school. All the excitement and expectations of her journey melted away at the sight of the tiny figure who watched their preparations without expression. Bending down, she drew his body to hers, as the thought of being separated from him seared through her with a pain that left her breathless.

"I know you'll be a good boy for Fiona, so I promise to bring you something very special when I return." Her words caught in her throat as she hugged him. His small arms tightened around her neck, and even when she set him on his feet, he refused to let her go. Gently, she pulled away, but when she saw a tear slip down the boy's cheek, she was ready to ask Andrew to take her bags from the carriage and leave her behind.

Sensing her dilemma, Fiona picked up Jamie. "Dinna ye worry, lass. He'll be fine with me. Without my usual duties here, I'll have lots of time to spend with him while you're away. Get on now, and have a lovely time."

Reluctantly, Varina climbed into the carriage beside the impatient Cordelia. Andrew snapped the reins, and they were off. Varina turned to watch until they rounded the bend in the bluff road and Fair Winds could no longer be seen. She knew she had grown too fond of the boy and that when she had to return to New Bern, it would be a thousand times worse than this parting.

The beauty of the day, the novelty of the journey, and the high spirits of her companions soon chased away her sadness at leaving Jamie behind. By the time they had passed through Dunedin and taken the Tampa Road, she found herself caught up in the pleasure of the drive and the anticipation of events to come.

"How far is it to Tampa?" Varina asked after they had traveled the deserted road for more than an hour without encountering any fellow travelers.

"That depends," Andrew replied. "If we had a straight road, I would say about twenty-five miles, but as you've already seen, this road is anything but straight."

Varina nodded, looking ahead at a curve in the road where drivers had wound their way around fallen trees, rather than clear them, until the course of the road itself had changed, zigzagging all the way.

"Because the road has so many doglegs, I'd say it's closer to thirty-five miles total distance. Still, we should be there well before dinner," Andrew said.

They stopped for lunch on the northern shore of Tampa Bay, spreading their blanket beneath a huge pine tree to shade themselves from the onslaught of the tropical sun. The tide was low, and from the high-water mark to the water's edge were yards of rippled sand, teaming with life, from the comic sidling shuffles of fiddler crabs to the graceful arabesques of long-legged water fowls.

Andrew sat gazing along the bay's shoreline which curved away from them to the right and left. The bay was frothed with white caps whipped up by the stiff onshore winds.

"You should enjoy all this natural beauty while you can," he said, "because in our lifetimes, most of it will disappear."

"Oh no, you can't be serious," Varina countered. "There is so much land here, it will take centuries to populate it all."

"Perhaps when we get to Tampa, you will understand better what I mean. Less than twenty years ago, Tampa was a small insignificant settlement of less than four hundred people. Since Henry Plant brought his Orange Belt railroad to town and connected it with the Port of Tampa, the population has grown to over four thousand."

"But does that necessarily mean it will continue to grow at that rate? New Bern's population continues to expand, but not in geometric proportions as Tampa's has. Won't the rate probably stabilize now?" Varina hated to think of the wilderness that surrounded her no longer existing.

"With growing industries, the best port facility in the state, and an unequaled climate, the influx of commerce and people will continue. And if war with Spain ever comes, the troops will disembark from Tampa most likely. And once they've seen how beautiful it is here, they'll return with their families. That growth is like an avalanche. There is nothing that can be put in its way to stop it now."

"Why would anyone wish to?" Cordelia asked. "Such progress can only bring all the goods, services, and amenities that civilized people are accustomed to. Where's the harm in that?"

Andrew shaded his eyes with his hand, then pointed to the sky over the western shore. Circling in wide majestic sweeps was an American bald eagle, sunlight reflecting from its wings.

"No harm at all, as long as there remains a place for creatures like those and a habitat to support them."

Varina studied Andrew watching the eagle, struggling anew to understand the character of the man before her. It was as if seven years had fallen away and he was the young impetuous Andrew once more, his vital interest in the natural world shining from his face as his eyes followed the circling movements of the majestic bird of prey.

But even as she watched, the transformation she had witnessed many times before came over him, and he stood as if disgusted with his surroundings, anxious to move on.

As they drew closer to the city, they began to pass small farms, but Varina was totally unprepared for the sight which rose above the pines as they neared their destination. Thirteen graceful minarets punctuated the skyline with the glistening silver of their onion shapes and tapered spires. Even Cordelia, a seasoned world traveler inured to the exotic, gave a gasp of delight.

"What is it?" Varina asked. "It looks like a scene from *The Arabian Nights*."

"Those are the towers of the Tampa Bay Hotel. Henry Plant's architect, John Wood, employed Moorish revival style, and those minarets represent the thirteen months of the Moslem calendar," Andrew explained.

He slowed the horses as they broke through the trees and the remainder of the hotel came into sight, a fantastical building of domes and spires with huge doors and windows constructed in the keyhole shapes of the Middle East. Accenting the Moorish forms on the veranda that extended across the front expanse of the hotel was delicate woodwork of gingerbread trim, making the facade resemble an elaborately decorated wedding cake. The building stretched gracefully along the west bank of the broad Hillsborough River, and from the hotel's wide porches and generous windows, guests could view the emerging city of Tampa on the opposite bank.

The entire hotel complex bespoke a style of life that Varina had only read about. As they approached the main building, they passed a golf course, boat house, race track, kennels, stables, tennis courts, and rail sidings for the guests' private cars. Varina was fascinated by the sight of guests being carried in rickshaws through the gardens that bordered the river.

Andrew laughed at the expression of disbelief on her face. "They even use the rickshaws indoors to transport guests along the lengthy corridors."

"Whatever for?" Varina's eyes widened even further. "Are so many of them infirm?"

"Don't be silly," Cordelia insisted. "It's the height of luxury."

"Well, I'll do my own walking, thank you very much," Varina said. "Enough time when I'm old and feeble to have someone else cart me about."

But all these sights did not prepare Varina for the grandeur of the hotel itself. The domed ceiling of the immense lobby was two stories high, its surrounding balcony supported by massive double columns of polished marble. Wide graceful staircases wound upward, their newel posts the standards for bronze-cast statues in Grecian styles. The furnishings were as elegant as the guests who wandered amongst them. French antique chairs and sofas were grouped in conversational settings, and the table surfaces and walls were covered with Oriental art treasures and Venetian and Florentine glass.

A perky young maid, whose starched black dress and white apron crackled when she walked, showed Varina and Cordelia to their rooms and informed them that Mr. and Mrs. Plant themselves had toured both the Orient and Europe to find appropriate furnishings for the hotel. Then her voice dropped discreetly, and the black ribbons of her cap fluttered as she looked about to make sure she was not overheard.

"And they spent over a million dollars and filled eight boxcars with the furniture for this place."

"Now there's a shopping spree that warms my heart." Cordelia laughed.

Varina turned first one way and then the other as they traversed the long broad hallway, taking in every object of statuary and painting until her head swam with the extravagance of it all and her neck ached from exertion.

Proudly, the young servant switched on the lights in Varina's room. "This is the first fully electrified building in Tampa."

As she unpacked Varina's bag, the young woman chattered happily about the grand hotel and its two ballrooms, grand salon, solarium, dining rooms, and a feature that Varina was certain Uncle William would not approve of— a casino with an indoor heated swimming pool.

By the time the maid had finished and gone on to unpack for Cordelia, Varina felt battered by so much elegance and found herself longing once more for the simplicity of Aunt Mae's kitchen. Such grandeur and wealth intimidated her, and she hoped her manners—and her wardrobe—would suffice and prevent her from causing Andrew any embarrassment.

The gleaming white tile and fixtures of the modern bathroom were a soothing relief after so much baroque decoration and art, and Varina was wearily washing the dust of travel from her face and hands when someone knocked at her door. She opened it to find Andrew standing in the hallway, a bouquet of delicate pink and white lilies in his hands.

"These are for your room. Makes it seem less impersonal when you have your own flowers, and they also have a lovely fragrance. I know the concierge here well, fortunately, and he can supply me with whatever we need." He nodded toward the blossoms as he held them out to her.

Varina was momentarily speechless, for here was an Andrew she had not seen before, somewhat like his old self, but more mature and self-confident than impetuous. She took the flowers, then stood aside and asked him in. Filling a porcelain vase from her night table with water, carrying it nervously when she realized it was of Oriental antiquity, she placed the sweet-scented lilies in it as Andrew inspected her room.

"Is everything all right? You have only to ask if you need anything."

She was disconcerted by this new Andrew, who until now had always seemed distracted, his concentration riveted on matters having nothing to do with her, but who at this moment stood studying her intently, his scrutiny of her making her awkward and tongue-tied. She stammered that her accommodations were more than adequate.

"Then all is as it should be. I want you to be comfortable and well looked after here. You have come to mean a great deal to Jamie and me, and—" He crossed to the window, gazing out across the river at the lights of the town that were twinkling through the dusk. When he turned back to her a moment later, he was the old Andrew once more, barely looking at her and speaking over his shoulder as he crossed to the door.

"I know it's been a long and tiring journey, so I've arranged to have room service bring dinner to your room—and to Cordelia, as well. Then tomorrow morning you can make an early start on your shopping. I've arranged for letters of credit for whatever you need."

Varina experienced a wave of disappointment at not having dinner with Andrew in one of the grand dining rooms, but she reminded herself that there would be other nights and that Andrew was being sensible.

"Well, then, I'll see you at breakfast tomorrow. Rest well, Varina." He stood for an instant, his eyes holding hers, but so dark and unfathomable that she did not know what to read from them. Then he was gone.

Later, when she had finished the excellent

meal prepared, according to her informative maid, by a chef Plant had brought in from Delmonico's in New York, Varina stood at the window, puzzling over Andrew. He was a man of so many moods and faces that she felt she could never know which, if any, was real. The fragrant lilies perfumed the room, reminding her of him with each breath she took, and she studied the scene before her to block him from her mind.

She watched the lights being lit along the Lafayette Street bridge that stretched from the hotel grounds across the river to the town where she would shop tomorrow for toys and furnishings for Jamie.

"Dear God," she prayed aloud, "please help me to do what's right for that adorable child, and forgive my coveting him for my own. Surely it can't be sinful to love a child so deeply."

She was about to step away from the window when her attention was caught by a carriage that had stopped on the avenue below her. The grounds were lighted, but not well enough for her to identify the tall and vaguely familiar man, the brim of his hat pulled low across his face, who waited beside the rented hack. However, the identity of the woman who rushed to his arms seemed unmistakable as the lamplight reflected on her red-gold hair. Her hooded cape had fallen back as the man lifted her from her feet in his embrace, and her face was exposed as the woman returned his greeting with a fervor that made Varina's mouth drop.

Varina continued to stand agog at the window as the carriage with Cordelia and her mysterious male companion pulled away from the hotel and crossed the Lafayette Street bridge.

Chapter Sixteen

"I'm sorry," Varina pulled her thoughts back to the present. "What did you say?"

"I simply asked if you slept well," Cordelia replied as she buttered a portion of muffin and popped it daintily into her mouth, smiling all the while like a tremendously pleased feline who has been served the best cream.

"Yes, very well, thank you," Varina fibbed, remembering the hours she lay awake as pictures of Cordelia and her secret gentleman played through her mind like a magic lantern show. Had that man been Andrew? The thought of Cordelia in Andrew's arms had caused her a sleepless agony that made her rejoice to see the sunrise, even though she arose weary and confused.

"I slept like the dead myself. I was so

exhausted that after the exquisite dinner they served me, I went straight to bed." She gave a slight stretch, like a cat in the sun. "This really is the most marvelous place. I could live here forever."

Varina looked at the woman closely. Was Cordelia the world's most adept liar, or had Varina's imagination played tricks on her once more, as it seemed to do so often lately? She saw that Cordelia was aware of her scrutiny, so she tried to act naturally, but as she lifted her coffee cup, her hand was trembling. Now, as from the day of her arrival at Fair Winds, she no longer knew what was real and what was imagined. Was this constant uncertainty an indication that her grasp on reality was slipping? *"Non semper ea sunt quae videntur.* Things are not always what they appear to be." The words from Theodora's tombstone leapt into her mind, and she set her cup down with a clatter, wincing at the thought of cracking the magnificent Limoges china of the grand dining room.

"Good morning, ladies." Andrew seated himself at their table and a waiter appeared instantly at his elbow, pouring coffee and taking his order. Varina sighed, relieved that Andrew's arrival had broken the frustrating circle of her thoughts and distracted Cordelia's attention.

"Rauol is to meet me this morning and I will spend the day with him, so I have arranged for carriages to take you into the city to do your shopping."

"How thoughtful of you, Andrew dear," Cordelia replied. "I can't wait to find a decent dressmaker."

"The concierge will have some helpful suggestions for you, I'm sure," Andrew said. "And for you also, Varina."

Varina stammered and blushed in both guilt and confusion. *You silly twit*, she admonished herself. *Go ahead and ask them what they did last night, but then Cordelia has already said she stayed in her room, and you were so certain it was Cordelia you saw.*

Varina looked up to find Andrew's eyes observing every nuance of expression that flitted across her face. She felt naked and exposed, as if her thoughts were printed in tall letters across her forehead, proclaiming to Andrew that either she had caught him in a tryst with his sister-in-law, or, even worse, her imagination had led her past the bounds of sanity.

She smiled weakly. "My shopping list is ready," was all she could say before she returned her eyes to her plate and concentrated on finishing her breakfast.

So absorbed was she in her soft-boiled egg that she was startled when a strange voice spoke at her elbow.

"*Buenos dias*, my good friend McLaren."

"Rauol!"

Andrew jumped up from his chair and embraced the speaker, thumping him on the back enthusiastically. Rauol, a short plump man with skin as brown as coffee and hair gleaming like a crow's wing, radiated a cordial dark-eyed smile that took in both women as well as Andrew. He could have been any age. The nutmeg smoothness of his skin suggested youthfulness, but from the sprinkling of gray hairs above his ears, Varina guessed him to be at least forty.

"Cordelia, Varina, this is Dr. Rauol Garcia whom I've told you so much about." He motioned for Rauol to join them and signaled the waiter to set a place. Then he launched into question after question about Rauol's work in Cuba as well as the unrest among the rebels there, jumping from point to point so quickly that Rauol had no time to answer, but only watched his friend in amusement at his thirst for information. Then, seeing that Andrew's questions were excluding the women, Rauol raised his hands in a gesture of surrender.

"Please, Andrew. We have before us the entire day to talk of these things, and I promise to answer all your questions. But for now, let us enjoy the company of these beautiful *senoritas*." His expression held such geniality that Varina could not help contrasting this thoughtful and cultured gentleman with the arrogant and menacing Estaban Duarte.

"Before we go any further," Rauol was saying, "I wish to invite all three of you to spend the afternoon with me tomorrow. I will show you Ybor City and then you will dine with me tomorrow evening."

"A wonderful idea! We accept." Andrew answered for them all, without waiting for a reply from Cordelia or Varina.

Varina found the idea of seeing the Cuban settlement intriguing, but was surprised that Cordelia seemed interested as well. She waited for one of Cordelia's typical excuses, but Cordelia simply sat, smiling her feline smile.

Soon the women had finished their meal, and when they rose from the table, Rauol stood and bowed, kissing the hand of each in continental fashion as he bid them *adieu* until tomorrow. Glancing back as she left the dining room, Varina saw the two men in deep deliberation, their heads bowed close together over their coffee cups.

Later that evening as she dressed for her first formal dinner in the palatial hotel, she reviewed with satisfaction the results of her day's shopping. For Jamie's room she had purchased a gleaming brass bedstead; drapery material of pale yellow linen to complement the cream-colored paint Gordie would be using to cover the dark paneling; a military campaign chest with shiny brass fittings for the toy soldiers, puzzles, and other toys she had also purchased; and for Jamie's bed, a boldly patterned blanket in bright primary colors, woven, so the shop owner had claimed, by Seminole Indians; and an article that no nursery should be without, a bentwood rocking chair with caned back and seat.

Closing her eyes, she could visualize the

results of her efforts, a gratifying change from the predominant gloominess of the boy's surroundings. But something was missing. Then she remembered the small wicker bed for Arby that would fit snugly in the corner at the foot of Jamie's bed. And she would have Gordie build child-high shelves so that Jamie could start a collection of his treasures as Andy and Harris had, until the boards bowed from the load of books, birds' nests, smooth stones, seashells, beetles in jars, and all the other objects that small boys find so fascinating.

All of her purchases, including Christmas gifts for each member of the household, bought from her own funds, would be delivered next week by dray. In her excitement over her shopping, Varina had all but forgotten Cordelia's puzzling departure of the previous night—if, in fact, it had been Cordelia—until the maid knocked at the door with a box from the florist, containing a spray of ivory tea roses with a card that read "For Varina, who should always have flowers—Andrew."

As she smoothed the skirt of her green silk gown and pinned the roses in her hair, she decided she would not waste any more energy over what she had or had not seen. Whatever the truth was, it was none of her concern. But even as she attempted to convince herself, her hand strayed to the roses in her hair, and she knew that if Andrew loved Cordelia, that she had lost not only him, but Jamie, too, a thought too painful to bear. She picked up her bag and shawl and hurried from the room, anxious for any distraction to push such thoughts from her mind.

Andrew and Cordelia were waiting for her in the lobby, Andrew elegant in black and white evening dress and Cordelia breathtaking in a black brocaded silk that set off her pale complexion, white shoulders, and stunning hair. Pinned to her decolletage were gardenias which she was thanking Andrew for when Varina arrived. Varina had never felt more like a country cousin.

She felt even more gauche when they entered the grand dining room. Almost every table beneath the high-domed ceiling was filled with expensively dressed and bejeweled guests, yet the room was practically noiseless due to the discreet tones in which these scions of wealth and power conducted themselves. A string quartet played subdued Mozart, and the entire scene was a panoply of hothouse flowers, flickering tapers, sterling tableware, and delicate porcelain china that left Varina feeling hopelessly inadequate to cope with such august circumstances.

Andrew, as if he sensed her discomfort, took her by the elbow and led her to her seat, honoring her with a dignity that would have suited royalty. As she realized that he had taken control, leaving her no decisions in which she might feel unsure, she relaxed and began to enjoy her surroundings, taking in the details to remember for Jamie and Fiona.

As they progressed through the numerous gourmet courses, from sea trout to roast beef and duckling to an array of desserts, fruits, cheeses, and cafe demitasse, Andrew entertained them with the story of Rauol Garcia and how he had come to meet him.

Rauol, according to Andrew, had been one of fourteen children born to a Cuban peasant couple. As with all Cuban peasants, his family was extremely poor, and all the children went to work as soon as possible simply to supply enough food to feed such a number. When Rauol was nearly eight years old, he had gone to work for an American who owned a botanical plantation near the village where Rauol's family lived.

At first, Rauol carried water, pulled weeds, and raked the paths of the American's gardens, but the boy had not worked there for long before the planter was impressed not only by Rauol's quick mind and genial disposition, but also by the love the boy had for the flowers and plants that he tended. The elderly American and his wife had no children of their own, and they asked Rauol's parents if the boy could live with them. He was treated as their own son and given the education and training traditional for the upper class to which the American couple belonged.

When he reached an appropriate age, he was sent to America to the best preparatory schools and college and studied botany and horticulture as his adoptive father had. When his training was finished, he returned to Cuba to run the plantation for his adoptive father, who by now was too old and infirm to see to the job himself. Rauol had not been there many years when the American died, leaving all his holdings in Cuba to Rauol. Rauol continued to care for his adoptive mother until she, too, died a few years later.

By that time, having never forgotten his humble beginnings, Rauol had moved his own mother and father onto the plantation and provided his brothers and sisters and their families with work there. Andrew had met Rauol years ago at Edison's home in Fort Myers where the two botanists had traveled to consult with the inventor on plants that might provide natural fibers suitable for the filament for his electric light bulbs. Their shared passion for growing things and an agreeable compatibility of dispositions forged a friendship that had grown over the years, nurtured by regular visits and frequent correspondence.

"Because Rauol does not come from aristocratic Spanish stock, unlike most landowners in Cuba, he has firsthand knowledge of the plight of Cuban peasants and is passionately concerned for their welfare," Andrew explained. "He is here in Tampa to gain support for their cause from the Cuban expatriates who live here."

"Will we meet any of these tomorrow?" Cordelia asked.

Cordelia's interest took them both by surprise.

"Yes, I suppose we might."

Again the catlike smile, inscrutable and enigmatic, appeared on the woman's beautiful face. "Good," was all she said.

Later, as Andrew and Cordelia whirled about the ballroom floor beneath the blaze of light from the electric chandeliers, Varina was overwhelmed by a sense of isolation, even in the midst of hundreds of people. Her loneliness, she decided, had little to do with her feelings of estrangement from the wealthy with whom she mingled, their aristocratic faces carefully composed portraits of hauteur, or in many cases, boredom. No, her isolation sprang more from the sudden realization that not only Andrew and Cordelia, but also Fiona, Gordie, and even Jamie, all seemed to know something that she did not know, something of utmost importance that they guarded carefully, lest its significance be diluted or denounced; something that bespoke danger in its knowing, but even worse peril in ignorance of it. And suddenly, as if the fingertips of a ghostly Theodora had brushed across her face, Varina was the most frightened she had been in her short life, and the worst aspect of that gripping fear was that she did not know why.

Dr. Rauol Garcia was a gracious and well-informed tour guide. As they traveled through Tampa into Ybor City, headed for one of the cigar factories, they passed row upon row of neat frame cottages with deep porches and shuttered windows behind their picket fences. Rauol

Darkness at Fair Winds

pointed to the large nail protruding by the front door of each cigar worker's home.

"Each morning before the household has awakened, the long loaves of Cuban bread are delivered by the bakery and hung on that nail for the family's breakfast."

When they reached the three-story frame building that housed the cigar factory, Varina could smell the tobacco in the air, all of it, as explained by Rauol, the excellent clear Havana leaves grown only in Cuba. As they moved through the building, Varina saw that unlike other factories of the industrial age whose walls resounded with the whine and roar of machines, the cigar factory was a place of quiet, even contemplation. Workmen sat at their benches, using curved knives and the trained feel of their hands to roll the high-priced, clear Havana cigars on their hardwood boards.

"When the cigars are completed here, they are taken to the pickers, who sort the cigars by size and color, and then to the packers, who place them in boxes."

Rauol whispered to his entourage so he did not disturb the lector, a reader who sat on a raised platform and read to the workers from newspapers, labor publications, poetry, and novels.

"Their favorite author is Cervantes. Here it is possible to receive a very broad education while one works," Rauol explained when they had left the building. "This lector is paid by the workers themselves; therefore, the factory owner cannot control what materials he reads. But other company benefits the workers are granted include the privilege to smoke as many of the cigars as they want while they work, to have coffee served at their benches, and to take three cigars a day home or to sell, as they wish."

"Do they make a good living at such a trade?" Varina asked.

"Indeed," Rauol answered. "Their wages are determined by a system of piecework, so much money for every thousand cigars produced. This enables the worker to control his income, to some extent, and also to set his own hours and pace of work."

Rauol went on to explain that the needs of the cigar workers were simple, but that especially since the Cuban patriot and poet, Jose Marti, had made his first visit to Ybor City three years ago, the workers, through the Cuban Revolutionary Party, had contributed heavily from their earnings to the cause of *Cuba libre*.

"These people are good citizens. They love the country that has taken them in. But they are immigrants, driven from their homes by the cruelties of the Spanish, and their hearts will always be in Cuba."

The carriage had stopped before a small cafe on the main street of Ybor City. Manuel Menendez, the owner, opened the door for them, and in a flood of melodic Spanish, welcomed them to Las Novedadas, which Rauol explained meant "the novelties," a reference to the delectable Spanish pastries for which the cafe was famous. Menendez led them to a special table and waited on them himself, bringing paella and yellow rice, sangria, and later Cuban coffee and pastries.

Varina and Cordelia were among the few women there, as most of the clientele were cigar workers. Passionate discussions were being held at many of the tables, and often Varina heard the phrase "*Cuba libre*" repeated. The cafe, it appeared, was the gathering place for local revolutionaries.

As they finished the last of their pastries, Andrew returned to his former questions about Cuba, and Rauol answered them unflinchingly this time, although the indignities and atrocities perpetrated upon his countrymen were difficult for him to speak of, and difficult as well for the others to hear.

"Our greatest need is for ammunition," Rauol said. "We have the guns, but without the bullets they are of less use than our *machetes*. I have been making arrangements since my arrival to purchase powder, empty catridges, and reloading equipment so that I can set up a small ammunition manufacturing plant at my plantation. One of the greenhouses will do nicely for a workplace."

"Isn't that risky?" Andrew asked.

"My friend, today simply to live in Cuba is risky, as you call it. But with God's help, we will drive the Spanish from our homeland and live in peace once more." He leaned across the table toward Andrew. "But there is something

253

you can do for me to alleviate the danger that I face."

"You know I'll help if I can," Andrew assured him, and Varina saw that Cordelia was taking in the entire discussion as if she were afraid to breathe. Was it her love of him that made her so absorbed in Andrew's answer?

"My comings and goings are monitored by the authorities, for they know my sympathies," Rauol was explaining. "Therefore, it would be difficult for me to bring the materials I mentioned into the country myself." He took a large white handkerchief from his pocket and wiped his brow and then the palms of his hands, then signaled for Menendez to bring them more coffee.

Tension filled the smoky air of the cafe, a pulsating anticipation of portentous events, a setting in motion of forces that would gather such momentum that those who began them would not be able to bring them to a halt. Varina could sense Rauol's reluctance to ask his favor and knew that it involved great danger. Andrew waited, unwilling to rush his friend. Finally Rauol gathered his courage to speak.

"Although the materials are of great importance, they are not of great bulk. A boat such as yours could carry the equipment in its cabin and hold, and the powder and cartridges could be lashed to the deck. With such a sleek vessel, you could easily slip unnoticed into the inlet near my home, and the cargo could be off-loaded and transported under cover of night."

Andrew did not react to the request, but sat motionless, contemplating the importance and the dangers of what Rauol had asked. His face gave none of his thoughts away.

"When would this shipment take place?"

"The week of the New Year. It is hoped that with the authorities preoccupied with their celebrations that they will not be as vigilant as at other times of the year."

Cordelia's eyes moved from the face of one man to the other, awed by the gravity of Rauol's request and the suspense awaiting Andrew's answer. Here was a drama that she did not intend to miss. Varina, remembering her own lament about leaving historical New Bern, realized that the room in which she sat was a place in which the tides of human history now ebbed and flowed.

Andrew absently stroked his left cheek, emblazoned now with a startling white scar from the bullet wound he had suffered, almost as if he were contemplating injury again. Rauol's business was a dangerous game, one in which men could be killed, or even worse, left to rot away their remaining years in a rat-infested Spanish prison. Now he looked at his friend and smiled.

"Your suggestion is an action I have considered taking myself." His face twitched in amusement. "Being a gunrunner promises to be a most adventurous occupation. In fact, I have even gone so far as to engage a two-man crew from Clear Water Harbor, ready to leave at a moment's notice. It was simply a matter of obtaining the right material—which you have now graciously offered to provide."

His genial face wreathed in smiles, Rauol sat back, satisfied at having accomplished his task and knowing that he had not underestimated his friend. Varina envied the unspoken exchange of trust and admiration that passed between the two men, mourning the absence of such a relationship from her own life. In recent days, she had learned instead to trust no one.

The two men arranged a date for the delivery and loading of Rauol's contribution to the revolution before the group left the acrid smoke-filled air of the cafe with the hearty invitation by Menendez for their return ringing in their ears.

Outside on the pavement, Varina paused for a deep breath of sea air to clear the tobacco residue from her lungs before stepping into the carriage. Just as she placed her foot on the carriage step, her glance fell on a shabbily dressed workman leaning against the building in the shadows of the cafe awnings. He would have passed as any cigar worker had he not lifted his head at that moment to light his cigar. The glare from his match illuminated his face beneath his battered hat, and Varina found herself looking at the unmistakable profile of Estaban Duarte—or was it? When his cigar was lit, the man pulled the brim of his hat low across his face once more and neither moved nor made any sign of recognition.

"Varina, quit dawdling! We're all waiting for you." The sharpness of Cordelia's voice sliced through her thoughts, and she climbed hastily into the carriage, embarrassed at having kept the others waiting. However, as soon as she was seated, she looked back to the man she had thought was Duarte, but the space against the cafe wall was deserted and there was no one else in sight.

Chapter Seventeen

The trio traveled home in eerie silence, weighted down by an uncommon gravity. Andrew, Varina felt sure, was contemplating his imminent journey to Cuba and its accompanying perils. Would he regret the commitment he had made to Rauol, she wondered, and even more important, did he think of what would happen to his son if he was killed or imprisoned?

Cordelia studied the passing landscape with unseeing eyes, and could have been musing over anything from her new wardrobe, which would be delivered next week in time for the Christmas celebrations, to her sadness at leaving the shops and social whirl of Tampa. Varina was never certain what Cordelia was thinking.

As for Varina herself, she still struggled with the fear that she was losing touch with reality.

That night at Las Novedadas when she had finally entered the carriage, she had asked if Cordelia had noticed the man leaning against the wall.

"Of course I saw him," Cordelia had snapped at her. "I had time to study the entire district while we waited for you."

"Wasn't he Estaban Duarte, the man you met at the Yacht Club Inn when I first came to Florida?"

Cordelia had become motionless and stared at Varina oddly, her delicate nostrils flaring with a hint of fear. "You must be joking. The Estaban Duarte I met was a tall, elegant gentleman, nothing like that short grubby little man at all. Do you feel unwell, Varina?"

She had laid the inside of her wrist against Varina's forehead, checking for signs of fever, and her nervousness as they rode back to the hotel convinced Varina that Cordelia had strong doubts about Varina's sanity. Andrew and Rauol had ignored the entire exchange as they continued the conversation that they had begun that morning at breakfast and carried on throughout the day, and from the fervor of their voices, Varina had known they would probably continue until far into the night.

Now as the carriage brought them closer to Dunedin, Varina silently instructed herself that she must somehow bring to an end her flights of fancy which had become so frequent since her arrival in Florida, and in their place, comport herself according to the principles of logic and reason in which Uncle William had so carefully trained her. There must be no more ghostly visions or other wild imaginings. How could she expect to care for Jamie if she could not take charge of herself?

The thought of Jamie made her recognize anew how empty her life had seemed without him during her Tampa visit, and she watched eagerly for the first sight of him as they approached Fair Winds on the bluff road. When Andrew stopped the carriage in front of the house and Gordie came out to help with the baggage, Varina went off immediately in search of Jamie.

She found him sitting in a swing beneath the camphor tree in the back yard and ran to embrace him. However, the blank look that the boy gave her, showing no sign of recognition, much less happiness at her return, made her stop short of gathering him in her arms. She knew then that leaving him when she had just begun to get close to him had been a terrible mistake. He sat motionless in the swing as if totally unaware of her presence. Sadly, she went forward, gently kissed his cheek, and patted his yellow curls.

"I won't leave you again, Jamie. I promise. If I must ever go away again, I will take you with me." The boy gave no response.

Dejectedly, she climbed the back stairs, dreading the chores of changing from her traveling clothes and unpacking. But when she entered her room, she suffered a dizzying disorientation, similar to the state she had experienced when she thought she had seen Theodora's ghost on the dock and Estaban Duarte in Ybor City. For a moment she thought she was in the wrong room, for the room was not as she remembered it. Gone were the ugly dark paneling and thick draperies that blocked the light. In their places were smooth painted walls of creamy-white; fragile lace curtains that let in the golden afternoon sunlight; Boston ferns and ficus trees in gleaming brass jardenieres; and dozens of fragrant long-stemmed roses the color of old lace in cloisonne cachepots on the mantel and bureau. A large mirror, reflecting the oblique rays of the setting sun throughout the room, replaced the fusty landscape over the fireplace, and as she looked at it, she saw that Andrew stood behind her in the doorway, observing her bewilderment.

"I told you there would be surprises when you returned," he said, his voice as expressionless as his face as he waited for her reaction.

At any other time, she would have been elated at the room's improvement and the fact that Andrew had thought enough of her to have the changes made. But now she was stricken with an overriding sense of failure, a sickness of heart at having deserted Jamie at a crucial time in his recovery, and thereby unwittingly undoing all the good she had accomplished since her arrival.

That stinging disappointment, combined with the fear that she was losing her mind, knowing that she had on numerous occasions suffered from an overactive and deleterious imagination that had wreaked havoc on her reason, caused her battered emotions to overwhelm her. She collapsed into the slipper chair in uncontrollable sobs.

Andrew, who until now had stood by the door, started into the room, but when she lifted her tear-stained face to his, a scowling expression suffused his face, and he threw his hands up in a gesture of futility.

"I'll send up Fiona," he snapped at her, then turned on his heel and was gone.

Dismayed that she had now added insult to Andrew to her list of deficiencies, Varina continued to weep until she felt a soft small hand work its way into hers, and she looked up to find Jamie staring at her. She opened her arms to him and he climbed onto her lap, placing his chubby arms around her neck and squeezing tightly. Fiona found them there minutes later and quietly withdrew unnoticed from the room, leaving the two to sit before the open French doors in contented silence, watching the dazzling colors of the sky reflecting on the clouds and water as the sun slowly dove into the sea.

On Christmas Eve, Varina stood in the second-floor meeting room of Library Hall, now crowded with residents and visitors alike as the entire community gathered to celebrate Christmas. On the stage at the far end of the room was the gigantic short-leaf pine that

Duncan had cut on his land and brought in that morning for the Bairds, Varina, Jamie, and Marjorie to decorate. The group had worked most of the day, stringing popcorn, making paper chains, and attaching the aromatic bayberry candles in their tin holders to the branches. Tonight Varina viewed the results of their efforts with satisfaction, the evergreen now aglow with candlelight, and Jeremy Sommerville, one of the older boys from Beth's school, standing watch, ready to smother any smoldering needles in his cupped hands, or failing that, to use the bucket of water which stood at his feet.

Garlands of evergreens and holly festooned the windows of the room, and the tree's candles released the resinous smell of hot pine into the air to mingle with the odors of coffee, citrus punch, and fruit cake from the beribboned refreshment table.

Varina felt very festive herself in her best gown of claret-colored velvet trimmed with satin ribbons of the same hue. Music was provided by two of the locals on fiddle and concertina, and the floor was crowded with dancers. Varina had had no shortage of partners herself, including the stately Reverend Baird and the agreeable Duncan, but now she sat enjoying a respite from the energetic gavottes and polkas and observed the spectacle of so many others in holiday spirits. Duncan and Beth, in a whirl of amethyst silk, wheeled by her, but were so engrossed in each other that they paid her no notice.

Spotting Jamie sitting on the edge of the stage with Marjorie, swinging their short pudgy legs as they waited impatiently for the yearly appearance of St. Nicholas, Varina was reminded of their reconciliation after her trip to Tampa. Her absence had, in the long run, had a beneficial effect on the child. Overriding his dismay at her desertion, Jamie had been reassured, for she had ultimately come back, returning his world to the way that he had become accustomed to it.

If only she could amend her relationship with Andrew as easily. Embarrassed at her loss of control over her emotions, she had sought him out that evening to thank him for the redecorating of her room, but the damage was not to be undone so easily. He had remained aloof and coolly polite, thawing only days later when the dray had arrived from Tampa, and the purchases for Jamie's room had been put in place. Jamie's interest in all that Varina had selected for the nursery pleased Andrew, and for a fleeting instant, she had caught a glimpse of kindness in his eyes when he praised her excellent choices.

"*Senorita* Cameron?"

She looked up at the handsome Latin features of Estaban Duarte.

"May I have the honor of this dance?"

The musicians were now playing a graceful Viennese waltz, and the room took on the quality of a fantasy, the music and dancers slowing to a dreamlike pace as Varina looked about helplessly for someone to come to her aid.

"Come now, you must cease this foolishness of being afraid of me." Duarte had read the panic in her eyes. "There is an entire roomful of people here to rush to your protection if you so much as raise your voice. Please, dance with me so that I may show you that I truly mean you no harm."

His Latin charm was irresistible. That, combined with the spirit of good will generated by the season, melted away her anxieties and made Varina question why she had ever feared him in the first place. Perhaps she had, as Duncan had suggested, misinterpreted his intentions and his character. She accepted his invitation.

"What brings you to Dunedin, Mr. Duarte?" They waltzed past the refreshment table where Fiona stood serving punch and watching Varina and her new partner with open-mouthed interest.

"I work in New York City, a dismal place at this time of year, so I am here on vacation to escape the winter weather and enjoy some hunting and fishing." He danced with an accomplished smoothness. "And you, why are you here in this wilderness?"

"I came to care for my young cousin. His mother died last year, and his father . . ." She stopped, catching a glint of something in Duarte's eyes that belied what her other senses were telling her. In spite of all signs to the contrary, she knew, deep in the region beneath her ribs where reason never reached and intuition reigned, that this man was a threat to her. She felt panic and irrational fear rising in her throat and would have broken away had not Andrew at that moment tapped Duarte on the shoulder.

"May I cut in?"

Duarte released her and stepped aside with a bow. "You have a most beautiful relative, Mr. McLaren. You must watch over her carefully or some lovesick suitor will carry her away." Before Andrew could reply, Duarte turned and was lost in the circling crowd of dancers.

"What was that all about?" Andrew asked as he took Varina in his arms and continued the waltz.

"I have no idea," she replied truthfully, wishing with all her might that she knew what Duarte was up to. The only certainty she had was that his intentions were not good. She looked again across the room and saw that he now partnered Cordelia, stunningly dressed in her new gown of sapphire-blue taffeta. "All I do know is that the man frightens me, and I don't know why."

"Then I suggest you avoid him, if for no other reason than to save yourself distress." Andrew smiled down at her, and she saw before her once more the carefree Andrew from her childhood, and at that moment she knew without question that he had captured her heart. His arm tightened about her and his eyes held hers as they danced, and all reality seemed a universe away.

The spell of the dance was soon broken, however, by the shrieks of children at the arrival of St. Nicholas. Alexander Baird, resplendent in a flowing white beard of cotton batting, the same material that trimmed his red flannel suit, had entered the hall carrying a large burlap sack over his shoulder.

"Are there any children here who have been good all year long?" the reverend boomed in a hearty voice. Awestruck and silent now, none of the children responded.

"Oh, I see," he continued, stroking his false beard theatrically, relishing his role as the merry gentleman from the North Pole. "Well, then, are there any children who have been good for *most* of the year?"

At this the shrieks and shouts began once more, and Varina saw that even Jamie, although making no sound, was hopping up and down in anticipation.

"Now listen carefully," Baird instructed. "All those children who have been good for most of the year are to line up here by the stage, with the youngest first, because I have something for each of you in my sack."

While the children received their gifts and bags of candy, all other lights besides the tree candles were extinguished, and the adults, accompanied by the concertina, sang Christmas carols. Varina stood beside Andrew, keenly aware of his pleasant baritone voice as it sang out the carols, blending with her clear soprano. Fiona and Gordie, Beth and Duncan, and Henrietta Baird were all close by, and Varina felt her heart swell with affection for these dear people who had befriended her in this strange land. The possibility of peace on earth and good will to all seemed very real—until her Christmas mood was shattered at the sight of Cordelia slipping out the door on the arm of Estaban Duarte.

"Merry Christmas!" Varina went to Jamie's room early Christmas morning to awaken the tyke. "As soon as you're dressed, we'll go down and open presents."

She helped him into the suit of dark blue velvet that she had bought for him in Tampa, appropriate for the Christmas service they would attend after breakfast. Then the two hurried down the stairs to the front parlor, where Andrew had already lit the candles on their own Christmas tree and a fire of pine knots crackled and spat in the massive fireplace.

Days before, Gordie had shown Varina how to clip the stems of the bright scarlet poinsettia plants and plunge the ends in boiling water to seal them; then Varina had arranged the festive flowers in large containers throughout the house, adding color and cheer to the gloomy interior. This morning the carmine arrangement on the mantelpiece contrasted sharply with Theodora's portrait, the flowers the color of blood beneath the eerie whiteness. *Not this morning*, Varina begged her overactive imagination, pushing the distasteful image away.

Cordelia, Andrew, and Fiona and Gordie who had joined them now, were dressed in their holiday finery and issuing greetings of "Happy Christmas!" to one another. Andrew, as head of the household, made a great production of taking each tissue-wrapped gift from beneath the tree, reading the recipient's name, and presenting it with a flourish.

As the gifts were being distributed, Varina remembered Cordelia's leaving the hall with Duarte the night before, and in a low voice, leaned over to the woman beside her and asked what she thought of the man.

"Only that he was very kind. In my excitement over my new clothes, I was too stringent in tightening my stays, so that by the end of the evening, I thought I was going to faint from the crowd and heat. He accompanied me outdoors for a breath of fresh air until my head cleared. Hardly enough time to get to know anything else about him. Oh, thank you, Andrew dear," she purred as he presented her with a package.

Varina frowned at the picture of Duarte Cordelia had painted for her, again inconsistent with what her instincts told her about the man. But her thoughts could not remain focused on him amidst the cheerful chaos that was taking place all around her. Wrappings were ripped apart to reveal handkerchiefs, shawls, books, and tobacco. Only Jamie, in his usual compulsive way, opened his gifts slowly and carefully, doing minimal damage to the tissue paper. Varina watched as he uncovered the mechanical Indian chief seated at a tomtom, a toy that had delighted her in Tampa. She showed him how to wind the key, causing the Indian to beat the drum with a ferocious racket. Cordelia gave him a picture book, but there were no gifts for him from the Roths or Andrew beneath the tree. Jamie was so absorbed in his wind-up Indian that he didn't notice their absence, but Andrew was impatient to give his own present.

"Son, we must check the stable for your other gifts."

Obediently, Jamie took Andrew's hand, and the others followed the pair out into the yard. There before the stable stood a handsome pony cart, freshly painted in red and blue.

"This is your gift from Fiona and Gordie," Andrew explained, watching the child as he examined the vehicle with great seriousness. Then Andrew disappeared into the stable and returned, leading a sturdy black-and-white pony. "And this is my gift to you."

Jamie's mouth formed a perfect *O* when he saw the pony. Then he approached it tentatively, holding out his tiny hand until he gently touched the horse's muzzle.

"There's a saddle and bridle in the stable, too. Gordie and I will teach you to ride and to drive the pony cart. In a year or two, you'll be able to ride to school on your own," Andrew said.

"I've seen enough, and I'm freezing," Cordelia complained, turning to go back indoors.

The others stood enjoying the sight of a young boy with his first pony until the sound of an approaching horse distracted them. Duncan had arrived with a large wicker picnic basket, its lid wired shut, slung before him.

"Merry Christmas all." He slid easily from his horse with the basket in his hands. "That's a fine pony and cart ye have there, lad," he called to Jamie. "But it seems to me that on such a lovely Christmas morning there is one other thing that a wee lad would be needing. Come here and I'll show ye."

Reluctantly, Jamie turned from his pony and came toward Duncan, who had set the wicker basket on the ground and was unfastening the wire that held the lid.

"Go ahead, open it up," Duncan said.

Jamie reached slowly for the lid, too slowly, because Arby, restrained too long on the ride from Duncan's house, was anxious to be free. He knocked the lid back from the basket and hopped out, shaking his small body so that his gray fur fluffed out around him and the red Christmas bow around his neck almost flew off. Jamie had frozen at the sight of the feisty little dog, and Arby, when he saw the boy, wagged his tail so furiously that his whole body moved. When Jamie did not respond, Arby ran to him and jumped up, his front paws striking Jamie in the chest and sending him backwards into the dust. Arby was on him in a flash, licking Jamie's face with his rough pink tongue.

Varina had started forward when Jamie fell, but Andrew caught her arm and held her back. Helplessly, she watched Jamie's expression crumple as the terrier pounced on him. None of them was prepared for what happened next. A burst of noise escaped from the child, a sound so unfamiliar that at first they did not recognize it. Through the cool crisp air of Christmas morning came a gift they had all longed for. Jamie was laughing with delight, emitting squeals and giggles as he rolled in the sandy stable yard with the sturdy little dog.

Chapter Eighteen

"His name is Arby, short for R. B., Robert Bruce. Duncan named him after a famous Scottish king and warrior because he's a cairn terrier from Scotland," Varina explained as she brushed the sand and straw from Jamie's velvet suit and combed debris from his yellow curls.

The dog rested on its haunches, watching the procedure with bright button eyes, and when Varina, with Jamie by the hand, went inside for breakfast, the little animal trotted along at Jamie's heels, as if the boy had always been its master.

The household gathered in the dining room for Christmas breakfast, and Varina saw Cordelia scowl and start to speak when she spied the small dog, but something in Andrew's expression stopped her, and the moment passed. However, within that instant, Varina had sensed the tension between the two, an intensity of emotion that was almost palpable in the morning sunlight. But she could not be sure whether the feelings between Andrew and his sister-in-law were those of love, or equally strong negative currents of emotions.

She did not ponder long over the enigma, because Jamie's attempts to feed Arby surreptitiously beneath the table were exposed by the boy's smiles and giggles each time the dog licked his hand, and the adults were so enchanted with his response that none had the heart to chastise him.

Later that evening when she had retired to her room with a glass of milk and a plate of Fiona's shortbread, Varina reviewed the day with mixed feelings. Jamie's laughter had been the greatest gift of all, and she was confident now that it would be only a matter of time before he was actually speaking. Arby had worked a miracle. Moments ago, when she had gone into the nursery to check on the boy, Arby had raised his head from where he lay curled against Jamie's feet. The cushion in the wicker basket on the floor was unrumpled, and Varina doubted that the dog would ever use it. He had already adopted his little master with all the fierceness and loyalty of his breed, and if he had made Jamie laugh, allowing him to sleep on his owner's bed was the least Varina could do for a canine of such value.

But even as Jamie's problems came closer to resolution, Andrew became more and more a mystery. Her relationship with him always seemed to take one step forward and two steps back. Ever since their return from Tampa, he had remained indifferent and aloof, a strange contrast to whatever impulse had compelled him to have her room redecorated. His Christmas gift to her had been a book, a scholarly treatise on semi-tropical plants; he had remembered her desire to learn the names and characteristics of the specimens in his gardens. And on the flyleaf he had pinned a delicate gold filigree rose with a diamond nestled like a dewdrop in its petals, an expensive and personal gift, but with no message except his name.

To Cordelia he had given a shawl of Chantilly lace, but if her gift had contained jewelry as well, she had not shared it with the others.

They had all attended church, accompanied by the Roths, and upon their arrival, Duncan had deserted them to sit with Henrietta, Marjorie, and Beth in the pastor's family pew.

"Hmmph," Fiona had mumbled, trying to sound disapproving, although her plump face was a picture of happiness, "might as well write out an announcement and put it in the church bulletin!"

Varina was happy for Beth and Duncan and for the uncomplicated relationship they had with one another. No puzzles or ambiguities there. Each knew the other as well as any one could, for both had an inherent simplicity of character that was both admirable and reassuring. But as for Andrew and Cordelia, just as on the day of her arrival at Fair Winds, Varina was still struggling to understand them, and the more she knew about them, the more complex and indecipherable their personalities became.

Earlier that evening, the Roths, Andrew, Cordelia, and Varina, grouped cozily around the Christmas tree, had shared a Christmas wassail bowl, a strong pungent brew of cider, oranges, spices, dark rum, and brandy heated over the fire. They had all raised their cups in a salute to good health, and Andrew, encouraged by the progress he had observed in Jamie that day, had made an addendum to the toast.

"There have been dark and painful days at Fair Winds for a long while, but tonight I feel that this unhappy era is coming to an end. I truly believe that our luck has changed and good fortune now resides here with us."

Perhaps it was only the potency of the brew, or that and the flickering light from the tree candles and the fireplace, but as Varina lifted her cup and drank, the scarlet of the poinsettias on the mantel appeared to wash upward, bathing Theodora's portrait in blood. She experienced in an illuminating moment of precognition, triggered by the sanguinary illusion, a terrible certainty that Andrew had tempted fate by his proclamation, and that the gods were not amused.

* * *

She had forgotten that moment of prescience in the days that followed, filling her time and her thoughts with Jamie and Arby, enjoying her walks along the shore and treks through the woods with them as if she were herself a child again. But the Saturday after Christmas she remembered her trepidations. The weather had turned bitterly cold during the night with a drizzly rain and blowing north wind that whipped up a froth of white caps on the leaden gray waters of the sound. In the late afternoon, she and Jamie were on the floor before the fireplace in the second parlor, playing tug-of-war with Arby over one of Andrew's old socks, when Gordie burst into the room, his cheeks and nose raw from the cold.

"Leave the lad with Fiona, lass, and dress as warm as ye can. We need your help at the plantation. The bottom is dropping out of yon thermometer, and if it continues at this rate, we may lose everything tonight."

Fiona had followed him in from the kitchen to take charge of Jamie, and Varina, propelled by the urgency in his voice and expression, ran up the front stairs to her room. She dressed hurriedly, pulling on her heaviest woolen stockings, a thick cableknit sweater over her shirtwaist, and her riding skirt, and boots. Thankful that she had brought from home her sheepskin jacket that she had worn on winter mornings on the river, she searched her bureau until she also found the red woolen mittens and cap that

279

Aunt Mae had knitted for her. She had laughed when Mae had insisted that she pack such heavy clothing, but her wise aunt had replied with one of her favorite maxims: " 'Tis better to have it and not need it than to need it and not have it."

When she ran out the kitchen door to join Gordie, waiting for her in the wagon, the knife-like cold of the wind made her think that she would need even more clothing than this to keep from freezing before this day was over. The rain hit her face like tiny slivers of ice as Gordie cracked the reins and headed the team at a gallop toward the plantation. The gates stood open when they arrived, and they drove straight through to where Andrew stood before a fire at the potting shed.

"Thank you for coming, Varina. There was no one else to ask. Every man, woman, and child in the area will be working to save their own crops today and tonight." He walked to the thermometer that hung out of range of the fire's warmth. "It's already down to thirty-eight and there's still several hours of daylight left." The worry on his face made him look older than his years. "But if this cloud cover holds and keeps the warmth from radiating into the atmosphere, it might not be so bad. The worst thing that could happen now is for the sky to clear."

He instructed Varina in assembling kindling and shavings at intervals along the path. While she began that task, he and Gordie loaded firewood in the wagon, then followed behind her, building massive bonfires that needed only the touch of a torch to set them ablaze in an instant. Varina worked at a furious pace, stopping only for seconds to massage the aching in the small of her back or to pull out the splinters that had penetrated her mittens. She gave only a passing thought to Cordelia's absence. Of course, Andrew wouldn't have asked her to undertake such grueling labor, but even if desperation had driven him to request her help, Cordelia would never have agreed to it.

She laid the last pile of shavings and kindling, then stood to survey the scene before her. Andrew and Gordie worked now by lantern light, one throwing logs from the wagon as the other stacked them in the pathway. As she threw back her head to ease the pain in her shoulders, she saw above her the deep blue velvet of the winter sky, sparkling with a million points of light. The sky had cleared, the protective covering of clouds had vanished.

"Fire away," Andrew called to Gordie, and the two men on opposite sides of the garden started down the paths with torches, igniting each stack of wood until the plantation blazed with bonfires like an army encampment on the night before a battle. Except the battle now, Varina thought, was a fight against the mass of frigid arctic air that had swept south across Canada, dipping far beyond its normal reach into the southern United States with a killing cold.

As soon as all the fires were lit, the men loaded the wagon once more, then drove up and down the aisles again, depositing wood to replenish the fires. Varina's job was to tend the fires, adding logs as needed to keep the flames high. She had been working so feverishly that she was unaware of Fiona's and Jamie's arrival in the pony cart until she looked up to see Jamie with Arby in his lap, huddled in the cart, bundled in tartans so that only their faces showed. The dancing flames were reflected in the child's and dog's eyes, while Fiona unloaded flasks of hot coffee and soup, thick sandwiches of cheese and turkey, and wedges of Aberdeen cake.

"Ye must eat, girl, and make sure the men do, too. This cold saps your strength, and it'll be a long night for all of ye. Now I must get the lad out of this wind." She threw her arms about Varina and hugged her, then climbed into the pony cart, heading it back to Fair Winds. Jamie and Arby sat backwards in the cart, watching the frantic activity in the gardens until the cart was swallowed up by darkness in the woods.

As the three took a few minutes to eat before stoking the fires again, Andrew assessed the weather. "We've lost the cloud cover, but if the wind holds, we still might come through." As if the gods were taunting him, the winds dropped and a dead calm descended on the land. The only sound in the crisp stillness of the night was the sibilant hiss and crackle of burning logs.

With rugged determination, the three labored on, loading and unloading firewood and feeding the voracious appetites of the bonfires throughout the night and into the small hours of the morning. Just before dawn Andrew checked the thermometer as he had every fifteen minutes throughout the night, and the instrument read nineteen degrees, its lowest point thus far. As the sun rose over the hammock pines, the trio fed the last of the remaining logs to the fires. Then Varina collapsed in exhaustion on a tartan in the potting shed, rolled the blanket about her, and fell immediately into a deep sleep.

The aroma of freshly brewed coffee tickled her nose and awakened her, and she arose to find that Fiona had come and gone once more, leaving coffee, juice, fresh scones, and hot ham biscuits, which the men were devouring as if they had not seen food for days. As she watched Andrew and Gordie, she burst out laughing, for the soot from the fires had blackened their faces, making them look like coal miners just emerging from the depths of the earth.

Then the laughter died on her lips as she glanced past them into the plantation. Every plant, shrub, and tree looked as if torches had been held to them. Leaves hung limp and brown upon the branches in acre after devastated acre. She sat dejectedly on the closest hay bale and began to cry. She was bone-weary, even after her short sleep. She ached in every muscle of her body, her hands were pierced and bloody from splinters, her hair and clothes were filthy and reeked of smoke, and for what? The entire plantation was destroyed.

Gordie, hearing her sobs, left his breakfast and sat beside her, putting a comforting arm around her shoulder and pressing a steaming mug of coffee into her hands. "There now, lass, dinna cry. It's na so bad as it looks. Tell her, Andrew."

With fatique etched in every line of his face, making him appear older than Gordie, Andrew picked up his coffee mug and joined them. His voice was filled with weariness, but not defeat.

"Believe me, it looks much worse than it is, Varina. Although the leaves are frozen, that doesn't mean the plant or tree itself is destroyed. There's no way to be certain until the spring comes and new growth begins, but I think most of the damage we see is surface damage. Sometimes all of a plant above the ground can be killed by cold, yet in the spring, the roots send up new plants again."

He reached out and laid a grimy hand rough with scratches against her cheek. "We couldn't have saved any of this without your help. You can be proud of the work you've done here."

Varina smiled up at him through her tears, but believing him was difficult with the frozen evidence of dead leaves visible in every direction. Andrew turned to read the thermometer once more. "The temperature's rising with the sun," he said. "I think we can take some time now to go back to the house to get cleaned up and get some sleep."

Looking like refugees from a holocaust, the three climbed wearily into the wagon. Passing through the shade of the forest on their way back to the house, Varina felt the cold more severely than she had at the plantation, and she shivered violently, even with the blanket wrapped tightly about her. Was this the imminent disaster that she had sensed on Christmas night? Then she remembered all the others in the community who made their living from their citrus groves, and she felt sick at the thought of what last night's freeze had done to their lives.

"What does all this mean to the citrus growers?" she asked.

"Just as with my gardens, it will be a matter of months before the severity of the damage can be accurately assessed," Andrew answered. "I do know this. An orange freezes if the temperature goes below twenty-six degrees for more than four hours. It was well below that for a lot longer last night, so, at the very least, all the growers have lost their crops for this year. That translates into thousands of dollars, even at a penny an orange. Whether they have lost their trees, too, remains to be seen."

"What happens now?"

"We'll get cleaned up and rest for a bit. Then Gordie and I must shift firewood from the barn to the plantation for tonight. If the temperature doesn't rise above freezing today, we must repeat our fires tonight, because the mercury is sure to plunge again."

"Dear God," murmured Varina, overwhelmed at the thought of enduring another night like the previous one. In exhausted silence, they completed the ride home.

Duncan's horse was in the stable when they arrived, and Duncan was in the kitchen, sitting at the well-scrubbed table with his head in his hands. He looked as tired as Varina felt, another victim vanquished by the blast of arctic air, but when he spoke, his concern was for Andrew.

"How bad at the plantation?"

"We may have lost some of the most tropical specimens, but we managed to keep the fires going all night, which should save most of the others. We won't know for sure for a while. And you?"

"The crop is lost. Even after daybreak, the fruit was solid ice. But the trees are my worry now. At one point last night in some of the lower pockets of the grove that trapped and held the cold air, trees were exploding like rifleshots from the pressures built up by frozen sap. Those areas this morning looked as if they'd been bombed, with chunks of bark scattered in all directions."

Andrew shook his head in silent commiseration. Duncan raked his fingers through his thick red hair and straightened his shoulders.

"I may be down, but I'm na out." He attempted a smile, but his look was woebegone. "Everything in the greenhouse, including some vegetables I'd started, is fine. I kept the woodstoves there burning all night. And in the nursery area where I graft young trees, I wrapped all the plants in burlap and fired that area all night, too, so I'm in better shape than some, I'm sure."

"Aye, but there's still tonight to get through," Gordie reminded him.

"So there is, my dear brother. I'm off to get some rest, but when I return, I'll help you and

Andrew restock the firewood at the plantation."
He rose and donned his heavy coat and hat.

"You're a good man, Duncan." Andrew clasped his hand.

"It's what neighbors are for." Duncan touched the brim of his hat to Varina and was gone.

Later, after a hot soaking bath that steeped some of the achiness away, Varina crawled beneath her bedcovers more exhausted than she had ever believed possible without being dead, too. As she drifted off to sleep, she did not know if she dreamed it or if it was a memory floating up from her subconsciousness, but whatever the source, she remembered that Andrew had held her in his arms as she lay against the hay in the potting shed and spoken so softly that she had to strain to hear.

"I made such a mess of things with Theodora, and I'm afraid of doing the same with you. I don't know how to make you understand, Varina, and it is so important that you understand."

Understand what? she wondered, but she was asleep before anyone could answer.

Chapter Nineteen

Impaled spiders, blood-drenched portraits, wraiths in white veils, Andrew's bleeding countenance, and leaping flames that threatened to envelope her had plagued her dreams, making Varina happy to awaken, ending the horrors that had filled her sleep. With the resilience of youth, a few hours of sleep, however dream-disturbed, had refreshed and revitalized her, and she arose strengthened to do battle once more against the freezing weather.

She found Cordelia sitting before the fireplace in the second parlor with her crocheting, a tea tray beside her and her new lace shawl about her shoulders. Though Andrew had not asked her to assist in the efforts to protect his plants, neither had it occurred to Cordelia to volunteer.

She reminded Varina of an indulged household cat as she basked contentedly before the fire.

"You seem to relish the role of common laborer," Cordelia said with a wrinkle of her patrician nose at the acrid odor of smoke that still clung to Varina's jacket and skirt. "Honestly, I cannot understand why you are wearing yourselves out this way. Let the twigs and sticks freeze! Andrew already has more money than he can spend in a lifetime. It isn't as if he can't afford to start over."

Varina opened her mouth to reply, then bit back the words, perceiving the futility of trying to explain to Cordelia how Andrew felt about his work. With a noncommittal nod, she went on to the the kitchen where Fiona was serving Jamie lunch, while Arby lay beneath his chair, waiting patiently for the morsels that dropped like manna from heaven from his little master's hands. Varina helped herself to one of Fiona's meat pasties, tucked an apple in her pocket, and went out to join the men.

The frost-seared grass crunched like paper beneath her feet as she crossed the yard to the barn where Andrew, Gordie, and Duncan were loading the wagon with firewood. The frenetic desperate pace of the previous night was gone, replaced by an efficient methodical quickness that enabled the men to do the job yet conserve their energies for the long night ahead.

Returning to the plantation, they set about reconstructing the bonfires and stacking piles of logs for replenishing them. In late afternoon as the sun dipped low over the pines, Andrew gave the signal and the fires were relighted against the plunging mercury of the thermometer. Duncan had gone home to tend to his greenhouse and young citrus trees, and Fiona had returned to the house after bringing them dinner. As night fell, the only sounds that could be heard on the crisp air were the occasional thuds and crashes of logs tumbling to the ground as they disintegrated in the fires, sending a glittering spray like fireflies shooting up into the darkness.

Andrew leaned back upon one of the hay bales, lighting the pipe that Varina had given him for Christmas, enjoying a smoke before the night's work began in earnest. The sweet scent of tobacco mixed with woodsmoke in the air; the stars, some mere pinpricks of light, others pulsing points of brilliance and color, sparkled like distant bonfires in the velvet darkness of the clear winter sky. Flames of iridescent blues and greens surged against the shadows, lighting the paths throughout the garden. Only the unexplained barren patch surrounded by its white picket fence remained unilluminated, a heart of darkness amidst the flames.

Varina pushed the black plot from her mind, focusing instead on the cold beauty and tranquillity that surrounded her. She felt bound with Andrew in a common struggle against the freezing temperatures. Sitting in comfortable silence, she savored each moment of a time she knew she would remember for the rest of her life.

Then through the cold night air came the haunting and melancholy call of an owl, an eerie, mournful sound that caused the hair to rise on the back of Varina's neck, breaking the spell of peace and contentment.

Gordie stood, stretched his arthritic legs, pulled his hat down about his ears, and turned his collar higher against the cold. The superstitious Scotsman looked about uneasily as the owl called again.

"I dinna like the sound of that," he grumbled.

"Why?" Varina asked. "It's sad, but there's a certain beauty to it."

"It's more than sad, lass." Gordie looked nervously behind him. "It's a warning. Some'un is going to die."

Andrew cupped his hands over the match he held to his pipe, hiding his smile at the older man's fears.

But all Varina's nightmares flooded back at Gordie's words, and not until she became busy once more feeding logs to the flames was she able to push the horrors back. But only for a time. Later she would have cause to remember his words well.

Two days later, Varina stood on the veranda of Fair Winds, watching cigar workers from Ybor City unload their cargo from a gigantic dray and carry it down the length of the dock to be stowed on Andrew's sailboat. After a ferocious fit of barking at the men's arrival, Arby had accepted their presence and was now playing catch with Jamie on the front lawn. The weather had turned warm and fine, almost summerlike, an ironic contrast to the days before.

She had worked through that night with Andrew and Gordie until almost four o'clock in the morning, when Andrew had suddenly straightened from shifting firewood, licked his index finger, and held it aloft. He gave a whoop of delight and threw his hat into the air.

"The wind's picked up, and it's coming from the northeast. The worst is over." He had checked the all-important thermometer to make certain and found that the temperature had indeed begun to rise from its earlier low of twenty-three. "If we can keep these burning until sunrise, we should be home free."

Encouraged by the fact that the crushing cold was finally breaking its grip on them, the three had experienced a burst of energy that carried them through the remainder of the night. Then Varina had stumbled home to fall in bed, this time without a bath, and had slept the entire day and the next night, too, totally unaware that she had missed New Year's Eve until Fiona greeted her the next morning with cries of "Happy New Year!"

Now she thought of Rauol Garcia and his family and what 1895 would bring for them and other Cuban patriots as they fought against Spain's oppressive rule. The boxes and crates being loaded on the boats carried reloading equipment, cartridges, and powder for making bullets to be used against the Spanish, and Varina shuddered as she pictured the bloodshed those bullets would bring.

However she thought of it, war was a stupid and foolish endeavor. Why couldn't men simply sit down and reason together? Then she remembered Uncle William's sermons on the existence of evil and its manifestations in men and women in the form of greed and jealousy and the lust for power. Sometimes, she supposed, it must take bullets and bloodshed to rid the world of those sins, but war still seemed an inhuman and inefficient solution.

Beth's arrival turned Varina's thoughts from philosophy as she welcomed her friend. Jamie and Arby also ran to greet her, and Beth was effusive in her admiration of Arby, much to Jamie's delight. The woman's lovely amethyst eyes misted with tears when Jamie smiled at her.

"I can see that you have not only a very fine dog here, but a great friend, too. You are a very lucky boy to have such a dog."

Jamie nodded happily in agreement.

Beth, after studying the activity on the dock, turned to Varina. "What's going on?"

Flustered, Varina did not know what to say. Andrew had insisted that no one be told of Rauol's shipment, but Beth had now seen it with her own eyes. She settled on a half-truth.

"It's a shipment of equipment and material for Dr. Garcia, a Cuban botanist, who is a friend of

Andrew's." She hoped Beth would infer that the crates contained botanical supplies.

With no reason to question her friend, Beth accepted her explanation, then turned to the reason for her visit.

"I'm worried about Duncan. I haven't seen him since the freeze, so I thought perhaps you and Jamie would walk up with me to visit him."

Varina was anxious, too, to see how Duncan had fared. So after telling Fiona where they were going—and being given a tin of shortbread to deliver—the three set out on their short journey through the pine hammock toward Duncan's. Arby trotted happily at their heels, except for occasional side excursions in pursuit of squirrels and swamp rabbits.

The palmettos and evergreens of the hammock showed little damage from the cold, but as they reached the clearing where Duncan's land began, the group stopped short, dumbstruck by the destruction that stretched before them. The neat rows of citrus trees still stood, but every leaf hung brown and lifeless, a dull contrast to the brilliant ocher of the fruit. As they stood observing the devastation of the groves, they heard repeated sounds like the irregular beat of a distant drum or the thud of an erratic heart. It took a moment or two before they realized the sound was that of oranges dropping one at a time from the trees into the sandy soil.

When they reached Duncan's grove house, however, he came toward them with a hearty welcome, seemingly unbowed by the ruination of his crop. He explained his optimism as he showed them through the healthy flowers and vegetables of his greenhouse.

"There's enough here, what with flowers and produce, to sell to the inn and to Sommerville's store. That should earn me enough to meet my debts until next year's crop."

"Next year's crop? But weren't your trees killed, too?" Varina said.

"Aye, some of them were, but being so close to the warm waters of the Gulf, most of them appear to be alive beneath the surface damage, so I should have at least a partial crop next year." His ruggedly handsome face lost its cheerfulness. "Others further inland weren't so lucky. Na only did they lose their trees, but because they had been farming on credit, they've lost everything."

Beth shook her head in commiseration. "Father has been visiting the growers to offer what comfort he can, and he says that some families just walked away after the freeze hit, leaving their homes, their furniture, everything, to go back north where they came from."

"I can thank God that so much of my livelihood was spared," Duncan said, "because now we can go on with our plans for the spring."

At this Beth, blushing a most becoming shade of pink, told Varina that she and Duncan would be married in May, as soon as the school term was completed. As the two friends walked back toward Fair Winds, Jamie and Arby trailing behind, Varina was comforted by the fact that even in times of disaster, life somehow goes on and good comes from trouble.

The next morning after Andrew had returned from taking Jamie to school and bidding the boy farewell before his sailing trip, he called Varina into the deserted second parlor.

"I won't be leaving until later today, but I wanted to be sure to give you these to keep for me until my return." He pressed two large bulky envelopes, both firmly sealed, into her hands. "If I should not return, they are to be opened. They are marked, one for William, the other for you."

Varina looked up at Andrew as if memorizing his gentle brown eyes, the aristocratic planes of his handsome face marked forever by the vivid scar on his left cheek, and the soft curls of his dark hair, only lightly sprinkled with gray. Knowing that the world would hold little attraction for her if Andrew was not in it, she refused to consider the possibility.

"How long will you be away?"

"A week and a half, two at the most."

"Then I will hold these for you until then," she spoke defiantly, as if she could return him safely by the strength of her own will.

"I know you will take good care of Jamie for me. See that you care for yourself as well. It is most important to me that you both be well and waiting when I come back."

He pulled her into his arms and kissed her softly, but before her startled senses could respond, he released her and was gone. Through the day, she watched from her window as he supervised the loading of supplies for the journey, burning every feature of him into her heart to hold while he was gone.

Later that afternoon, the two-man crew had arrived and they were preparing to cast off when Varina realized that it was almost time to pick up Jamie from school. As she passed through the kitchen on her way to the stable, Fiona stopped her.

"Here's a list of what I need from the store, if ye dinna mind shopping on your way to pick up the lad." Fiona handed Varina a page with the needed articles written in her feathery script. "You'll have to take the pony cart. Miss Cordelia took the carriage."

As she drove toward town on the bluff road, Varina felt as if the light had gone from the day, even though the sun was shining brightly. She could not imagine Fair Winds without Andrew. She would have to think of ways to make the time pass quickly until his return.

She stopped at the general store to purchase the items on Fiona's list, but she was so distracted by her thoughts of Andrew that she was back in the pony cart when she realized that she had forgotten the spool of white thread. Placing her purchases beneath the seat, she got down from the cart and slipped back into the store, walking quickly toward the dry goods counter. A large display of gardening tools stood between her and the cash register, where a customer chatted with the storekeeper. Lost in thought, she did not at first perceive the significance of their conversation.

"She's a purty little thing, but I shore do feel sorry for her."

"Why's that, Miz Cranston?"

"Living up at that big house with all those strange goings-on."

"You talking about Fair Winds?"

"I ain't whistling Dixie, Sam. They say McLaren killed his wife. If that's so, I reckon this un's next."

"Go on, Miz Cranston, you know she died of yellow fever."

"That's what they'd like us to believe, but I know he murdered her. A cold-blooded killing, it was."

Varina's heart was pounding and her mouth was dry with fear. She knew she should leave, but she was unable to walk, as if her feet had been nailed to the floor. She dreaded what she would hear next and wanted to run from the store to avoid it, but she had to know, so she did not move.

"Now, Miz Cranston, you know what the minister was telling us in church the other day about gossip. That's a turrible thing to be saying about a man without proof, that he killed his own wife."

"I got all the proof I need, Sam. Ruby, Doc Thompson's wife, told me that Doc said 'tweren't no fever that killed Miz McLaren. No, not fever, but poison. And he not only poisoned her, but he

Charlotte Douglas

beat her up afore she died. The man's an animal. Oughta be shot!"

Varina did not wait for Sam's reply, but flung the thread back on the counter and ran from the shop, hearing nothing else over the blood pounding in her ears. Shaking so that she could barely hold the reins, she drove the cart at a breakneck pace down Main Street and onto Jerry Lake Road toward the schoolhouse.

As soon as she had left the town behind, she stopped the pony and sat, trembling with fear and disbelief. Or was it disbelief? Did not what Duncan had told her support what Mrs. Cranston had said? And then she was seized by a thought so sickening that she retched over the side of the cart. Had Jamie witnessed this atrocity? Was this the cause of his muteness, the knowledge of a horror too terrible for words? And all the while, in her heart where her images of Andrew were treasured, a voice cried out in anger against such a heinous charge. A murderer? A wife-beater? Not Andrew! Not the Andrew whom she loved. And she could not love him as she did if what the vicious, trouble-making, tongue-wagging woman had said was true.

But what if her instincts were wrong? What if he had killed Theodora? She was back on the dizzying emotional trapeze that she had ridden for so many days when she first came to Fair Winds. But how could she know the truth? It would be days before she would see Andrew again, but when she did, she would have to ask him, even at the risk of her own life, if the terrible gossip was true.

Jamie. Her thoughts were disconnected, tumbling like beads from a broken string. School. She must see that nothing disturbed the progress Jamie had made. He must not see how upset she was. Slowly, she smoothed her hair back from her face and straightened her clothes, while trying to calm herself by breathing deeply. She focused her thoughts solely on Jamie, on the diminutive golden-haired child whom she loved as her own. She must keep him safe and happy above all else.

Fortunately, Beth was preoccupied with two quarreling students when Varina arrived in the schoolyard, so she did not have to face her observant friend in her current state of emotional disarray. She hugged Jamie to her when he climbed into the cart, then turned the pony, and headed quickly for home.

For once, Jamie's silence was a blessing, for there were no questions for Varina to answer. She focused all her thoughts on the small boy beside her, vowing never to let him hear the things that she had heard that day. Her concentration was so diligent that she did not notice the carriage in the road before them until Jamie pulled on her sleeve. As they drew nearer, she saw Cordelia seated behind the team.

"What's wrong?" Varina cried, fearing a disaster of the worst sort in her present frame of mind.

Cordelia smiled her feline grin. "Why, nothing is wrong, dear Cousin Varina." Her voice

dripped with sarcasm. "In fact, as of now, everything is going to be very well indeed."

Estaban Duarte stepped into the road from
amongst the trees, a small silver derringer shining in his hand. "*Buenos dias, Senorita* Cameron.
Did I not tell you these woods are dangerous?
Too bad you did not listen to my warning and
return home, but now it cannot be helped."

"I don't understand," Varina said, placing her
arm around Jamie and drawing him to her as her
mind struggled to reconcile Estaban's appearance with Cordelia's.

"You don't need to understand!" Cordelia
snapped. "Just do as you're told."

Varina now noticed another man, one she had
never seen before, sitting on horseback behind
the carriage. Duarte motioned him forward,
then turned to Varina.

"If you do as we say, the boy will not be
harmed. It is up to you."

Varina nodded, her throat too constricted
with fear to speak.

"You will drive the cart to the church and tie
the pony there. You will leave the boy on the
church steps with instructions to stay there until
someone comes. Is that clear?" Duarte waved
the small gun, its barrels like two deadly black
eyes, toward her.

"Cordelia and I will follow in the carriage, but
Rigo will ride beside you all the way. You must
not speak to anyone or give any sign or you are
both dead. When you have left the boy, you will
join us in the carriage."

Again Varina nodded, then slapped the reins against the pony's rump when Duarte waved her on. She handled the reins with one hand, still holding Jamie close to her with the other, keenly aware of the dark rider just behind her.

"Jamie, look straight ahead and not at me, and listen very carefully." She kept her own eyes on the road, hoping those behind would not see her talking to the boy. "When I leave you at the church, you must watch until the carriage is out of sight. After it is gone, you must run next door to the manse to Henrietta and stay with her until I return."

She felt panic rising in her throat. How was she to know if he understood?

"If you know what to do, squeeze my arm."

Tears of relief filled her eyes as two small hands hugged her arm fiercely. Perhaps Jamie, at least, would survive.

When they reached the church, she tied the pony to the picket fence and led Jamie to the church steps.

"Remember what I told you," she whispered as she embraced him one last time. Then she turned and hurried to the carriage, where Duarte, with incongruous gallantry, assisted her inside.

"Do you not think it would be better to take the boy with us?" he asked Cordelia.

"No, there's no danger leaving him. The brat can't speak. Besides, we'll need him when we return."

As the carriage pulled away, Varina turned to

watch the pathetic tiny figure standing staunchly dry-eyed on the church steps, watching her as closely as she did him. She thought her heart would break as she remembered the promise she had made never to leave him again.

Chapter Twenty

Her abductors had timed their kidnapping well. With the men of the town still in the groves and the women beginning their preparations for the evening meal, no one else was in sight as the carriage pulled away from the church onto the road to Clear Water Harbor, leaving only a tiny mute boy to watch their going. Within fifteen minutes, they had reached the inlet at the mouth of Stevenson's Creek where a sloop waited on the high tide.

Still brandishing the small but deadly derringer, Duarte motioned Varina aboard, and he and Cordelia followed. The boat's crew of four rough-looking men stood awaiting orders.

Duarte turned to Rigo, still on horseback. "Return the carriage to Fair Winds. Tell the housekeeper that the boy is at the church and that Miss Vandemere and Miss Cameron decided to accompany Mr. McLaren on his trip to Cuba. If they ask any questions, tell them that is all you know."

Varina watched helplessly as Rigo drove the carriage away. She knew there was no escaping. Even if she dove into the water and swam away, any of the men on board could follow and restrain her. Comforting herself that Jamie, at least, was safe, she sank miserably onto the deck, thinking that life could deal her no worse hand than this.

It did. The crew raised the vessel's trim sails, which immediately filled with the strong breeze, propelling the boat briskly across the sound toward the pass between two barrier islands and into the Gulf of Mexico. Once on a southerly course down the coast, the crew raised the spinnaker, which puffed into life like the bosom of a well-endowed dowager, increasing the boat's speed, causing it to heel in the water until the deck slanted at a precarious angle.

Waves of nausea washed over Varina as seasickness attacked her violently. Cordelia, showing no sympathy, took her by the arm and led her below to lie on one of the narrow bunks in the cabin, settling herself on a bunk opposite Varina.

"Why?" Varina managed, her physical distress incapacitating, yet insignificant compared to her mental turmoil.

"I suppose there's no harm in your knowing the whole story. You won't be able to use the information, and my telling it will pass away the time until we catch up with Andrew."

Cordelia positioned herself on the bunk so that she could keep an eye on her prisoner and keep watch through the porthole, too. She arranged her skirts comfortably about her, as naturally as if she sat in the second parlor taking tea. Meanwhile, Varina fought against the sickness that battered her, gathering every inner resource to concentrate on what Cordelia was saying, knowing with a dreadful certainty that her very life might hinge on what the devious woman had to tell her.

"It all started over two years ago, before Theodora died," Cordelia began, sounding very pleased with herself. "Estaban and I met at a party at the Spanish embassy in New York. He is attached to the consulate there."

Her voice continued, rising and falling like the motions of the sloop, weaving a story as fantastic and unbelievable as the situation in which Varina found herself. The beautiful Cordelia and darkly handsome Duarte had fallen passionately in love. Their attraction to one another, their passion for high living, and particularly Duarte's love of gambling had quickly exhausted Cordelia's substantial inheritance.

When Cordelia learned of Theodora's death, she had hoped for her sister's portion of the family fortune to revert to her, but it had gone to Jamie instead, with Andrew as guardian. Cordelia and Duarte had fretted long over their lack of funds, when Duarte was unexpectedly assigned to investigate the Cuban revolutionaries operating out of Tampa. It was then that the couple worked out their scheme.

Cordelia would come to Dunedin and insinuate herself into Andrew's affections, while Duarte conducted his investigations. At the appropriate time, the two would arrange a fatal "accident" for Andrew, leaving Cordelia in charge of Jamie and his money. In time, another "accident" could be arranged for the boy, too, and the couple would have the money and Fair Winds to themselves.

Hearing this, Varina experienced a rage that swept aside her sickness, but she continued to lie still, absorbing all that Cordelia told her in hopes of finding a way of escape. Her resolve was magnified and strengthened by the fact that not only her own life, but Jamie's and Andrew's were also at stake.

Preening with self-satisfaction at her well-conceived plan, Cordelia continued her story. "You, Varina, were the fly in the ointment. I had no sooner arrived than I learned that you were expected. Estaban went to intercept you, planning to lure you from the train and dispatch you before you ever reached here, but you caused such a scene, drawing so much attention to both him and you, that he had to dispense with that plan."

Anger and terror blended in her mind until Varina felt that she might faint. Duarte had planned to kill her before she reached Dunedin! She forced her attention back to Cordelia, who was still telling her tale, relating horrors as if describing a Sunday picnic.

"We decided then that it might be best to try to frighten you away. First I tried something simple. I watched as you studied Theodora's portrait when you first arrived and knew you must have noticed the ivory fan. Mama had given us matching fans when we were young girls, one of her last gifts to us before she died, and I had brought mine to Florida with me. When you were asleep that first day, I put it in your room for you to see, then removed it when you left."

Cordelia turned from the porthole and smiled at Varina, the beauty of her expression a startling contrast to the evil of her intentions.

"Your reaction was not what I had hoped, so I knew that more drastic measures would be necessary to scare you into returning home. I had brought my wedding dress with me, fashioned after Theodora's. The night of the storm I arranged the pillows of my bed to look as if I slept there, dressed in the white gown and veil, slipped downstairs, climbed to the upper veranda, and then into your room. After you had seen me, I stayed hidden on the veranda until you stopped prowling about and finally went to sleep once more. Then I returned to my room. But my efforts, as you know, were ineffective."

Varina could hear the exasperation in Cordelia's voice as she went on with her narrative.

"We thought then that our original plan was best, so Rigo was sent to kill Andrew. But the fool, who is supposed to be an expert marksman, missed and only wounded him. Still attempting to frighten you home, I left the spider on your pillow, but all to no avail. Estaban, too, did his best to scare you into leaving, but since you would not be frightened—"

"You don't really believe that my Uncle William will let you get away with all of this, do you?"

Cordelia was unmoved by Varina's question, brushing it away as inconsequential. "There is nothing your uncle can do. Jamie is my sister's son, and any court will award a small boy to his closest female kin, knowing that he needs a mother. Besides, since I have made it my business to know that Andrew has not made a will, the fact that most of Jamie's money came to him through Theodora's inheritance from our parents also stacks the cards in my favor."

Varina sat very still, remembering the letters, one to William and one to herself that Andrew had given her before he sailed. She had placed them in her bureau, and now she had the hope that if she and Andrew did not survive Cordelia's plot that Fiona would find Andrew's letter to William. Varina was certain that it contained a will, and just as certain that the guardianship of Jamie and the overseeing of his inheritance had been left to William's wisdom. Varina kept this information to herself, holding onto it as a

Darkness at Fair Winds

last hope for Jamie. But even without a will, she had no doubt that Uncle William would prevail in looking out for Jamie's welfare. However, as long as Cordelia had convinced herself otherwise, she and Duarte would go through with their deadly scheme.

"When we realized that you would not be frightened away, we decided that you must be killed." Cordelia's voice droned on, chilling in its dispassionateness, describing how she had lured Varina onto the dock that foggy night, then hit her with an oar, knocking her into the water, then untying the boat's boom to make it look like an accident.

"That would have worked, too, if it hadn't been for that damned hermit, fishing you out as he did. But no matter. Things have a way of working for the best, for when we went to Tampa, I discovered Andrew's connection with Garcia, and now we have found a very satisfactory way to rid ourselves of all of you and satisfy Estaban's superiors at the same time."

Varina's mind still struggled to assimilate all that she was hearing. Then the pieces began to fall in place. "So it *was* Duarte I saw in Tampa. And it was he you met the night we arrived!"

Cordelia stretched like a cat and smiled haughtily at her captive. "You are so slow to understand this, for all your fine education. But now the actors are all in place, and the play will go on. It is unthinkable that this will not succeed."

311

"What do you plan to do to me?" Varina asked, fearful yet knowing that her wits were all that could save her now and that she must learn as much as she could wring from her loquacious jailer.

Cordelia told her of their plans, plans of murder and intrigue, as calmly as one might read a grocery list. "When we overtake Andrew's boat, he will have to let us on board, because we will threaten to kill you if he does not. We will substitute our own crew and sail to meet Garcia. But we will alert the Spanish authorities first, so that they will be there to meet him, too. When we are through with Andrew as our decoy to lure Garcia, we will kill you both. Then it is back to Dunedin to claim Fair Winds and Jamie's money."

Varina tried to stay calm. She knew that if she let the rage she felt building within her take control, that she would not be able to help herself or Andrew.

"Won't people be suspicious?"

Cordelia laughed. "I will tell a very convincing story of the tropical storm that destroyed Andrew's boat as we were all sailing to visit our good friend, Dr. Garcia. Unfortunately, I will be the only survivor."

"Fiona and Gordie won't believe you!"

"Perhaps not, but what can they do? What proof will they have?" Cordelia laughed again, a brittle sound, like glass breaking.

Defeated, Varina lay still. Now that she knew the facts, she felt like a fool for not having seen it all before, but castigating herself at this point would get her nowhere. She had to think of a plan of her own.

The sun was setting when she heard a voice ring out in Spanish above them, but she did not understand what was said. Cordelia, however, leapt up at the words, smoothing her skirts and grabbing Varina by the arm.

"We must go on deck now. They've spotted Andrew's ship."

They sailed alongside and called to Andrew to let them board, but he refused until he saw Varina, her arms twisted behind her by one of Duarte's crew. The sea, as if in conspiracy with her abductors, calmed at that point, easing the transition of Varina, held by two of the crewmen, and Cordelia and Duarte. The sloop which had carried them, manned by the other two crewmen, turned back toward Tampa.

"Let her go." Andrew spoke with such authority that the two sailors released her at once, and she ran into Andrew's arms.

"Remember that I am paying you and you'll take your orders from me," Duarte barked at his ruffians. Then again waving his derringer, he directed the two men from Andrew's crew forward. Andrew, sensing too late to warn them what was to happen, pulled Varina to him and covered her eyes.

"Bastards!" Varina heard him say as two shots rang out, amid screams and groans and then the sound of bodies hitting the water, followed by a furious splashing and churning of the sea.

Charlotte Douglas

Varina, pale and shaken at the cold-blooded murder of Andrew's crew, looked up to see Cordelia staring over the side with glittering fascination.

"Sharks." She smiled at Duarte with satisfaction. "No incriminating bodies to wash ashore."

Duarte was calmly reloading his tiny pistol. "Keep an eye on them."

The sailors shoved Andrew and Varina against the cabin, instructing them to move at their own peril, as Cordelia and Duarte went forward, while the new crew got the ship underway once more. The clink of a bottle and glasses and low laughter could be heard coming from among the cases stowed near the bow. Duarte and Cordelia had begun an early celebration of the success of their plan.

Varina was shivering violently, and even wrapped in Andrew's jacket with his strong arms holding her close, she could not get warm. Her chill had nothing to do with the climate, for the night was mild and pleasant, but instead emanated from deep within her at the thought, not of her own death, but of those she loved more than life itself, Andrew and Jamie.

Slowly, her trembling ceased, even though with the setting of the sun, the temperatures had dropped. To the west was nothing but the wide expanse of gulf waters, stretching unbroken by land over a thousand miles to Mexico. To the east was another string of barrier islands, like those offshore from Fair Winds. Andrew followed her gaze.

"Anna Maria Island and Longboat Key." His voice was unperturbed as he identified their location. This was an area he knew well, having traveled it many times on his trips both to Rauol in Cuba and to Edison in Fort Myers.

"Now," she heard him say, "can you tell me what's going on?"

Quietly, not wanting to call attention from the crew or the couple that sat in the boat's bow among the lashed crates of powder, Varina related to Andrew all that Cordelia had told her. His only response was an occasional tensing of the muscles in his arms that still embraced her, but he, too, gave no reaction, wishing to stay as inconspicuous as possible.

When she had finished, he sat back, pulled his pipe and pouch from his pocket, and deliberately lighted his pipe. Varina could tell from his face that his mind was working actively to assimilate what she had told him and struggling, as she had, to find a solution.

"I do not say this to frighten you any more than you already are," he finally whispered, "but only to steel your resolve at what we must do. They *will* kill us, you know. Their murder of my men proves that."

Varina nodded. She had no doubts that she would be killed. The only questions were where and when. She leaned back in Andrew's arms, feeling an unnatural peace for one who was about to die, but she had accepted it. There was nothing more that she could do. Watching the moon rise over the dark outline of the islands,

Charlotte Douglas

she wondered why she felt so numb, why so little pain at the thought of her life ending when it had barely begun. She had read that one's life was supposed to flash through one's mind before dying, but her mind was blissfully blank, filled with neither poignant reminiscences nor foreboding terrors.

Beside her Andrew stirred. "It's time."

"Time?" Varina had not thought death would come so soon.

"Time to spoil their plans," Andrew whispered. He pointed to the southeast where broad beams of light sliced through the darkness. "Sanibel Lighthouse. There are people there who will help us." He placed his fingers against her lips. "Please, don't ask questions. Just do as I say."

He hefted the small tin of matches for his pipe before slipping them back into his shirt pocket. Then he stood slowly, holding up his hands in plain sight as he approached the crewman at the helm.

"I need to relieve myself. May I move to the other side?"

With a smirking grin first at Varina, then back to Andrew, the sailor, nursing a bottle of whiskey in his own private celebration, jerked his head toward the starboard side, and Andrew disappeared behind the cabin.

When he returned a few minutes later, he settled quickly next to Varina, speaking in hushed tones. "In a moment all hell is going to break loose. We'll have the element of surprise on our side, so when it does, leap to the rail and dive in. We'll swim for the lighthouse." He stopped short as a thought occurred to him. "You did say you could swim, didn't you?"

Varina nodded, casting an apprehensive glance toward the lighthouse which seemed far away over the blackness of the gulf waters.

"*Fuego!*" The sailor's scream split the night air as Cordelia's echo came from the bow. "My God, the boat's on fire!"

"Now!" Andrew whispered, pulling her to her feet and roughly pushing her up over the rail, then leaping off himself. She dove deep into the water, weighted down by her boots and petticoats, her lungs straining to the bursting point as she held her breath for what seemed forever. Fighting her way through the dark depths toward the top, she struggled to kick off her boots, and when her head broke the surface, she tread water, attempting to untie her crinolines.

"Swim," Andrew hissed, "as fast as you can!"

Streams of unintelligible Spanish passed between Duarte and his men, and above it all, Cordelia could be heard screaming, "Water, throw water on it! For God's sake, you stupid men, there's water all around us!"

Varina was swimming as fast as she could against the drag of her wet skirts, Andrew keeping pace beside her. Somehow the two managed to put about fifty yards' distance between them and the burning boat before they heard Cordelia shriek, "They're getting away!"

Looking back toward the boat even as she swam, Varina could see the four of them silhouetted against the flames as they pressed against the railing, distracted from their firefighting to search the dark waters for their escaped captives.

"I see them!" Cordelia cried, pointing in their direction.

Duarte fired his derringer but had no hope of hitting them at such long range. He was reloading to fire again when the entire boat appeared to lift above the waves. A huge geyser of water shot into the air as the boat erupted in a series of explosions, sending flames, debris, and bodies high into the air.

When the rain of water, sparks and debris ended, the boat and its passengers were gone; scattered planks, some still aflame upon the silent sea, the only record of their passing.

Chapter Twenty-One

Andrew and Varina swam to shore along the silvery path of moonlight cast across the water. For long minutes after the explosion, they had tread water, waiting to see or hear any sign of life or survivors. But the only sights were of flotsam and jetsam on the moonlit waves, and they could detect no sound but the surf pounding the distant beach. Everything, from her abduction by Duarte to the violent destruction of Andrew's boat and the people aboard, had such an air of unreality that Varina believed she must be dreaming, living in an illusion that would soon evaporate, placing her safely in the comfort of her own bed and the world as she wished it to be.

But the cold that was creeping into her body from the deep gulf waters was real enough, biting deep into her bones.

"We've got to get to shore," Andrew insisted, coughing up salt water with a sputter. "If we swim due east, we'll hit the beach sooner, then walk the rest of the way to the lighthouse. Get rid of as much clothing as you can." He dipped his head beneath the surface as he removed his boots.

Varina's teeth were clicking too hard for her to respond, but she managed to unfasten and kick off her petticoats, then joined Andrew in the long swim toward the island. The exertion gradually spread a comforting warmth through her limbs, but when they struggled through the surf onto the beach itself, the night air hit her skin and soaked clothing, causing her to shiver violently.

Andrew looked toward the reassuring beam of light that flashed like clockwork against the southern sky and estimated they were almost two miles north of the lighthouse. Checking his pocket, he found he still had his matches in their waterproof tin and set about gathering driftwood to build a fire in the shelter of a dune.

"We'll rest here until daybreak, then hike to the lighthouse for help."

Varina knew she should be experiencing a gamut of emotions from terror to rage to grief after all that had happened in the last few hours, but her only feelings were of numbness, a paralyzing cold throughout her body and a blessed absence of thoughts or other sensations. Her one overwhelming desire was to lie down and sleep. While Andrew was building his fire of driftwood and other debris, she curled in the sand close to the flames and was soon in a deep slumber.

She awoke with a start and the knowledge that someone slept beside her, their bodies joined like spoons. She lay curled against Andrew, his back to the dunes, her face to the fire. The heat from the fire and from Andrew's body had warmed her and dried her clothing, but her body and hair were covered with salt and sand.

She rose quietly so as not to awaken him, walked to ease her knotted muscles, and looked around her. A sparkling beach of sand as fine and white as sugar stretched north and south as far as she could see. Scattered along the water's edge were piles of seashells, heaped like treasure, rosy pink and beige shells in forms and shapes that Varina had never seen. Behind her, the island, covered with sea oats, mangroves, and cabbage palms, was seemingly devoid of habitation.

She had walked into the breakers to wash the grit from her face and hands when a long serpentine object wrapped itself about her ankles. She ran from the water, screaming in surprise and fright, then crumpled on the sand in tears as she unwound Cordelia's lace shawl that had tangled about her feet. Even from the depths of a watery grave, the woman reached out to haunt her. With the numbness of shock wearing away, the impact of all that had happened turned her tears to hysterical weeping.

321

Suddenly she found herself in Andrew's arms, his voice murmuring comforting words in her ear, but her hysteria deepened as she remembered the charge she had heard against him: wife-beater and murderer. Yes, murderer. He had killed four people last night with the fire set aboard his ship; he had known that the powder would explode. What kind of monster was this man?

The slap of Andrew's hand across her face brought her to her senses long enough to realize that she had babbled her thoughts aloud and that Andrew now stood watching her in disbelief.

"Are you going to beat me, too?" she asked.

He flinched, as if she had landed a physical blow.

"Because of all that you've endured, and what is still before us, I'll ignore that for now. But it is time, my darling Varina, that we talk."

He led her back to the fire by the dune where she sat reluctantly, fearful of what was to come, but knowing there was no escape.

"We'll deal with first things first," Andrew began. "Yes, I knew that the powder would explode, but we were in a desperate situation. Duarte had already killed two innocent men. Not only were your life and mine at stake, but if Duarte and Cordelia had been allowed to carry through with their plan, Rauol and all of his family would have been executed by the Spanish authorities. Then that murderous pair would have returned to Fair Winds with Jamie next on their list of victims."

He had picked up a branch of driftwood, and as he spoke, snapped it into smaller and smaller pieces. "They didn't have to die. If they had been less foolish—and less drunk—they could have jumped ship, too, as we did."

He threw the driftwood to the ground and fell to his knees before Varina, grasped her by the shoulders, his fingers digging hard into her soft flesh, and forced her to look him in the eye. "It would be a lie to say I did not want to kill them. I'd like to have broken them both into bits like that piece of branch. But with God as my witness, Varina, if I could have thought of a way to save ourselves without hurting them, I would have done it."

His gaze was so intense that she could bear it no longer and lowered her eyes. Could she believe him? One part of her wanted to, wanted to throw her arms about him in gratitude for rescuing her, but another part, the part of her that had swayed between reason and terror for the past few weeks, was not convinced. She would have to know more. Steeling herself for the worst, she raised her eyes again to his.

"How did Theodora die?"

Andrew sank back on his heels, covering his face with his hands. When he raised his head once more, his look was steady and unwavering. "How Theodora died is a very long story that must be told from the beginning . . ." He paused, licking the salt from his lips. "But the sun is getting higher and we have no water. We must get to the lighthouse before we dehydrate any more than we already have."

He stood, brushing the sand from his clothes. "If I promise to tell you as soon as we're out of danger, will you come with me now and trust me?"

Still warring within herself but having no other choice, Varina took Andrew's hand, and together they began the long trek toward the south end of the beach. How soon would it be before she knew the truth? Either this man, the only other human she knew of on this deserted island, was a heinous murderer, or he was not. And how could she be sure, even if the story he told vindicated him? Yes, he was Uncle William's brother, but that did not guarantee the fineness of character that her uncle enjoyed. History and literature were rife with examples of siblings whose characters mirrored one another, one bright and good, the other dark and evil. Had she escaped the clutches of one demon only to fall at the mercy of another?

But where was her faith in her intuition, in that deep small voice within her that kept reminding her that she loved Andrew? Was she capable of valuing someone who was not inherently good? Was it Andrew's goodness— or his evilness—that was not what it seemed? Her head ached from her inner turmoil and from the glare of the sun reflecting from the gleaming sands and the calm gulf waters. If she was going to reach the lighthouse, she must focus her energies on the journey and away from useless speculation. There would be time enough after they returned home to sort out the puzzle of Andrew's character.

Their bare feet slowed their pace. When they walked along the breakwater, broken shells sliced at their exposed skin like razors, and when they moved farther in along the beach, the soft sand shifted beneath them, sucking them deeper and deeper into the fine white powder with each step so that they had to extricate themselves before taking another.

Varina, weak from thirst and exhaustion, her face and arms seared by sun and wind, relied more and more on Andrew to pull her along and keep her moving. At last, before the sun had climbed to its zenith, they reached the mangroves that separated the houses of the lighthouse keepers from the sands. Above them loomed the metal tower housing the powerful lamps that lit the sea. Following a narrow path that led from the beach through the trees, they emerged into the yard behind the houses. A teenaged boy was chopping kindling, but he dropped his hatchet when he saw the two and ran to the house.

"Ma, there's people here! Looks like they was shipwrecked!"

A woman stepped onto the deep porch that encirled the house, shading her eyes with her hand to watch them as they crossed the yard. Her age was impossible to tell because her skin and hair had been dried by the sun and sea and her clothes were of rough but immaculately clean homespun.

"Ezra," she called to the teenager who also stood watching their approach, "go tell your father we have guests." Having decided that they were no threat, she waited with her hands rolled in her apron until they reached the foot of the porch stairs. "Welcome to Sanibel Island, folks," she greeted them. "Looks like you could stand a cold drink and a good meal."

Varina's last reservoir of strength had been emptied by her trek up from the beach, and as she raised her foot to mount the steps into the beckoning shade of the porch, the sun wheeled in the sky, and her world went black.

She knew she must be dreaming. She could feel the softness of a mattress and pillow beneath her body and the sheet that covered her. And she could hear the voices of Gordie, Duncan, Andrew, and another she couldn't identify. It had to be a dream. Gordie and Duncan were at Fair Winds, not here, almost two hundreds miles to the south at Sanibel. Then another possibility occurred to her. Maybe she was dead. If so, she thought, being dead was wonderfully comfortable.

When she awakened again, she thought for a fleeting instant that the room was on fire, filled as it was with the reddish glow of a magnificent Florida sunset. She looked about with interest at the room's high ceiling and large windows, built for coolness and ventilation, and its sparse furnishings, beautiful in their simplicity. Then she saw her clothes, freshly washed and ironed, draped across a chair beside the bed, and realized that the woman must have undressed her, bathed her, and clothed her in her own best nightgown, a soft handsewn creation of cotton batiste edged with a pale blue ribbon.

Swinging her legs over the edge of the bed as she sat up, Varina frowned at the multitude of cuts and scratches on her feet and gingerly tested her weight on them before rushing to the water pitcher that stood on the washstand. She gulped down the refreshing liquid as if her body could never get enough of it again.

Then she removed the woman's nightgown and folded it carefully across the foot of the bed, and pulled on her own clothes, wincing when they touched the sunburned skin of her arms and face. The woman must have been listening for signs of her awakening, for she slipped into the room, closing the door behind her.

"Feeling better?" she asked.

"Yes, thank you. I'm grateful for all you've done." Varina indicated her clothes and the rumpled bed.

"We're happy to have visitors. We don't get them often." The woman's brown eyes were as soft as her voice. "My name's Ellen. I already know you're Varina." She reached into her apron pocket, pulling out a comb carved from a shell. "I know this ain't much, but Ezra made it while you slept. Thought you might be needin' it."

"You're very kind. Thank you." Varina, touched anew by the woman's thoughtfulness, accepted the comb, pulling it through her rebellious curls.

Ellen looked down at Varina's feet and with a hint of embarrassment apologized for not having a pair of shoes to offer her. Varina saw that Ellen's own boots were old and worn. Impulsively, she went to the woman and hugged her.

"I couldn't wear shoes now anyway with the state my feet are in."

"Then if you're finished dressing, I have some supper ready. And your people are waiting for you." She was out the door before Varina could reply.

Her people? Did that mean there had been other survivors from the ship? Her knees buckled from the terror that thought instilled in her and she sank back onto the bed.

A knock at the door broke through her fright, and Andrew stuck his head in just far enough to speak.

"We're waiting for you. Come on!" Then he, too, disappeared. But he hadn't sounded as if anything were amiss. If anything, Varina would have described his tone as jubilant. Curiosity overcame her fear, and she rose and left the room.

The bedroom door opened onto a central hallway that traversed the length of the house, and Varina followed the sound of voices to an open door where the lamplight spilled into the hallway. When she stepped into the room, she almost fainted again with surprise. Gathered around the kitchen table as Ellen served them supper were Gordie, Duncan, Andrew, and Ezra, and two men whom Varina had never seen before. Their conversation stopped when they saw her in the doorway.

"How—what?" She knew she was standing there with her mouth open, but her brain didn't seem to connect with her voice, so she couldn't find the words she wanted to say.

Andrew rose from his chair, took her gently by her sun-blistered arm and led her to a seat at the table. "It's an incredible story, and a lengthy one. I suggest you have some of Mrs. Burton's excellent chowder first." He pulled out a chair between Gordie and Duncan and gently pushed her into it. She moved like an automaton, so stunned with surprise that she had no will of her own.

Andrew returned to his own chair, but before continuing his meal, he introduced Varina to Mr. Burton, the lighthouse keeper. The other man he introduced as Cyrus Downs, captain of the *Caladesi*.

"He'll be taking us home," Andrew explained.

Ravenously, Varina ate fish chowder and cornbread, her hunger for the moment overriding her curiosity over how the Roth men had reached Sanibel so quickly. The men talked of boats, fishing, and the unrest in Cuba, and Varina realized that Andrew, Gordie, and Duncan were keeping their business to themselves and accepted the fact that she would probably not be told any more until they were out of range of their hosts. When the meal was finished, the men thanked Ellen for her hospitality and stood to leave. Varina took the woman's weathered hands and kissed her sun-dried cheek.

" 'I was a stranger and you took me in.' God bless you, Ellen Burton."

Then Duncan swept her up in his strong arms and carried her back to the beach along the path she had traveled that morning. He waded into the waters where the *Caladesi* was anchored and handed her up to Andrew, who was already aboard, with Gordie and Captain Downs. She settled down onto the deck as the sails were hoisted and filled with wind.

"We'll be home in time for breakfast," Andrew promised her. "You can sleep in the cabin, if you like."

"Oh, no, I'm not moving from this spot," Varina threatened, "until someone tells me what is going on. When did you arrive? How did you get here? How did you know where to come?"

She threw questions like stones at Duncan and Gordie who had joined them on the deck while Captain Downs took the helm.

Gordie chuckled at her ferocity and nodded toward his brother. "You'd best tell her, lad, or we'll na have a moment's peace the whole way back."

Duncan cleared his throat, self-conscious in the role of storyteller, then launched into a recounting of the events that had occurred at Fair Winds after Varina's abduction by Duarte. The Roths had been having tea in the Fair Winds kitchen, when Henrietta and Jamie arrived in the dog cart, accompanied by the constable.

"Henrietta said she knew something was wrong when both Jamie and his cart had been left abandoned at the church, so she had stopped in town to ask Wilbur Clyde, the constable, to ride out with her to see what the trouble was.

"We had no sooner heard her story than Duarte's man, Rigo, arrived with the carriage. He wasna expecting the welcome he received. Wilbur Clyde is na man to have angry at ye, believe me. He threatened to drive Rigo to Tampa himself and turn him over to the Cuban Revolutionary Party there if he didna tell us where Duarte had taken ye."

The Roth brothers, looking at each other, chuckled appreciatively at the memory of the effectiveness of Wilbur's threats.

"When we learned that Duarte was sailing to overtake Andrew, Gordie and I rode to Clear Water Harbor and hired Captain Downs and the *Caladesi* to help us catch up with him. We knew that Andrew would sail straight down the coast, and that even if we missed him, we might reach Rauol in time to warn him."

Duncan paused uncertainly, unused to delivering long narratives.

"You're doing fine, my friend," Andrew said. "Just tell her as you told me."

"We were fairly optimistic about reaching ye in time to help somehow, until we came across the wreckage of Andrew's boat. That was a dreadful sight, let me tell ye. We sailed back and forth, looking for any signs of life, but found naught but widely scattered pieces of wreckage, all indicating a terrible explosion.

"We were about to give up all together when Captain Downs suggested we check the islands, in case anyone had managed to swim to shore. He put us ashore at the north end of Captiva and we walked its whole length, looking for signs of survivors. When we found naught there, we started at the north end of Sanibel and did the same thing, only there we found the remains of your fire, and followed your tracks to the light-house. Ye know the rest."

Varina's eyelids drooped. Even after her sleep that afternoon, her body still cried for rest after her ordeal. But even as she drifted once more into unconsciousness, the deep small voice within her kept insisting that something was missing from Duncan's story. That even now, all the pieces did not quite fit.

She was aware of nothing else until hours later when Andrew shook her gently. "We're coming through the pass into the sound. We're almost home."

The sun was lifting above the horizon, and the wind and water were so gentle that the boat glided smoothly up the sound, and Varina realized with surprise that she had not experienced any seasickness on this voyage. When they passed the long pier at the end of Main Street, Captain Downs began to blow an announcement of their arrival on a large conch shell, its low full tones echoing back to them from the shore. As they came to Fair Winds, he eased the boat alongside Andrew's dock.

Andrew and Duncan leaped to the pier to secure the lines, then with Gordie's assistance, pulled Varina up onto the wooden planks.

A tumult of noise erupted as the wide front door of Fair Winds burst open and Arby scudded across the lawn, yapping happily at the sight of them. Fiona and Jamie followed close behind, their happiness at the safe return of the travelers shining in their faces.

With his short legs pumping as hard as they could, Jamie reached them before Fiona did.

"Papa! Papa! You brought Varina back!"

Varina stopped, unable to move from the shock of Jamie's speaking. Gordie was at her elbow, and she turned to him in amazement as Jamie threw himself into his father's arms.

"There was one thing Duncan didna tell ye," Gordie admitted. "We thought we'd save it as a homecoming present. 'Twas Jamie who told Henrietta, and then us, everything that happened to the two of ye yesterday."

Chapter
Twenty-Two

Varina's hands trembled as she pulled on her riding boots. She was dreading her ride with Andrew this morning. Last night as she had mounted the stairs to bed, he had caught her by the elbow.

"Ride with me in the morning. There's a story that I promised to share with you."

His countenance was rigid, its contours carved from stone, and his eyes had burned black and dark, a startling contrast from the man who had laughed and smiled the day away with his newly talkative son. He had promised to tell her of Theodora's death, and it seemed he intended to keep his word. Now Varina feared what she was about to hear. As Duncan had once remarked, the truth couldn't be good. Why else would it have been a secret from so many for so long?

Why couldn't things have remained as they were yesterday, she thought wistfully, a day of joyful celebration, both of their own rescue and of Jamie's decision to speak again? The only grim note in the day had been Andrew's trip to the railroad station to send a coded telegram to Rauol to warn him of the authorities' suspicions and to inform him that his shipment had been lost.

The Roths and the Bairds had joined in their festivities, and they had picnicked on the lawn in the summerlike January sun, and played croquet and lawn tennis. It had been a day much like the ones Varina remembered from her youth in New Bern, carefree and fun, with no shadows or puzzles to mar its perfection.

But today the piper played a different tune, and squaring her shoulders as she pulled on her gloves, Varina prepared to dance to it.

She met Andrew at the stables and they mounted their horses in silence, heading them at a slow walk toward the plantation.

"It's hard to know how to begin," Andrew said, looking at the path ahead, avoiding her eyes.

"There's no hurry." Now Varina was not sure she wanted to hear his story, remembering the old cliche that what she didn't know wouldn't hurt her.

"Theodora only came to the plantation once—the night she died." Andrew began. "But I'm starting at the end. I must go all the way back to when I met Theodora, if I am to make you understand."

His voice was low and hesitant as he told of meeting Theodora when she had attended a lecture he had given in New York City, but as he progressed, his voice strengthened and the rhythm of his speech reflected more confidence.

"She seemed terribly interested in my work, and invited me to her home for dinner the following evening so that I could share my experiences with her father, who was confined to the house by arthritis. When I arrived there that evening, both of them plied me with questions about the places I'd been and the plant life I had discovered. Their fascination was quite intoxicating for a young man so long a stranger to civilized company.

"And Theodora herself was a beautiful woman. You remember, don't you? You met her right after we were married."

Varina nodded. Oh, she had definitely remembered.

"In the ignorance of my youth, and my own pride in the importance of my work, I was certain I had found the perfect woman to spend the rest of my life with. Not only was she lovely, but she was supportive of me in my travels and my research.

"But as soon as we were married, it was as if she had become another person. She wanted to hear nothing of my work and resented that it had brought her to what she always referred to as 'this Godforsaken place.' She was somewhat appeased when we built Fair Winds and she could spend her time going through catalogs to order its furnishings, but still her temperament worsened.

"I had hoped that Jamie would make a difference, but she resented him, too, from the day he was born, and was happy to have Fiona accept full responsibility for him. It took me a long while to understand that she had only pretended an interest in my work to get me to marry her. Her inheritance from her wealthy mother would not come into her control until her marriage, and she was anxious to get her hands on that—and to cast off the strict rules of living under her father's roof. Ironically, the old man died only months after we were married, and she could have had both her parents' money and her freedom then—without me—if she had only waited. I think she always held that against me, too."

He brought his stallion to a halt and turned to look at Varina.

"Don't think I am blaming only Theodora. Much of this was my fault as well. If I had been less vain and more perceptive, I would have known that I couldn't bring a wife used to the social whirl in New York City to the Florida wilderness and expect her to be happy.

"From the very beginning of our marriage, there was something else about Theodora over which I had no control. She was insanely jealous of anything and everything that took even one second of my attention away from her. My first hint of it was when we visited all of you in New Bern. She wanted me to have nothing to do with my own brother or any of his family. Later, my plants, Jamie, my friends, my trips were viewed by her as indignities forced upon her, requiring that she give me up to something or someone else."

He paused, clearly not wanting to say what was coming next.

"In the end, that jealousy unbalanced her, causing her tenuous hold on sanity to snap. In retrospect, I know I should have acknowledged her problem and sought help for her long before, but at the time, I honestly didn't know what to do."

He put his horse to a slow walk once more. Varina, not knowing how to respond, said nothing.

"She had become so irrational that she began to shriek and scream at me even when I stayed at home with her. Nothing I did pleased her, so I escaped by taking as many trips as I could. The day of her death, I returned by boat from my trip to the Everglades to find every light in the house blazing but the house itself empty. I knew that Fiona and Gordie were probably at church, but I didn't know if Jamie was with them or Theodora. She hardly ever left the house unless she took a trip to Tampa to shop, so I set out to look for her.

"When I reached the stable, my horse was missing. Having no idea where she might have gone, I decided to check the plantation first. If she wasn't there, Gordie and Fiona would be back home by the time I returned, and they might know where she went."

Once more he reined in his horse on the path and looked about as if searching for something.

"There"—he pointed to a spot in the path ahead—"there's where I found the horse, its saddle lying beside it. She must not have fastened the cinch strap securely. I knew for certain then that she must be at the plantation. The gates were standing wide—they were never locked until after her death—and when I entered the gardens, the place looked as if a tornado had ripped through it. Flowers and shrubs had been slashed, and their blossoms and branches trampled upon."

They had reached the plantation now, and Andrew unlocked the gates for them to enter. Today the gardens bore evidence of their latest disaster, most of the plants limp and brown from what was already being referred to as the Great Freeze. However, here and there, along a sheltered wall, or close to where a fire had provided protecting warmth, a plant thrived in verdant health, some even blossoming, bright spots of color and hope among the destruction.

The two dismounted, and Varina followed Andrew to where he stopped before the barren plot enclosed by the three-foot picket fence.

"This is where I found her. Seeing this fence around the tree that was planted here must have convinced her that this plant was in some way

very special, and she attacked it with a venge-
ance. It was hacked to the ground, its branches
torn apart. She had the *machete* Rauol had given
me clasped in her hand, and bits of the leaves
and branches were found in her mouth. She had
even ripped into it with her teeth in her fury."

Varina's mind struggled to comprehend what
Andrew was saying. "But I still don't understand
how she died."

"The fence *did* mark this tree as special." He
laughed, a dry sound tinged with bitterness.
"Life is full of ironies, some more intense than
others. In this case, it was as if the plants had
claimed their own retribution. The tree that was
here was strychnine, fenced for the protection
of children and animals, because its leaves and
branches are deadly poison."

Now the missing pieces were beginning to
fall into place. Theodora had died at her own
hand, a victim of her own obsessive jealousy.
But there were still unanswered questions.

"But why the lies about how she died?"

Andrew raked his fingers through his hair, visibly uncomfortable over Varina's query.

"I took Theodora back and carried her to our
room. I wanted to cover her so that Jamie would
not see her. She had been badly bruised by her
fall from the horse, lacerated by the plants, not
to mention the horrible effects of the poison
itself."

That explains the doctor's wife's gossip about
her having been beaten, and about the charges
of poison as well, Varina thought.

"I hadn't any thought then except to tell the truth about her death. When we found Jamie in that catatonic state, we could only imagine what he had seen or heard to have had such an effect on him. In fact, we may never know."

His voice shook with emotion as he spoke of his son. "Even though he is speaking once again, I will never ask him about it unless he decides to discuss what happened. I can't risk his slipping into such a state and losing him again."

He stopped, lost in memories of the dreadful year of silent agony that the small boy had endured. "I'm sorry, where was I?"

"You were explaining why you lied about what killed Theodora," Varina said, feeling his pain as her own as she watched him struggle with his tale.

"When we saw how badly affected Jamie was by whatever he had seen, or whatever had happened to him, we—Fiona, Gordie, Doc Thompson, and I—decided that the story of yellow fever was best."

"Why?" Varina was still having difficulty following Andrew's reasoning.

"With Jamie the way he was, silent and unresponsive, we feared that people might think he was insane, like his mother, if the truth of her death were known. We also didn't want to say anything to Jamie that would disturb him any more than he already was."

"Fiona told me that you burned everything of Theodora's because of the fever. If there was no fever, why did you destroy all her belongings?"

Andrew shook his head. "We acted as if the yellow fever story was true. Gordie and Fiona even refused to tell Duncan the truth, freeing him from having to lie as the rest of us did." Then he looked at Varina, his eyes bottomless pools of pain. "But the real reason I destroyed everything of Theodora's was that I could not bear to have any reminders of her after all that had happened. I suppose it was a way of striking out at her with the anger and hurt that I felt."

He turned and walked away, not wanting her to see the shame he suffered.

Varina followed and grasped his arm, forcing him to face her once more. "But the portrait—why didn't you destroy it, too?"

"I truly loved the Theodora of that picture. The girl in that portrait was not the madwoman who died here. And I wanted Jamie to be able to remember his mother, so the portrait was the only thing of hers I didn't burn."

He looked about sadly at the barren plot of earth, burned at regular intervals to keep the deadly strychnine tree from reseeding or springing up from any remaining roots. Then he turned back to Varina.

"In hindsight, I can see perhaps I handled everything wrong, including the lies about Theodora's death. But in my own defense, I can only say I did what I thought was right at the time."

"Oh, Andrew," Varina cried. "If only I had known. I thought—"

"You thought what?" His eyes burned dark as he waited for her answer.

"I thought that you had killed her." Her words were soft and ashamed, and she could not look at him. "Can you ever forgive me?"

"Forgive you? Varina, don't you know by now that I love you? Since the moment you stepped into my life again that November day at the railroad station, I have watched you care for my son and heal him with your love. I've seen you hunger to learn all that you can about the work that I do. I watched you work yourself into exhaustion to save my plants." He pulled her into his embrace. "And I've seen you smile and laugh and turn my gloomy house into a home. I love you, Varina, but I've been so afraid to tell you, afraid that I would make a mess of things as I did with Theodora."

He kissed her long and hard, and her arms reached up to encircle him. He had answered her questions, laying Theodora's uneasy spirit to rest. Gladly, Varina set aside her former fears and misgivings and returned his love.

Three weeks later, Varina, Andrew, and Jamie sat on the northbound train, viewing the marshes of Glynn as they sped by the window.

"Tell me again, Papa. Where's Arby?"

"He's safe in his comfortable kennel in the baggage car. The porter will let us check on him at the next stop," Andrew explained.

"And where are we going?"

"We're going to New Bern to see Uncle William and Aunt Mae and your cousins, Andy, Molly, Margaret, and Harris." Varina estimated that he had answered this question at least six times now.

"And why are we visiting them, Papa?"

"So that Uncle William can marry Varina and me," Andrew answered for the innumerable time, accustomed to the repetitious litany of Jamie's questions, until the next question, a new one, gained his full attention.

"Will that make Varina my new mama?"

"Yes, son."

"That's good. I didn't like my old mama. She frightened me."

Varina, aware that this was the first time Jamie had mentioned Theodora since he had begun to speak again, tread carefully.

"How did she frighten you?"

"She came into my room with Papa's big knife, and she was very angry. She said she was going to kill everything that Papa loved, and since I knew that Papa loved me, I thought that she was going to kill me, too."

Jamie's relating of these events was almost offhanded, as he gave part of his attention to the passing landscape, enjoying his first journey by train.

"What did you do then?" Varina asked.

"I ran away from her and hid in my own special place. And from then on I stayed very quiet and very small, so she couldn't ever find me. But

I don't think she's coming back again now, do you?"

"No, I'll be here to look after you from now on, my favorite boy."

"I know." Jamie smiled up at her with adoration shining in his bright brown eyes. "That's why I talked to Henrietta, so those bad people wouldn't keep you away."

Varina looked at Andrew and knew that he was sharing her thoughts. Although Jamie had solved part of the puzzle, explaining his former silence, they knew they would never know whether Theodora had really intended to destroy Jamie as well as Andrew's plants or whether Jamie had tragically misinterpreted her words.

"Do you know what else, Papa?"

"What else, son?"

Jamie looked out the window, around the train carriage, and then at the couple seated across from him. His face glowed with smiles. "I'm the happiest boy in the whole world!"

Andrew took Varina's hand and tucked it through his arm, pulling her close.

"So am I, son. So am I."